JEZ

Jez Lowe was born in C   and writer of songs, inspir   England. Much covered   , he has around twenty albums of original songs to his credit. His first novel "The Dillen Doll" was published in 2017. He has been a principal writer for the award-winning BBC Radio Ballads series since 2006, and is currently engaged in writing songs for a project for The National Theatre on London's South Bank. This is his second novel.

Also by Jez Lowe

The Dillen Doll – 2017

THE CORLY CROONS
By

JEZ LOWE

Published by Badapple Books
PO Box 57,
York
YO26 8BN

www.jezlowe.com

Printed and bound in Great Britain by Clays Ltd., Elcograf S.p.A

ISBN 978-1-9998888-2-4

THE CORLY CROONS

THE PLACE

It wasn't a city yet.

A big river, so-named, with Newcastle on one side of it, facing down Gateshead on the other, but bearing none of the many bridges that came to connect the two of them in later years. Only a low span of crumbling stone existed to join them as friends, neighbours, sneering competitors. They each had their accomplices along the length of the Tyne: places like Wallsend, Byker, North Shields and Tynemouth on the northern side, and Blaydon, Pipewellgate – now vanished – Jarrow, Hebburn and South Shields on the southern side. And the river itself, clogged by ships, barges, keels and boats of every shape, size and country of origin. The people that came with them were just as mixed, just as varied, with a hundred languages rattling and roaring along the quayside and through the narrow chares and alleyways that ran into it.

THE TIMES

Any stranger arriving in mid-nineteenth century Newcastle would have been confronted by a town gripped by changing times. In this Northern heartland of the Industrial Revolution, things were moving on apace. Lavish new buildings and open spaces were replacing airless slum areas, railways were bearing down upon the place from every direction, sails were being replaced by steam on the River Tyne, and electric lights were illuminating whole lengths of streets, both inside and out. Coal's smoky presence was everywhere, and skilled workers set a world-class standard in glass-making and ship-building. Scientific and engineering advancements were almost common-place, but such grandness belied the poverty and hardship that most folk endured. History was being made elsewhere too, with war overseas and political upheaval at home, as ever, a constant backdrop to the times.

THE SONGS

But this was Tyneside, and underlying all this upheaval there was always music. A soundtrack of new songs and melodies was being written at a feverish pace, by people, mostly men, at all levels of society. The traditional music that had long been part of the North East of England was being developed into a unique repertoire that blended the old narrative ballad style with music-hall ribaldry and drawing-room sentimentality. People could barely get enough of it, and much of what emerged was being immortalised on paper, with printing shops and publishing houses churning out broadsheets and chap-books to a public hungry for every new verse, each new skit, each new ballad. And it's lucky for us, here in the twenty-first century, that they did so.

THE STORY

The four or five central characters in our tale are all fictional, but everyone they meet and speak about were real enough. Only one name has been changed, and with good intention. But it was someone real enough who makes a tiny appearance early on that was the inspiration for everything that comes later. A faceless policeman in London, who happened to share a name with a tragic figure on Tyneside, a man who was a gifted songster, who's lines gave a title to each chapter, but who's own story fizzled away, leaving behind only the character that he created in his songs. This is likely not his real story, but better this, I hope, than no story at all.

ACKNOWLEDGMENTS

Benny Graham, Corrin Bramley, Kate Bramley, Kerry Manning, Bev Sanders, Annabelle Polito and Steve Tilston. Special thanks once again to Kari MacLeod for her artwork and Lisa Kirkbride for her design.

THE CORLY CROONS
By

JEZ LOWE

About seven Ah gave ower workin'
Got beard off, and put a white sark on,
For Newcasslers, thought Ah,
If they don't see me braw,
Will say "What a gowk is Bob Cranky!"

Ah ran to the toon without stoppin',
And found every street like a hoppin',
And the folk stood se thick,
Ah sair wished for me pick,
To hew out a way for Bob Cranky.

From "Bob Cranky's Leum'nation Neet" by John Selkirk.
Published in The Tyne Mercury, June 1st 1814

CHAPTER 1

"And when to Newcassel I gang"

The town seemed to be tumbling down that day. Its stones and bricks and boards were being hacked and scratched and chewed at. Men, swarming like river-rats, climbed across its jagged crust, biting at its edges, and spitting out the stale mouthfuls in hideous heaps upon the scarred ground. Eaten away from the inside, its ribs and bones reached up painfully from the rubble, while merciless hands with picks and hammers beat its poor body to death in the cold early morning drizzle. They tugged and tore at it in a frenzy, ripping it apart, twisting it, torturing it, in an orgy of dust and destruction. Nearby, a church steeple, spared from this only by the grace of God, looked down in sadness at the massacre, but made not a sound of sympathy. The deafening noise of demolition thundered on like the world's end, and the Lord chose to ignore it.

Evan Piper strained his neck upwards at the sight of two men on high, swinging long-handled hammers in rude rhythm at a single stubborn piece of wall that was still reaching up tall and proud at one end of the building that it used to be. As if in some mad air-borne dance, the men wielded their weapons in pendulum swings and cracked at the brickwork like skilful spiders fighting over a web laden with yesterday's prizes. Piper felt himself catch his breath as he watched a chunk of it suddenly break free, taking with it a sizeable piece of masonry as it hurtled down, and causing both men to stagger back and fight for their balance, a full thirty feet or more from the ground. He heard their torrent of curses echo across this urban battlefield, as fellow-warriors down below called out words of abuse and ridicule, in a language that meant nothing to him. The acrobats above him rested for a moment on their unsteady perch.

By a lower wall, at the other end of this scene, a short but darkly handsome man suddenly raised his voice in song, as he pulled whole bricks from a pile of debris at his feet. His voice was high and almost tender, in full command of the long, swooping notes that the melody demanded. Remarkably, a paltry few of the words he sang reached Piper's ears intact: they spoke of pig-tails, jackets and garters, and were seemingly in celebration of a man called Bob Cranky, a hero whose name was certainly unknown to him. Then at once, from all around this broken-brick doomsday, other voices arose in chorus with the first, as if in some mad staging of a dawn-lit operetta with a cast of performers whose face paint was grime and dirt, and whose costumes were mud-caked rags, torn coats and sodden headwear.

The song bloomed gloriously, but then was suddenly destroyed by ear-splitting strokes of picks and axes on stone from another corner of this curious theatre. Piper stood for a moment longer in thought, then moved on.

His own steps were surer now, his balance more certain. The heavy sky was reluctantly allowing the meagre light of the new day to pare back the strangeness of these dark narrow streets. People were emerging from unseen doorways and jagged entries, and moving with lazy purpose to and fro. A shawl-covered figure with a woman's bare arms glided across his path a few yards in front of him. She gave a quick furtive glance in his direction, before scurrying off into the overhanging shadows. He straightened his back at the sight of her, and tried to sense her features from the brief flash of her face that he'd caught. She was already pretty to him, with wide eyes and red, parted lips, her hair dark and long beneath the wool, her body strong but full of softness. He imagined her voice, and it emerged not in the hard-edged clamour of the local street noise, but in the familiar roll and swoop of his own home town, at whose heart flowed a friendlier, smoother river. Beneath its coat of city filth, The Thames had a noble history, a royal patronage and borders of classical delicacy. What he had seen of this town's river, the sludge-grey spittle of water that they called the Tyne, filled him with the dismay of distance and despair. For not the first time that day he asked himself what he was doing here.

His ship had docked in darkness, and his quivering legs had found dry land at five o'clock that morning, on a strange quay already bustling with carts, barrows, sea-dogs and dock-hands, high-collared clerks and sturdy colliers, all hurling throat-wrenching language at each other, in an accent that blended Dutch, Scottish and old English into one indistinguishable jabber. It left Evan Piper's tired mind bruised and exhausted. There'd been no sleep for him that previous night, when the waves had pounded the old steamer mercilessly as they rolled on their way towards the near shore. The grinding machinery beneath his berth had fought a breathless and noisy combat with the sea. The structures of the side-housings had creaked and groaned, and the world had lurched and shuddered angrily in rhythm with the swell. Time and time again, lights from the land had promised a smooth entry to a river mouth, but on and on they'd battled through the darkness, until they'd made a wide sweeping turn into port, and gradually a soothing calmness had mercifully descended.

He'd stood on the quay at last, aware of masts and yardarms towering like a forest around him, the stink of the river catching his throat, the madness of voices that made no sense to him, and the tall blackness of warehouses and store lofts bearing down, as if trying to push him back to the very water that had only just delivered him. He had stumbled over ropes and chains, slipped on unspeakable detritus and wet iron rails, his legs still caught in the motion of the sea. Then he'd lurched for the first set of steps he'd seen, in the hope that they would lift him out of this insanity and into a higher, more civilised world. Breathlessly reaching their summit, he'd found that the tottering structures and smooth cobbles there were quieter, but offered no real relief. A church bell had sounded twice, and he'd sought the sanctuary of its open door with a fugitive's haste, and flung himself into its stone heart. There he had sat, his dignity bruised, his body shivering with weariness and confusion, like some beached sea creature gasping for the familiarity of the waves.

The long face of a soldier, his eyes wide and woeful, his head lowered in the sorrow of defeat, looked down from on high, captured forever in glass. All stain of colour had faded from him, dulled by too many winters and by the soot of a town choked by chimneys. A cold, century-old stare was all he offered to the congregation. The sword clasped in that delicate hand leaned limply by his side, never to be raised in battle. Only the serpent crushed beneath his clenched foot showed any mark of defiance, with a determination that the warrior himself would never know.

What meagre light the morning had to offer stood little chance of soothing this fragile image, nor bathing the sad grey flagstones of the cold floor in brightness. A high altar of dark oak loomed in a hideous arch across this austere landscape. The gloom all but devoured a single candle glowing earnestly beneath a faceless saint in dull marble. Only the faded blue wrappings of a sleeping statue of the Virgin, her tiny hands turned in supplication, offered any hint of colour. Even the cross of brass that claimed pride of place here was of no comfort.

For a moment, Evan Piper had felt himself search in his heart for some feeling of devotion, or perhaps humility in the face of this bleakest of scenes, as if a holy duty called upon him to do so, but he was suddenly distracted. A painfully twisted man in a filthy pea-jacket, carrying a blue seaman's cap respectfully in a loose hand, struggled into a pew on the other side of the aisle. It was a different brand of duty that urged Piper to look closely at this crippled figure, in case something might be learned from it. Indeed it was that very same duty that had brought him to this town, surely as far from God's kingdom as could ever be reached; it was a duty which to him was much more sacred, much more meaningful, than any holy obligation that might be expected of him in this inglorious place.

The cold draught from the wide stone arch behind him caused him to regret his decision to slide himself into his chosen spot to the rear of the nave. He sat hidden in the near darkness of a shadow cast by a sturdy buttress, its plaster façade crumbling with age. He couldn't move now, he felt, without drawing attention to himself, and that was the last thing he wanted to do. He pulled his long rough coat over his legs as best he could, tugged at his collar, and pulled his hat and bag of belongings closer to him, as if he could draw some warmth from their familiarity. At least from this position, he could observe everyone who entered, every bare-headed man, every shawl-draped woman, every shivering, wind-blown figure that might dip itself into this holy gloom.

As the moments passed, he clawed at some kind of order in his mind. He found himself rubbing one hand into the other, pressing fisted knuckles into open palm, tightening and kneading them like a worried widow. His back was arched and his body tight and cowering, as if the weight of these sacred walls was his alone to bear. He leaned back purposefully and groaned audibly. He heard the sound echo across the stone, and it startled him, though no-one else showed any notice of it. His eyes were wide now, his breath caught in his chest. He let it out slowly. Outside beyond the doorway, a wind blew in a low moan, as if it too shared his troubles. He chuckled at the notion, and felt suddenly calmer. The fear of the night's stormy waters left him, and he fought against the tiredness that had surely cast this weakness over him.

An old woman in black weeds appeared and swayed silently at the end of his bench. She hesitated when she saw him, then moved herself into the row in front of him, casting what he imagined was a withering look in his direction before she puffed to her knees in prayer. He smiled to himself. Even here, he was an interloper, a cuckoo in a penitent's nest, unwanted, an outcast. Strangely, he found comfort in the thought. He didn't belong here, he didn't need to be here. He was merely sheltering in the Lord's house from the early morning storm, and he would soon move on and be about his business. And it was there that the true purpose of his presence here surely lay.

A clergyman, a black shape in the greyness, with a white holy-man's collar hanging at his throat, emerged from a vestry door on the right. He strode up the steps of the chancel with an extravagant bound, then knelt before the altar, his head raised as if he had been chosen for the task. He held the position for some moments, then dropped his head, as if in shame. The helmeted knight stared down at him from his glass limbo, as if he shared in that same guilt. Piper peered around at this meagre gathering of lost souls. Did even God himself dismiss this fearsome town and its North Country desolation? Where was the ceremony, the singing that he recalled from his boyhood, his mother's squat certainty at his side, the mischievous boys and squinting girls, the psalms bouncing madly around the vaulted beams and the mumbling of long prayers from old men, unashamed of their beliefs and devotions. Had he ever found any comfort in those beliefs, even as a boy, even before he'd abandoned them? If he had, he had no memory of it now.

Piper dug deep into his coat for his time-piece and though his wariness prevailed upon him to wait, the gloomy oppression within this place convinced him that to confront the drizzle and chill without was somewhat preferable. The throaty voice of the pastor was rising into matins as Piper slid from the bench and stepped towards the open archway. The bitter widow twisted her neck contemptuously at him as he glanced back, and then he was out into the bleak November dawn.

He had had a destination in mind, but he was reluctant to reach it at this still-early hour. The noise of hard labour had attracted him to the site of falling walls and breaking buildings, and he unwittingly witnessed the early signs of a feverish change that was taking hold of this ancient town. Tightly knitted streets of stone, wood and daub were being razed, allowing fresh air to wash through for the first time in centuries. But soon they would be replaced by taller, nobler structures of Coade-stone finery. The people who had known this place as home were now scattered elsewhere, in anticipation of the influx of a grander, richer populace. Piper found a curious relief in this, having watched such callous changes devour his own native city. It was as if a wave of civilisation had finally splashed upon this far-flung shore. But then he remembered how, in that city of his, the careless sweeping-aside of humanity from its moorings had brought turmoil and chaos along with it, in a jumble of crime and desperation that was currently gripping those very streets that he had left behind three days previously. For him though, crime and desperation were very much the stuff of life.

Still deep in thought, he turned a sharp corner into a broader street, and suddenly found himself in uncanny brightness, as if some magical trail of fire was falling away, back towards where the river lay. A score or more of gas-powered flames, housed in high glass boxes danced their way downwards, the furthest of which were already being dowsed by brown-hatted men in matching green coats, in readiness for a daylight that was still battling with the thick grey sky.

Piper had seen street lamps before, but never in such numbers, and had certainly not expected to see them here in this unproven town. Their brilliance, even in the face of such dismal weather, cheered him immensely.

The coarse snort of a nag, drearily hauling a half-filled cart of small coals up the rise towards him, made him start. The pipe-smoking carter gave the animal a half-hearted slap with a willow twig and addressed Piper with what he took to be a sharp greeting. Piper smiled, nodded, and retorted with a dry-throated "Good morning," which itself brought a further, even less discernible reply from the other man, before he busied himself with guiding the whole endeavour, horse, cart and coal, around the sharp corner from where Piper had just come. A short man in white, with a flat board of loaves on his head, crossed the street towards him, and he too offered up a guttural greeting before disappearing down the same street. A few paces to his right, two lads were hauling wet sail cloth onto a warped barrow, only to watch it slip slovenly off again on the other side. He envied their lithe, boyish energy, as they leapt to rescue it time and time again. On the opposite side of the road, the columns of a tall expansive building dwarfed an aproned woman throwing a bucketful of black water across the paved footway, which she then proceeded to brush furiously with a broom made from thin twigs. There were bright hoardings on the wall behind her, with words in red and blue, and agile figures drawn around them. It was undoubtedly the exterior of a grand theatre, another surprise to Piper in this den of Philistine iniquity, and he made to cross the street to investigate what was on offer. As he approached, a tall-hatted man in a familiar-looking blue outer-coat emerged from a side entry beyond, with curious glances in both directions, up and down the thoroughfare. He was greeted cordially by another passer-by, some distance away, and responded in kind, and then his eyes turned to Piper, his curiosity obviously aroused in an instant.

Evan Piper advanced, his mind made up. "Good morning to you, mister," he said, briskly, but awkwardly. "Do you have time for a word?"

The police constable hesitated, and nodded slowly. "Of course, mister," he said, the suspicion obvious, even in those few words. Piper recognised it, and chose to ignore it. He forced a smile.

"I'm newly arrived on the morning steamer from London," he said. "Bad weather delayed our arrival from late last night to early this morning. My lodging was arranged, but isn't likely to be open at this hour, I suspect. And so I find myself aimlessly wandering the streets in anticipation of it."

"Your lodgin'," the other man enquired. "Where was that to be?"

"With Mrs Dixon, at The Unicorn," Piper replied, readily. "Situated in the Bigger Market Place, I believe."

The policeman smiled with condescension. "The *Bigg* Market," he said. "Yes, a worthy lodgin' for a man so far from home." His tone softened somewhat. "But you won't get entry there before noon I daresay," he continued. "And I certainly couldn't influence that, if that's what you expect of me."

"No, no, not all," Piper said, "But I do have an early appointment this very morning, which I intend to keep, despite my dishevelled state." He laughed cautiously. The policeman looked him up and down, but made no comment. "And that's something you could perhaps help me with."

The officer nodded again, but still looked curiously unconvinced. "Possibly so," he said. "Where exactly is this appointment of yours?

Piper laughed again. "Well there's the heart of the matter," he said. "My appointment is with Chief Superintendent Turnbull at the police house, which is why you and I meeting like this strikes me as so fortuitous."

The policeman lost all signs of thawing. He raised his head warily and peered at the stranger in the heavy morning air. "And why might I ask would you need such an appointment with Mr Turnbull?" he muttered, "Who I may add is a very busy man, and whose door is not open to admit every wanderin' stranger from stormy sea journeys, no matter how early in the day he happens to arrive in port."

Piper was tired. His patience was already wearing thin. Why had he even approached this man? He could surely have found his way to the police house by asking directions from any common tradesman in the street, of which by now there were many, striding with familiar routine about their morning business.

He pressed on with measured politeness. "I'm sure he's very busy," he said, "But I do have an appointment, as I say. I am expected, and I wondered perhaps if you can assist me by pointing me in the direction of his office?"

"Well, perhaps I could do just that," responded the other, sensing the subtle change in tone towards which this conversation was listing, "if perhaps you could indicate to me just what this exactin' business of yours might be about."

Piper breathed heavily and ground his heel into the stone beneath his foot. He looked about him warily.

"It's private business, and somewhat sensitive in nature," he said slowly. "I merely need to be directed to the place of which I speak. A simple request. I'm sure you can sense its delicacy, if not its urgency."

The constable stared back, then took a deep, thoughtful breath. Piper sensed movement under the man's long coat, as if unseen hands were reaching for surety in the face of uncertainty.

"Can I ask you for your name, sir?" he said at last, his voice almost tuneful with restraint.

Piper's mind raced, weighing up and deliberating with a trained speed that fatigue eventually overpowered with an audible sigh. He succumbed to it with distaste.

"Certainly," he said. "My name is Piper. Inspector Evan Piper of the Metropolitan Police of London, Aldersgate division."

CHAPTER 2

"When aw pat on my blue coat that shines se"

There was a fire burning in the grate of a black range that stood in the corner of the upstairs room of the Police House. A handful of men were in various stages of undress, donning singlets, undershirts, and tailcoats, making ready to join the dayshift that would very soon depart to relieve the night-watch. All of them turned to look as, following the constable that he'd met on the street, Evan Piper entered. He instinctively made for the fire. One man with extravagant moustaches and side-whiskers sat nearer to it, brushing soot into the worn leather of his boots. He stopped in mid-rub, and looked up, first at Piper, then at his companion, who in return muttered something about "Mister Turnbull", in a sharp growl, then exited through a further door. Piper laid down his bag on the floor and held his hands up to the fire, his back against the silence. He turned at last, and saw the other men going about their business with only an occasional scowl in his direction.

A red-haired individual, with cheeks to match, filled a brown drinking cup with black tea from a cracked pot on the table by the window. He took a long gulp from it, and stared menacingly at Piper as he did so. No drink was offered to the visitor. By now, all of those around him were dressed in their blue coats, with grey winter trousers beneath, all except for the flame-headed one, who stood almost defiantly in a coarse green jacket, into the pocket of which he stuffed the handle of his wooden crake-rattle. One by one, they collected their tall hats from shelves near the entrance and filed out down the stairs. Sharp clangs of hammer on metal began to echo from below, where earlier Piper had passed a brass fire pump being closely examined by its four-man crew. As he'd followed the policeman in through the open doors from the street, the men had only briefly turned their attention towards him. There'd been another heavy door, this one with a tell-tale barred window, from behind which a man's voice sang a tuneless lament in the darkness, and then the stairs that had led him here.

The Police House was smaller than the one he was used to in Aldersgate, but not dissimilar. This room was made more homely by the crackling fire, which was not a feature of his own station. There was a passage beyond the inner door likely leading to offices and other rooms, and to where the constable who'd brought him in had headed some minutes earlier. An ink-written roster on a board was propped up on a chair, in front of a line of printed posters nailed to the side wall with regulations and reminders in bold, blue letters. The other walls were bare, except, curiously, for a framed portrait of a dark-haired woman with tender features, hanging carelessly at a slant on the side between the windows.

Piper caught sight of the jug of tea still on the table, and made a move to peep over its brim in the hope that he could claim a sly mouthful, but at that moment the sudden appearance of yet another, older officer at the inner door stopped him in his quest. Their eyes met for a brief and wordless moment.

"Come along here," the man said at last, with an air of tired authority. Piper picked up his bag and followed him through the doorway, and down a long passage reeking of stale tobacco-smoke and damp coats. They passed two closed doors, and then walked through the third, into a high-ceilinged, narrow space lit by a large window at the rear, in front of which an unvarnished table laden with sheets of paper and ledger books was tilted awkwardly. There was a chair beyond it, but the man to whom it belonged was standing off to one side, his face silhouetted by the grey daylight behind him. He looked towards Evan Piper in silence. The officer who had ushered him in turned on his heel without a word, pushed past him and left them alone together.

The silence stretched out between them, until Piper broke it.

"Mister Turnbull is it?" he said, adding quickly, "Apologies for burdening myself upon you at so early an hour."

The other man stretched his neck to one side before responding. "What time is it? I've been up all night, and…" He trailed off into a stifled yawn.

Piper restrained himself from drawing his watch from inside his coat, and replied with a hopeful smile, "It's not yet eight o'clock. I've missed a night's sleep myself, due to a heavy storm on the last part of my journey. I'm not a sea-going man by nature."

There was a replying smile. The other man pulled back his chair noisily and slumped into it. He rubbed his eyes hard with the fore-fingers of both hands. Piper took the opportunity to look around the room as he did so. It was

15

sparse, the grate of the tiny fireplace long without spark, the painted walls peeling and the floor scored with muddy boot-prints. A chalked scrawl upon the open door at his side announced "Superint Turnbull" in an uneven hand.

Turnbull spoke again. "There was an incident at the new roadway yesterday, near to the ferryboat landing. A landslide, caused by a severe frost they say. Somewhat beyond my usual spread of duty, but it was the railway company who was pioneering it, and some men were embedded in the fallen mass. My own constables were keen to attend, as a few of them had at one time been employed by the same company, the Newcastle and North Shields, and were familiar with some of the injured." He paused, and gazed off, momentarily in thought, then continued.

"We were there until around four o'clock, when the men were reached. Sadly three souls were lost, including one who worked in this very building up until not long ago. A scoundrel, not cut out for law-keeping, but a likeable chap all the same. Hence the sombre atmosphere that greeted you just now."

Turnbull's slow, tired drawl bore all the sharp corners and harshness of the local dialect, but was much more measured and restrained than anything Piper had heard in the hours before this. It was almost like following a dance that he had yet to learn.

The Superintendent was maybe ten or so years older than Piper, in his late forties perhaps, with thinning hair, streaked with grey at the sides. His neat beard created a stern impression, as did his firm eyebrows. He wore day clothes, not a uniform, and his black jacket, though neat

16

and brushed, showed signs of age and wear. His collar too was yellowed with age.

Piper himself suddenly felt conspicuously shabby. He hadn't washed or shaved for two days and nights, and his own black hair was flat to his head from rain and sea-spray. His light grey top-coat might blend in with London street fashion, but here seemed dandy-like and frivolous. Even his tall hat, much celebrated and admired by the men on his watch in Aldersgate, seemed laughingly out of place with its light-grey smooth pile and pale silk band. It had been one of his late father's last purchases, and Piper cherished it, and occasionally even revelled in its garishness. He sensed that Turnbull, and likely all the other men that had witnessed his entrance moments before, had studied his appearance, and already formed their own judgements.

Turnbull rearranged a pile of papers on the desk in front of him, and pulled out a sheet that Piper recognised from the crest at the head. Turnbull glanced at it.

"Tell me, Inspector ..." he paused and consulted the page in his hand, "Inspector Piper. Do you have miscreants and rogues amongst the men in your own police-house in..." He looked down again, but with unseeing eyes. This little charade was not amusing Piper in the slightest. "In Aldersgate?"

"I have no doubt," he replied, "but our division is somewhat longer-established than yours. It was among the first that Mr Peel initiated, so maybe we've learned more about sniffing them out and casting them back from where they came."

Turnbull glanced up at Piper and let the letter fall from his fingers. He nodded slowly, and leaned back.

"Your superior Mr Banks frames this as a letter of introduction, without really explaining the nature of your visit, or what you might expect by way of assistance from me and my men. Relative novices we may be compared to your own squad, but we're no less busy because of that." He paused and resumed his cold stare, adding, "You've endured a long, and I'd imagine, expensive journey, and yet I'm provided with no information as to what has inspired such an undertaking. Forgive me if I display some…" He searched for a word, "some concern, or indeed some mild suspicion at your arrival at my door."

Piper returned the stare, and leaned gently against the open door. He was ready for this reaction, but feigned polite surprise.

"Suspicion?" he said, arching his brows. "Why suspicion? It's my turn to be intrigued by your words, I have to say."

Turnbull loosened slightly. "Come, Mister Piper. Our force here in Newcastle is only seven years established, with no major accomplishments, and with little or no public credit. On the contrary, my men and I are faced with resentment and disdain by a good section of the very populace that we have been appointed to protect. And now, suddenly, with little explanation, an officer is sent three hundred miles to nestle into the bosom of our enterprise, to witness first hand our standards of efficiency and organisation, not to mention our honesty and dedication, and then presumably to make a return journey with all such information in hand to be shared and reported upon to those who sent you. You see my point, Inspector?"

Piper smiled. "Ah! A spy in your midst," he said. "A Judas. I do indeed see your point, and it's one I anticipated, which is why I have permission from Inspector Banks to bring you, and you alone, into my full confidence from the outset. I know of no other way to prove myself and rise above this awkwardness."

"If your confidence is so exclusive a commodity then, should I feel honoured to have a share in it?" Turnbull tried to keep the sneer out of the words, but barely succeeded in doing so.

Piper let out a long breath. He was suddenly tired again. He'd imagined such a conversation from the outset, but not at so early an hour, and without rest from his journey. Nevertheless, he thought, he'd have to make the best of it.

"I see you have only one chair," he said, "Perhaps there's somewhere we can go to continue this conversation in comfort. And a warm drink and a crust of something wouldn't go amiss, for my part. The effect of the tossing sea is beginning to wear off on my empty stomach."

Turnbull stretched in his seat and stood up. "There's a bread-maker on the High Bridge. He's used to allowing us a quiet corner and some privacy, and his girdle-scones are a particular favourite with the constables. We can go there."

He stood and emerged from behind the table. Piper noticed his mud-caked boots and soiled gaiters. The hem of his overcoat too was similarly stained. Once he'd put it on, Turnbull led the way out through the narrow passage, across the warm day-room, and down the stairs. They were soon back in the dank cold of the busy street. Piper glanced at the shuffling men and swaying women that thronged before him. The northern climate had weathered them. The stink of coal had narrowed their eyes and shortened their breath, and here in one of the wider streets of this warren of a city, their hardiness stood out in the pale morning light. Turnbull noticed Piper's roving eye and slowed his pace to engage him in conversation as they walked.

"You took the steamer?" he said. "Which boat runs here in mid-week?"

"The Innisfail," Piper replied. "Under Captain Murray. A determined man. There was talk of us sheltering at the Humber, but he ploughed on. I didn't thank him for that. It was quite a storm."

"He has a timetable to worry about, as we all do. But count yourself lucky. The Apollo left the Wear a week ago, for Amsterdam, and is reported lost with all hands yesterday." He turned with a grim look. "On your journey back to the south, perhaps a coach would suit you better."

Piper allowed himself a smile. "A colleague of mine went by coach to Doncaster last April, when the long routes were still in place. On his return he took to his bed for a week with back-pains and aching joints. Ten hours of torture is how he marked it."

"Soon you'll have the option of the railway, wherever you need to go. There's talk of a direct line from here to London within the year. How that'll affect the traders and businesses up here is much discussed. There are those who'll fight it, much like the keelmen did, when the first paddle steamers sailed up the Tyne. Those keelmen a rare breed now, in all their yellow finery and high living. All those years of struggle with Hostmen and coal companies don't count for much when the engineers and architects get a firm grip on things. The changes come thick and fast, and the best we can do is try to keep up with them."

Piper pressed on with this line of talk, hoping that it would smooth a path for what was to come. He also sensed he might have a liking for this fellow, despite his sullen attitude.

"I saw much hard labour and demolition happening on my way to see you this morning," he said. "Yonder, through that lane, I believe, away from the river."

"To the west there? Yes, they're tearing down the old rows and promising us tall terraces and stone blocked halls, with an ornate square around a flower garden, right here in the middle of the town." He smirked, knowingly. "Well, we shall see, but at least those hovels and middens will be cleared away. The very air was putrid around them. There'd have been another rush of the cholera before long, if something hadn't been done. And there's none of us who lived through the last one that could cope with another such thing."

He quickened his pace, and pushed through a group of gossiping women in poke bonnets and shawls that had gathered at the entry of a narrow lane. Piper followed him into a narrow-windowed shop, from which the warm smell of bread oozed forth into the morning. Without a word, Turnbull caught the eye of a squat man in floury white, busy stacking a pile of long trays behind a low counter. He raised his eyebrows and pointed towards the rear of the premises, and in response the baker gave a wide toothless smile and an elaborate nod of his head. Turnbull pressed his way on, and Piper followed him into a tight space where a flour-dusted table and two chairs were pushed against a wall. No sooner had they sat down, than a breathless woman, also in white baker's livery, arrived with a tray bearing two cracked cups full of tea, and two flat, round dough cakes on a tin plate. A lump of beef lard was on a sliver of paper in the middle of it.

Turnbull nodded his thanks and motioned for Piper to take his share. The tea was only just warm, but was the first thing that had passed Piper's lips since the day before. The cake was thick to the taste, but the lard helped it down. The two men ate in silence for a few minutes, then finally, perhaps for the first time, Piper felt Turnbull look him straight in the eye.

"So tell me, Inspector Piper of London," he said gently, with an amused and sardonic smile upon his face, "What could possibly be so important to have brought you all this way through stormy seas and foul November weather, if it not be murder, treason, or the threat of war for our beloved nation?"

Piper returned his smile, and very gently put down the empty cup that he'd been holding.

"Oh, it's actually all of those things," he said, "And likely more besides."

CHAPTER 3

"Sic verra fine things"

Evan Piper's part in this chain of events was somewhat incidental, accidental even, and, moreover, a relatively recent development. On top of that, despite having been handed what he took to be a significant role in a larger investigation, he was fully aware that many of the facts, as known to his superiors, had not been shared with him. Now, faced with the need to explain the situation to a less-than-sympathetic outsider, a trust in whom he had yet to establish, it seemed like a very big step was about to be taken.

When he had first heard a certain name mentioned, in passing, at the assize court of The Old Bailey, a mere three weeks ago, he had been involved in a completely different case. It was one concerning an Aldersgate street gang, a foolhardy set of ruffians who met at the local Shakespeare Tavern to organise forays to Mile End, with an intention of terrorising local stallholders into parting with money and goods, in order to allay the threat of violence against them and their wares. It was a simple ploy, set up by simple men, and Piper had found little difficulty in seeking out the main perpetrators and slamming the door of justice in their face.

One morning at their court-hearing, Piper had had cause to confer with a middle-aged constable who had played a not insignificant part in the operation, by the name of George Selkirk, officially noted in court proceedings as PC G327. Selkirk was not part of Piper's regular watch, but had proved trustworthy and reliable in this case, and while waiting for the court session to begin, Piper had found it no trouble to start up an amiable conversation about less official business with his junior-ranking colleague. It was in the course of this friendly chat, that PC Selkirk had mentioned in passing the recent death of a cousin, John Selkirk by name, in a tragic accident in his native town of Newcastle. A drowning, no less. Upon offering condolences, Piper had been thanked, but the other man had admitted that he had only met the deceased on a very few occasions, when this cousin had himself been living in London some ten or more years before. It seems that at that time, the company that the man had been keeping was far from desirable, in the opinion of a newly recruited member of Mr Peel's police force. The constable had thus kept his distance from his northern relation, and he and the rest of the family had eventually lost track of him. The last he had heard, he told Piper, was that John Selkirk had returned to Newcastle a ruined man, thwarted in business and addled by drink.

Then, he said, a few days before, Constable Selkirk's uncle had come into possession of a Tyneside newspaper, copies of which were regularly brought to the capital by traders on the collier brigs, and shared amongst their displaced kinsmen. It had been in one of these papers that notice of the tragedy concerning the lost cousin had been reported, and consequently the rest of the family had been informed.

At that point in the conversation, Constable Selkirk was called to give his testimony, and at day's end the two men had parted with a handshake. Later that evening, while

24

walking back to the police station at Aldersgate, the name of John Selkirk had begun to ring vague bells in Piper's mind, and it was in this way that the present chain of events had begun to take shape. It hadn't taken long for him to trace the source of those bells.

Now, sitting in a baker's backroom three hundred miles from home, the banality of this somewhat domestic saga, along with the combination of vague chance and coincidence which was the background to it, caused Evan Piper to be cautious and circumspect in divulging the nature of his mission to the cynic of a man with whom he was now sharing a table. Turnbull's face showed no trace of emotion as Piper began to unravel his tale. He stared into Piper's eyes blankly from the moment the latter first spoke, as if determined not to be daunted, impressed or convinced by anything he said.

Piper spoke firmly but cautiously. "On the twelfth day of this month," he said, "a mere two weeks ago from today, a man called John Selkirk died here in Newcastle, in particular and somewhat tragic circumstances." He raised a hand in emphasis. "You'd have likely had no cause to be aware of it," he said. "The man was a drunkard, and wastrel, and when he was found, floating face down in the river that day, there were few who mourned him, and fewer still who were surprised at how he had met his end. There was an inquest, as required by law, and a mention in the local press, and that was the end of it. Then, by chance, news of the incident reached London, where the man had relatives, and by an even more unlikely series of events, that news reached the office of my superiors, where the name of John Selkirk of Newcastle had already made itself known in a very different light."

Instinctively, Piper pulled in his chair and leaned forward towards Turnbull as he continued his story.

"You'll be aware of course of the attempt upon the life of the Prime Minister, earlier this year," he said, "Resulting in the death of Edward Drummond, his secretary?"

Turnbull broke his silence. "Death, through negligence on the surgeon's part, it was said."

Piper shrugged. "Be that as it may. A man was arrested for the crime, and charged."

"McNaught, or McNaughton was it, some such name? A Scot, and a maniac. He's led by illusions and insanity. There was nothing more to it than that, so we're told."

Piper nodded. "And that is possibly true, and it's certainly the official attitude." He paused, choosing his words carefully. "But there's another train of thought, one that could maybe warrant more investigation. The man McNaught is surely guilty of pulling the trigger, but he has had certain associations in his life that suggest that a wider enterprise was at work in spurring him on to his actions, and that perhaps that work is not yet done. As we speak, the country is riddled with radicals, extremists, Irish zealots, Chartist sympathisers, and others, none of whom have much fondness for Mr Peel and the Whigs. The French are still smarting from their drubbing, and indeed it's known that the man McNaught has travelled in France." He paused. "As also, we're informed, did the recently deceased John Selkirk."

Turnbull shook his head in obvious disbelief.

"Wait a moment," he said. "Are you telling me a ragged drunkard found floating by the banks of the Tyne last week was somehow involved in a heinous assassination attempt upon our Prime Minister in our capital city, some ten or eleven months ago?" He smirked in undisguised contempt at the notion, then leant back with a look of disdain. His features then gathered a more troubled look. "So, you have come all this way to tell me this," he said. He let out a long, contemptuous breath. There was a silence between the two men. Turnbull's face gradually grew more serious. "So let me ask you, Inspector Piper," Turnbull said slowly, "What then are you *not* telling me?"

Piper stared back at him. "What I'm not telling you," he said, "is what I do not know. I'm acting under the direction of men with more insight and more information than you or I. They gave me instructions to investigate the man Selkirk, here upon his home ground. He's been in their sights for some time I gather, but his whereabouts have been unknown to them. His possible connection with recent events is unlikely to be the only reason for my enquiries. Indeed, it's a full twelve years since the man lived in London, but even then he was of interest to certain offices, mainly due to the company he was keeping. However, the details of most of this affair are deemed to be not my concern. I'm here merely to add to the information that is presumably already known."

Turnbull's face looked puzzled suddenly. "And why you? Why were you chosen for the task?"

Piper smiled. "Because I'm cursed with wide ears and an unforgiving memory. The name of Selkirk was mentioned, among scores of others, when the assassination

27

happened last January, and then when I heard it again in passing, only a week or so since, it rang a vague and distant bell. I rashly raised the matter with my superior Mr Banks, and he in turn mentioned it to others. Thereupon he came back to me with the orders that led me here. More than once, especially on the sickening sea-journey that I was forced to endure last night, I questioned the sense of this entire escapade, but the gravity with which my orders were delivered causes me to treat the matter with due care and concern. You yourself can take the whole thing as you choose, but I was obliged to acquaint you of the details as I know them, seeing as how I'm now stepping into your realm."

Turnbull rubbed his eyes again, and sighed heavily. "I think sir, that you've been sent on a fool's errand." He paused. "But I'm in sympathy with your position, knowing that you act under solemn orders. I'll give any assistance I can, within the boundaries of my own pressing duties. I can't afford the time to simplify your task, any more than I have time to ridicule it. Keep from under my feet and I'm happy to tolerate your presence." He chewed his lip as he considered it all, then continued. "I'll inform my men that you're working as agent to your own Superintendent on a personal matter. They too may have sympathy with that burden, and treat you accordingly. As far as the police house is concerned, come and go as you please." He stood up and pulled his coat about him. "I must return there myself now. Do you have lodgings?"

"Yes, and I'll spend the rest of the day there." Piper was suddenly exhausted. "I might need a few pointers from your sergeant as to the layout of your town and its various procedures, but that can wait until tomorrow."

"Yes, my sergeant will advise you on that. His name is Fitzsimmons. He's a solid and astute man. Some of the others you'll encounter at the police-house are less trustworthy, as I say, but that need not concern you. I'll tell Sergeant Fitzsimmons to offer you any assistance you need."

Outside, they parted with a curt nod from Turnbull, and Piper found himself once more alone in this strange place. The cold breeze cut deeply into his fatigue. He walked diagonally across what he knew to be Pilgrim Street, and through a dismal alley, where street-scavengers were sifting through a mound of their spoils. The cobbles rose up in a gentle slope, with anonymous shop windows and door-less entries at either side, and then suddenly gave way to a wider street sloping sharply upwards to the right. On the path in front of Piper, hollow-cheeked women were raking through heaps of old clothes laid out on canvas sheets stretched out upon the ground. A tall, thin man wreathed in unknown misery was watching over them suspiciously. Further up the street, wooden stalls and trestles were lined in formal rows, though most were empty of wares, save for an amply-filled vegetable display in the centre.

Piper looked about, and saw a faded sign fastened to the wall above him, which read "Bigg Market". A few steps further on, he caught sight of a board swinging above a wide-windowed frontage, upon which a unicorn was depicted, raised on its hind legs, with its principle feature, a long and pointed horn embossed impressively in gold, plain to see. He passed through the meagre crowd and resisted the temptation to buy anything from the stall. As he approached the hostelry, a woman in grey skirts and a startlingly-red blouse came out of the door with a broom in her hand. She was about forty years of age, but with little grey visible in her glossy black hair. Her skin was the colour of the gipsy women that hung around the London thoroughfares of Pick Hatch and Clerkenwell on mornings such as this. Her dark eyes too betrayed similar origins. She immediately saw him approaching, and eyed the bag in his hand, and then the hat upon his head, with wary curiosity.

Piper raised his stovepipe in her direction.

"Mrs Dixon?" he inquired of her.

"Aye, that's me", came the reply.

"I have a room booked, through the agency of a Mr Jack Rowtledge, from the Town Clerk's Office, though I'm afraid I'm a day late in getting here."

She leaned her head to one side in what he felt was a dangerously attractive manner, much practised, and wiped down the front of her apron with her hand.

"They all talk like that where ye come from, d'they? Charm and that?"

Piper smiled. "Well, no," he said, "Only the polite ones like myself, who find themselves a long way from home and in dire need of rest and repose."

"Mister Pipe, is it?" she said.

"Piper, Evan Piper. My ship's arrival last night was delayed. I made my way here as directly as I could, in the hope that the room's still vacant. I've had a long and somewhat eventful journey, and I'm sorely in need of sleep."

She looked at him for a long moment, then her eyes softened. "Why man, how can Ah resist such a sad tale?" she said at last. "Get yoursel' inside, and Ah'll get ye settled."

Evan Piper followed her in through the tall doorway, and immediately up a narrow flight of stairs. Mrs Dixon pushed open a door at the top of the landing and led him into a dark space, which brightened as she drew back a single brown curtain. It was a sparse but tidy room with a washstand, a wide bed with a patched green woollen blanket cast over it. There were four hooks set in the near wall, two of which had long since been deprived of their points of usefulness.

The landlady garbled in some detail about the rules of the house, the times of access and the urgency of payment, most of it in as strong an accent as Piper had heard since his arrival. Fatigue was about to overpower him, when at last Mrs Dixon closed the door with some effort behind her, and dropping his coat onto the floor and his hat on the washstand, he sank onto the bed.

As he closed his eyes, the sounds outside could just as easily have rattled a London window. A cawing street-vendor's cry, the high whine of an infant, the pointless bark of a dog, the chatter of children and the carefree laugh of a young woman, all sung to the tune of a low-whistling wind and gentle patter of rainfall.

He was asleep within moments, and tramping with heavy feet through dreams of home.

CHAPTER 4

"Gaun to keek at lunnin"

To a small boy, London was merely four or five streets, leaning into one other, filled with voices and smells, and swarming with older children, making mischief, being scolded by faceless mothers in faded skirts and thinning woollen shawls. Unwashed and often unwanted, always thin and ragged, the children glared and stared and then erupted into squealing confusion and destruction, or shuffled back and forth together, in exclusive bands of tiny outlaws. Their mothers and fathers inevitably kept a distance from each other, and instead hunted in packs. The men could be seen standing listlessly on corner-ends smoking pipes, their moustaches masking any individuality, their voices low and measured. The women stood in doorways, chattering and keening, whispering and cawing, all with drawn, anxious looks on their faces, and resentment in their eyes. The children bothered around the mothers, squabbled with each other, tripped, bled and cried and then threw stones and sticks at invisible demons. At day's end, everyone would reluctantly dissolve into family groups once more. With rarely a word between man and wife, the air instead would rattle with the sound of hunger, of tiredness and of hopelessness.

It changed little as Evan Piper grew to be an adult. He was a lanky young lad, thin and quiet, but dark-featured and not without a boyish handsomeness. His tendency to be often deep in thought, however, caused unease among many around him. There did come an age when girls began to take a liking to him, but he was wary of them, and oblivious to any approaches that came his way. Eventually they turned their gazes elsewhere. When any particular face took his fancy, he was clumsy and awkward, and habitually took a step back that he was never really courageous enough to retrace.

Luckily, he wasn't morosely sentimental, as his mother always claimed his father had been. Evan took each day as it came, but smouldered with an undefined ambition. The future may have scared him, but the past only bored him. Occasionally he'd find himself reminiscing over a forgotten face or a missing place, but by and large, there were few memories that occupied him. He had no recollection of the epidemics and illnesses that took away the small bodies that he'd once seen scurrying around past his own mother's door, and not even the one that almost took him. He was a survivor in a world where so very many did not survive. He'd known everyone, and sometimes ran alongside them, sometimes joined in their wrong-doings, but more often just wished he'd dared to do such things. His sense of right and wrong lay heavy on him from an early age.

His father had been a clerk for a hat-maker in West Cheapside, and was a kind man. People liked him, Evan knew that. If there was trouble in the street, a drunken husband, a lost child, a debt that couldn't be paid, Mister Piper was the man that people turned to. The wisdom of his words and his sure concern for the well-being of others were a real balm that sustained many in their daily struggles. His own worries and cares, he kept to himself, and he was indeed a quiet, inward-looking man, even to his own family. When he'd died of a swift fever, Evan was sixteen years old, and the street was a crowd of silent mourners and sombre faces, all looking lost without their Mister Piper. Evan was enraged by it. The man should have been his alone to weep over. They had no right to be moved by his departure in such a way.

Evan's mother was a seamstress, and worked as a slop-trade stitcher at their old wooden kitchen table, a teetering candle as the only light, her bent fingers sore and bleeding, her eyes squinting and scowling. Twice a week, she bundled up the shirts and linen that she had worked on, and carried them to an upstairs loft in sight of the old city walls, with a tall grey tree outside it, where she would swap them for a small bundle of coins wrapped in a calico patch, and another round of linens to be worked on. Evan often went with her, and remembered the widest street, with juddering omnibuses pulled by unhappy horses, and rattling carts and flat-backed barrows, and rushing, angry people, and soldiers proud of their uniforms, their scars and their missing limbs. The women there were slim and hatted, the men suited and haughty. No children ever came to this street, he realised, and he always worried about his own presence there.

Once he'd seen the dome-topped cathedral, hiding at the end of a long row of tall, chequered buildings, and another time there'd been a crowd of folk surrounding a tall man with a silver beard, standing higher than everyone, with his hands raised and his head thrown back in anger, shouting about God. Evan knew why the man was shouting. God was far away, high in the sky, through the grey smoke and the scudding clouds, waiting for Sunday's bells to call him down to the church at the end of his Aunt Alice's street. His mother would take him there every week. He liked it, though his father never went near the place. The strict shadow of the chapel in the Welsh valley of his childhood had sucked a love of God, and maybe even a belief in Him, out of his father's life forever. Evan began to feel ashamed that he went to church at all, and despite himself, eventually refused to accompany his mother, much to her bewildered disappointment. He would watch her go, longing to walk off beside her, but conscious of the presence of his father, silent in his ungodly stubbornness, almost daring him to succumb to piety. It would be a long time before Evan entered through the door of a church again.

At the end of the French Wars, when Evan had been ten years old, there had been a victory parade in one of the new parks, too great a distance for most from their district to travel to, but his father had woken him in the darkness of an early morning. The pair of them had walked and walked as the night turned from grey to light, and somewhere far away, flanked by high, wide houses and smothered by laughing, wide-eyed people, Evan had seen soldiers in red and gold, flags of white and blue, heard music from shining brass and thumping drum, and had been transfixed by the perfect march and step of straight and noble men, young ones, old ones and ancient ones, in pointed hats and dangling feathers.

Evan had scraped their images with stone on stone, on walls and on footways up and down their lane, and told everyone he met what a sight it had all been. One had been

Wellington, he claimed. Another had been the King himself, he was sure of it.

A long time later, there had been a riot at the docks of Mile End, and Evan had woken to hear the clatter of a hundred horses' hooves pass by the end of the street. He'd rushed out to see the last of the Bow Street Horse Patrol, decked out in their blue top-coats and scarlet waistcoats, making their way to establish order and normality once again.

From that moment, his ambition in life was to wear that uniform. There were no more wars to tempt him into a tunic, but he'd be a soldier nonetheless, one that looked after the people around him, much like his own father had done, protecting them from rioters and robbers and footpads instead of Frenchmen and Corsicans. So at the age of seventeen, after a succession of local, menial jobs, he'd walked with a crowd of other lads from his neighbourhood into the Bow Street Magistrates building, and signed his name onto a list for recruitment and training. He'd spent a long two months cleaning out stables and chopping firewood for a shilling a week. Then one by one, the other lads had drifted off, while he'd persisted through a heavy winter. It would be nearly two years before he was given the black coat and tall hat of an officer of Sir John's Runners, and allowed to accompany a long-serving officer, named Joseph Watts, on daily patrols along Barbican and down to Threadneedle Street. Watts had once been a paid Thief Taker, and was sly and opportunistic, as were many of the Runners in those last few years of the squad's existence. He tried to ensnare young Piper into his shady antics and slovenly approach to their task, but somehow

Evan had remained aloof from it. Watts was eventually dismissed for his dubious pursuits, and Evan soon found himself as a trusted assistant to Rupert Banks, the Chief Handler at Bow Street.

His dedication and thoroughness was overwhelming. It had been a good deal of time before he realised that he had no life of his own, outside of his role as a Runner. His position and responsibilities came at a high price. His old acquaintances had begun to avoid him. Neighbours no longer looked in his direction when he returned to his mother's house at day's end, and the one girl that he had set his eyes upon, now scorned him and barely acknowledged his presence when he approached her.

The very tunic that he had coveted had become a curse and a stigma. Poverty had forced everyone to adopt a life tinged with dishonesty and shadiness, and Evan Piper was regarded as a cuckoo in the nest, never to be taken into a confidence, never to be trusted, a man whose allegiance to the law far outweighed his loyalty to those who had grown up and lived around him. But even when the truth of this dawned on him, he refused to go back. Rupert Banks had recognised a skill in him, and nourished it. He found him a room to move into, above a shipping office in Newgate Street, and never hesitated to lay responsibilities in the young man's hands.

But it was a lonely life. Piper was tall now, fresh-faced with wavy black hair, and readily adopted his late father's formal mode of dress when out of uniform. More than once he sensed interest from young women who passed him by on their way to the cloth-shops beyond the old city walls. They'd walk haughtily past him, arm in arm, aloof and silent, then burst into giggles and glance back when he'd passed. But this was only when he was in his street clothes. When he was in his Bow Street tunic and hat, they would cross the street to avoid him.

His accent also became an issue for him. His mother had retained much of the West Country burr in her speech, and his father often fell noticeably into a Welsh lilt, though never the Welsh tongue itself. Evan had naturally picked up flavours of all these things as a child, and the rough tongues of the street had failed to knock it out of him. By the time he fell under the influence of Rupert Banks at Bow Street, his words came out in an unwieldy sing-song form, which plainly caused amusement among his fellow Runners. Defensively, rather than pretentiously, he began to emulate Mister Banks' own way of speaking, and had soon developed a rather flat but never-strident cadence which suggested an education which he was frankly lacking. This too he tried to remedy, over long, candle-lit nights with a table-full of dusty books and periodicals that he'd found in a store-cupboard at the magistrates building. Those around him noticed all this. Some encouraged it, some ridiculed it, but almost all admired it, either secretly or overtly.

Evan Piper eventually made his professional mark when he was actively involved in the arrest of a man known as Black Eyed Jack Stirabout, one of the notorious London Burkers. This was a gang of grave-robbers-turned murderers, who were supplying corpses to the new medical school at Greenwich. When the gang had finally been exposed, Jack Stirabout was the last to be apprehended, until Piper himself had spotted him, he was sure of it, outside the Pavillion Theatre in Whitechapel, just as the patrons were leaving late one Friday evening. Stirabout was loitering with a view to dipping his hand into a careless purse or pocket, when Piper had emerged from the shadows and grabbed him. He managed to restrain the villain with the help of an elderly, but still sprightly ex-army officer who had just enjoyed a night of staged melodrama, and was seemingly in the mood for some real-life thrills of a similar sort.

The London Burkers case was a much celebrated triumph for the Runners, and underlined the need for a more organised approach to law-keeping in the rapidly expanding and increasingly busy streets of the capital. When Rupert Banks was personally asked by the Prime Minister Robert Peel to help initiate a metropolitan police force, Evan Piper was one of the first to be invited to be part of the new force. He accepted and was almost immediately given the rank of Inspector, a new title, which had been adopted to avoid any militaristic overtones that might breed suspicion and wariness among ordinary folk. When Banks had warned that the rank would preclude the wearing of a uniform, Piper feigned a slight disappointment, but was secretly relieved. The boy in him had outgrown the outward show of officialdom, and he suspected the job ahead would be made easier by the wearing of plainer clothes.

Piper had been living in that upper room in Newgate ever since. He had settled into the solitary life. There were a couple of young Peelers that he occasionally shared a drink with in an alehouse at Aldersgate market, but as he outranked them, it was never an easy, relaxed gathering to be part of. Female company was something he longed for at times, but he was resigned to being without it for the foreseeable future. His life and career seemed mapped out for him in plain, ordered terms, and he had surprised himself by being so focused on duty and ambition. What routine he had was governed by the vagaries of the criminal classes, the petty and chance-taking members of which tugged at his own sympathies, more often than not. It was the increasingly active, newly emerging professional criminal that he abhorred, most of whom preyed as much on the poor and defenceless as they did upon the rich and privileged.

Beyond this, he found himself at the centre of an increasingly changing world. There was a new, young queen on the throne, and though her empire was vast, it was under siege from many sides. Even her own country was scorned and threatened from both without and within. The sense of triumph from the French Wars soon faded into distant memory, as anarchists and radicals skulked in shadows and cellars, in the very streets where Evan Piper had previously only sought out thieves and burglars. There was talk of bombs, of kidnapping, of treachery and subversion, and these were increasingly becoming a major source of preoccupation for the still fresh-faced Police Force, as yet untried and untested, and certainly still distrusted by the population as a whole.

Meanwhile, the rest of his native land was unknown to him. He had no desire to see it or acknowledge it. The rest of the world though, was making its way to his doorstep. Refugees and immigrants from across Europe and beyond had sought sanctuary in the great metropolis that London had become, and though Piper himself had no axe to grind with any of this, the diverse nationalities had brought with them all the pride and the prejudices that they had inherited from their ancestors. The melting pot of languages and religions and customs that had boiled over in the eastern ends of London, had cast a dangerous and volatile cloud of menace that hung around at every street corner, every thoroughfare, every public house and every workplace in the district.

Somehow, Evan Piper had ended up with much of this under his personal care, perhaps because he seemed to have also inherited much of his father's skill at diplomacy and persistence. Alone among his fellow police officers, Piper seemed to have a knack of establishing trust between himself and the many diverse factions that Peel's force was having to deal with on a daily basis. Strangely attired men with thick, awkward accents would ask for him by name in times of strife in their community, from whatever direction. It was a joke among his colleagues at the police house, and he himself often laughed at the position of trust in which he had unwittingly found himself. But at the same time, he relished it. He was fascinated by the dark, brooding faces and deep voices of the older men, the silent devotion of their plump wives, the jittery mistrust of their sons and the exotic beauty of their daughters. They would all watch him warily whenever he encountered them, but then bow respectfully as they went their separate ways.

So it was, as the century raced towards its mid-point, that Evan Piper was honing his skills as an enforcer of law. His territory was well-known to him, as were his enemies, and as he was to them. London was the centre of his universe, though it was now an overwhelmingly bigger, louder and more wayward London than that cluster of tiny streets which had once been his whole world.

CHAPTER 5

"But they mak a sang, man"

Evan Piper awoke, his boots still on, his body tightly tangled in coarse bedding, and a rich darkness all around. His left arm was stiff from being beneath him, and it now tingled painfully into life. The air was cold in his nostrils, but his first sensation was one of relief at not having spent another tortured night in physical and mental turmoil upon the roaring seas. The thought of another such journey to take him back to his own city, was acutely troubling for him. Why he was affected so, he couldn't understand. There had been women, old men, and even a child on the same boat with him, and they had chatted and dozed as if on a calm lake in summer, while his imagination had played evil games with him, and his insides had churned with every pitch and fall of the vessel. The nights had been worst of all, peppered with sweat-drenched waking nightmares, then alternating between head-spinning half-sleep in a cramped bunk with a snoring fellow-traveller across from him, and a petrified staggering along the rolling decks, where the quest for fresh air only brought cold spray and salty tangs that did nothing to sooth a troubled belly.

In the still steadiness of this early morning, Piper pushed all such thoughts from his mind and considered his position, following his arrival in this town. Having explained his mission aloud to Superintendent Turnbull the day before, Piper was now questioning the worth of this whole unwieldy enterprise more heartily than ever. Had he overplayed its importance, and indeed his own role within it, in an effort to be taken seriously by the other man? Turnbull's cynicism was probably justified, especially when he rightly pointed out that the only feeble link between the late John Selkirk and the events of the previous January, hinged on a full ten years gap across what was already a flimsy connection. The pathetic end that the man had come to did indeed make the entire affair quite laughable when set out in plainly-spoken conversation.

Piper's instruction had been simply to check on Selkirk's recent affiliations, to surreptitiously take note of any associations that he might have had of late, and to summarise any radical or subversive movements currently active in Newcastle and the surrounding area. It was too late to incriminate the dead man himself. Selkirk was merely a stepping stone that had to be tested, given the current political turmoil, as Piper's commander had spelt out with some feeling, following the attempt on Robert Peel's life.

Inspector Banks had sat at his desk in the high upper room of the Aldersgate police station and coldly set out the situation for Piper, a mere four days since, though it seemed like a lifetime ago from where Piper now found himself. It was clear, Banks had said, that the man Selkirk had spent time both in France, and with malcontents in London a dozen years ago, and that his associates from that time were still very much active today, even though Selkirk himself had returned to his native town. But for what purpose had been that return? How politically active had he remained in a region far from the wary gaze of national law and security, and where Irish, Scots and Continentals mixed and mingled together in a melting pot of social upheaval. Old Banks had got more passionate as he'd continued, whether through his own political leanings, or due to internal pressure that was being felt by the police force as a whole, from a higher official direction. After all, the force had been initiated by Peel himself, so there had undoubtedly been a sense of embarrassment when their role as keepers of the law had failed to protect their very own figurehead and benefactor, in the face of an assailant.

Inspector Banks had stood up as Piper turned to leave his office that day. A new age of industrial strength was dawning, he'd said, and the coal-rich, railway-linked northern towns could very easily soon reach a position where they could even unseat the elected power of London itself. Ambition had to be reined in and controlled, he'd said, and every effort had to be made to ensure that it would be.

Piper had turned all this over in his mind many times during the following few days, and did so again now, but he could not muster the same level of determination or concern for these eventualities as his superior officer had done. If men could work for a wage and feed their families, he thought, if new ideas were encouraged and developed, and if life could be made better for both rich and poor, then why stifle such enterprise in order to maintain a struggling political order?

Opinions such as these though, he knew, were best kept to himself. Crime was his concern, and he knew that crime was a commodity that thrived at every social level, high and low, rich and poor, in the north and in the south and everywhere in between.

From somewhere below him, a woman's voice rose in a swooping melody. It moved from room to room below him, and when eventually it formed itself into words, Evan Piper remained as baffled as ever as to their meaning. The singer had seemingly married poorly, and her good days were done. Her husband evidently had an ugly body and bubbly body, and the man himself was 'an ill-faced hideous loon'. And yet the melody that the song employed, betrayed a curious joy in the knowledge of all this!

Evan Piper smiled and braced himself to face the day. The light of a lamp shone briefly under his door, and then the sound of heavy feet clumping down the stairs merged into a muffled conversation, punctuated by laughter.

The curtain was still pulled open across the window, and Piper peered through the grimy glass at the day outside. The clouds were barely lit by the oncoming dawn, and looked bothered and threatening as they rolled past. He washed in the cold water from a jug on the nightstand, and defied the chill air by changing his underclothes, shivering as he did so. He fastened his overcoat and brushed dust from the rim of his hat, then spent minutes on the dark landing, forcing his door into a position that would agree with the lock. He pocketed the key and descended the stairs. The noise he made had alerted Mrs Dixon, who hailed him from the inner room below, a small parlour that looked on to the main saloon bar.

"There's a heel o' bread and some potted hough at yon table," she said, drying her hands on a grubby cloth. "And help yoursel' to tea from the pot. Ye got some sleep then? It was quiet down here last night, so no wonder ye slept through."

Piper nodded. "Yes, thank you," he replied. "I was indeed tired. I feel a lot better."

She watched him cut the bread and sniff gingerly at the fatty lump next to it. It was mainly grease, but with some remnants of meat speckled through it. He took a slice of it on a knife and spread it on the bread. It actually tasted wholesome and good. He mimed his thanks to her through a mouthful.

"So y'er from London?" the woman asked. He nodded again. She continued. "Ah had a man from London stayin' last year. His name was Roberts. Rupert Roberts. A surveyor for the railway. D'ye know him?"

Piper shook his head. "The name doesn't ring a bell with me, I'm afraid."

She pressed on. "A shortish chap, with fairish hair and a dark beard. Dressed well. He said he was a London lad. Ah thought maybe ye'd bumped into him."

Piper shrugged, "Well it's a big place. Like here, but much bigger. Swarms of people. I don't think I've ever come across him."

Mrs Dixon stared at him for a moment. "Well Ah know it's a big place," she said with an edge to her voice. "Ah just though ye might've run into him, seein' as how y'er in the same business." Piper looked up quizzically. "The railways," she said. "That's why y'er here isn't it, for the new line to the coast?"

Piper jolted slightly. "Oh yes," he said quickly, "But not in surveying. I'm more an office planner. I rarely meet up with surveyors." She continued to stare at him. He ploughed on regardless. "That accident yesterday," he said, remembering his conversation with Turnbull. "What a tragedy. Not my concern officially, more of a surveyor's problem, but a tragedy none the less."

Mrs Dixon softened slightly. "Aye," she said. "One of those lads used to spend evenin's in here, though Ah can't place him meself. There was a gent talkin' about him last night, and a few of the regulars knew him. But Ah can't mind him at all. It was the frost, they reckon. That's what caused the slide. Of course, Ah remember the big frost, when Ah was a girl. A terrible winter, that. The Tyne was froze for a week. The whole toon came to a stoppage. A lot o' deaths, poor bairns, old 'uns, watermen an' all. Ye have to dread that happenin' again. And it's only November!"

Piper listened to her, nodding his head. He felt he had avoided suspicion to some extent. Obviously Mr Rowtledge, whoever he was, had given him a mild alias as a railwayman when he'd been asked to book the room, by letter from London. There'd been no time or opportunity to discuss it.

"I have the room for the week, I think?" he said as he rose.

"As long as ye like," came the reply. "There's no custom for it at this time o' year. There's two others taken, but they're acquaintances. Ye can come and go as ye like as well, but Ah bolt up at eleven o'clock. Join us down here for a drink o' summat' if ye have in mind this evenin'."

Piper smiled. "Thank you, I might do that." He straightened his coat, and then added as an afterthought, "Actually, I did meet somebody in London who knew the town, only a few weeks ago. He'd had family up here and there'd been another tragedy. A Mister Selkirk. A drowning accident I believe, by the bridge."

Mrs Dixon stared back at him, her eyes wide. "Old Johnny?" she said, in some amazement. "Ye heard tell o' him all the way at London?"

Piper pulled back slightly. "Well, a cousin of his mentioned it. The family had been contacted I suppose. There was no closeness, but a tragedy like that makes a mark on kinfolk, I'm sure. Was he someone you knew?"

The woman leaned back against the table behind her and nodded her head in sadness. "Well, he was a sorry sight in recent years, with the drink," she said. "Ah have to say, Ah wouldn't have allowed him in my door, looking as he did, but he was known well enough at the taverns on Sandgate, and at the quayside. They thought nowt about takin' off him what little he had. But he was a popular lad at one time because of his poetry. That was twenty years ago, Ah reckon, and everybody was singin' his verse at that time. Then he went off, to London as well in fact, so Ah heard, to make his damn fortune. But he came back spent and wasted. Even his own brother neglected him after that. An awful condition, Ah'm surprised he lived as long as he did, poor little bugger. Ah saw him at the pant, not six weeks since, hardly recognised him but for his thick toppin' o' hair. Dressed in rags, filth on him, sleepin' in the wood-shop, somebody said."

Evan Piper listened, perhaps too intently, to her words. He restrained himself as she finished, and then tried hard to conceal his interest.

"So he was a poet of some sort, this man?" he said. "With some reputation?"

"Well, of course he was!" came the reply. "D'ye not hear of 'Bob Cranky' and his adventures? Why, man, he was truly comical, and sharp as a needle with it. Ye still hear folks singin' them. At Balmbra's, at The Wheatsheaf, even in me own sittin' room here. He was as talented as any of them. But whereas some o' them have kept at it and have been more popular because of it, Old Johnny just drifted away, as he always did, and folks forgot. They remembered the songs, but forgot the man that cast them!"

Piper listened with some amazement. "I had no knowledge of all that, I have to say. And he has a brother? I did mention to the cousin of his that I'd pass on any sympathy to any relative I happened to come across during my stay in the town."

Mrs Dixon stood up with a sigh. "Aye," she said, "His brother Jimmy is a clerk at Bell's Court, at the top end o' Pilgrim Street. They're a good family. His own father was a hairdresser in the Close, where the mayor's residence stands now." She stared off into a middle distance, in some thought, adding at last, "Here Ah am, peddlin' drink, and all to add to the ruination of folk like Johnny." She shook it off. "Well, a body has to make a livin'," she said as she marched out through the doorway and into another room beyond.

It was after ten o'clock when Evan Piper finally sidled into the police house at the bottom end of Pilgrim Street. The morning had threatened rain, but when none came, he had taken the opportunity to explore the byways and

52

alleys, known locally as "chares", as he soon learned, that led him away from his lodging and back towards the river. The quayside was even busier than it had been when he first saw it, and he'd stood at one end of the stone bridge across the river, leading to the town of Gateshead, nestling like a younger sibling on the opposite side. It had been there, on the Gateshead side, that John Selkirk had met his untimely end. No ship ventured this far up the water, but fast-flowing barges filled with coal, known as keels, were plentiful, deftly skimming under the stone arches and weaving their way about in the skilful hands of powerful young men in flat tar-hats and short jackets. Whether their skill would outlive the advent of the powerful, larger steam-powered vessels that were already berthed downstream, as if in waiting of their destiny, it was impossible to say. The old bridge was the hurdle that the newcomers were unable to pass. Talk of a new, higher bridge was already rife, which would mean that access to coal stathes further up the river would be open for all-comers, no matter their size.

Piper gleaned all of this in a stilted conversation with two old men in matching woollen caps, sharing a pipe of tobacco between them, as they sat on the edge of a stone trough by the dockside. He had resisted the temptation to ask them about the death of John Selkirk, which had occurred within sight of where they now were. In truth, the circumstances of how the man had died had no bearing on his enquiries, as far as he was aware.

All was quiet inside the police station when he finally arrived there. The constables were already out on the streets, and the fire-grate was cold and lifeless. He took the time to study a large chart of the town, mapped in grey with all the major streets named, and a key below for numbered side streets and back alleys. It was a flat blur to him at first, but at last he managed to trace the path of his excursion of that morning, and the layout began to make sense at last. He tore a page from his London duty-book, as ever in his pocket, and with a pencil he picked up from the table next to him, he scrawled a basic plan of the immediate district on the north side of the river, between his lodging at The Unicorn and the place where he now stood.

He was aware at once that someone had entered the room behind him, and he turned about. It was the sergeant that he had seen very briefly the day before, and who had led him to Turnbull's office. Fitzsimmons, if he correctly remembered the name that Turnbull had given him.

"The Superintendent isn't here today sir," he said stiffly. "You would catch him tomorrow morning, a bit earlier than this."

Piper raised his hands in apology. "No, sergeant, that's not why I'm here. I merely needed to gather my thoughts and see the lie of the land. I noticed the chart yesterday, and took the chance to consult it without interrupting the flow of the station."

The man nodded and turned to leave. Piper stopped him.

"Actually, Sergeant," he said, "I don't suppose I can take a quick look into the duty book, just for a particular incident that happened two Saturdays ago, by the bridge? It involved a relative of a constable in London that I'm acquainted with, a man called Selkirk. It was his cousin, John Selkirk. An accidental death, of some concern to him, and to his family. They're obviously anxious to know the tragic details."

The sergeant was clearly thinking of some reason to deny the request, but Piper was already advancing across the room, so the officer turned and led the way, with a curt, "Follow me, if you please."

They filed through the first door in the gloomy passage, and into a narrow office. The duty book was already open on the table, and the sergeant cautiously approached it. He gave Piper a glowering look, and began to leaf through its pages.

"Saturday, November 12th," he muttered, his eyes scanning the length of the paper. "Here it is. Constable Ramsay reported the incident, though it was likely the night watch who attended the scene. It reads, 'The body was brought from the water at seven o'clock, having been sighted from the Gateshead side of the bridge by Mr Craddock and Mr Harris, two passers-by at four o'clock. The man was identified by Dr Rossiter, and taken to the Dead House.' That's all there is, sir. Will there be anythin' else?"

"Constable Ramsay, is he on duty today?"

The sergeant hesitated, and then looked up at a roster on the wall next to him. "Not at this moment sir. He worked Earlies for the last two days of this week, so is due to report for duty at two o'clock this afternoon. He was the man who escorted you here yesterday morning, I believe."

Piper nodded, "Oh yes, I remember. And this Doctor Rossiter, where would I find him, should I need to?"

The other man eyed him narrowly and again hesitated. "I wouldn't know sir. He's a Gateshead man, I believe. He often attends incidents at the river's edge, though he's no longer in general practice as far as I'm aware. I've seen him mentioned several times at incidents such as this."

Piper rubbed his chin thoughtfully. "I see," he said. "It's probably unnecessary to bother him then." He paused. "Thank you. It's Sergeant Fitzsimmons, isn't it? I appreciate your help. I'll try not to bother you anymore. I know you're busy enough without this trivial stuff."

The sergeant closed the book and straightened it on the table. "That's all right sir. It's undoubtedly a tragic business." He looked up slyly. "And it's a long way that you've come to ask about it. The least I can do is tell you what you need."

The words hung in the air for a moment. Piper gave a laugh. "Oh it wasn't exactly that which particularly drew me here. It's just that Selkirk, Constable Selkirk that is, is a good man, and a reliable man to boot. It's a favour to him, that's all. You know his type, Sergeant, I'm sure of it. Joined the service almost at the beginning, and works hard without the reward that lesser men in higher positions are handed." Piper looked hard at the other man. "Forgive me for saying that, but I think you will take my meaning."

Sergeant Fitzsimmons softened and smiled. "I do indeed sir, and it's gratifyin' to hear a man in your position recognise it." He hesitated a moment, then continued. "My oldest brother knew this man Selkirk, the dead man, years ago. He mentioned it to me when the report was in the Journal after the inquest. The fellow was a writer of songs, and well admired for it. Everybody knew of him, maybe twenty-odd years past. My brother Tom is nearly seventy now. He didn't know him well, but he was on speakin' terms with him, that much is true. Selkirk was known for his poetry, and his humour, long before some of them who are popular now. And folks could buy the verses in print, up on Grey Street. Those songs of his, you'd still hear them sung when I was a lad, when I was first goin' into the taverns, like The Black Boy and The Flying Horse, down at The Side and past the Sandgate. He was quite the name amongst those with an ear for such things. Then he'd gone off to London for business opportunities. That was years ago. Our Tom didn't even know he'd come back. He was affected sorely to hear what had happened to him."

Piper thought about this for a moment. "Yes," he said, "Everybody who's spoken about him is of a similar opinion. A sad case indeed. So he entertained, did he? On the music halls, is that what you mean?"

"I don't think he entertained as such, not personally. He just wrote the verse and the songs, like a lot of them do, and then the players and singers learn them and put them in their act. It's a going concern, it truly is. Very popular. They opened a new music hall at The Wheatsheaf, upstairs, just last year, and folks are flockin' to it. And not just the ordinary folks, mind. The gentry too, they see a real artistry in it, that's what they say. It's just a daft carry-on to the likes of me and you, sir, but there's moneyed folks, livin' in them big houses out on the Durham Road and up in Jesmond, they used to present it in their drawin' rooms and parlours like it was true poetry, if you can believe that. And even now, there's verses printed in books and clippin's just about every week."

Piper stared at the man.

"So it still goes on, does it, this verse-writing and song making?" he said, somewhat perplexed by this information.

The sergeant nodded.

"Certainly, certainly," he said, "More popular than ever. One of the lads here, Charlie Ramsay in fact, the man that you met yesterday, he's very taken with it, and has written a good few himself, though I don't think anybody has picked up on them yet. In fact he's come up with a corker about Superintendent Turnbull…"

The sergeant stopped himself suddenly. "Oh excuse me sir, I didn't mean to say that about Mr Turnbull. He's a good man, no-one can say otherwise."

Piper smiled broadly. "No harm done sergeant, none at all. This is all so interesting, I had no idea I was in the company of poets and songsters and the like. I'm somewhat astonished by it all, to be honest."

"Oh yes sir," came the reply. "It's a busy thrivin' concern. There's poets and writers around every corner. Everything that happens, every day of the week, someone turns a verse or two out about it. The Bards of the Tyne they call themselves. Everybody's tryin' to get a hand at it. And who wouldn't do? Better than hewin' coal for a livin', you must admit."

Piper nodded his head. Better indeed, he thought. Still, he was somewhat taken aback by all this. It hadn't escaped his notice that everywhere he'd been in the city since his arrival, people had been raising their voices in song. Jobbing workmen on builders flats, street merchants, his own landlady, and now even one of the constables, so he was informed, all thought nothing of launching forth into a ditty at any given opportunity. The regionalism of it intrigued him somewhat, the deeply home-grown nature of the popular verse, delivered in this obtusely slanted lilt and arcane language. Such an under-current of literary and musical enthusiasm, and one that was evidently so ingrained in the very fabric of the town, was not what he had expected. The drab and rather abrupt greyness that he experienced thus far belied such a hidden character. None of this surely had any bearing on his own case, yet the fact that the central figure in his enquiry had once played such an integral part in this curious culture, surely meant that Piper would have to dip into it himself in the course of his work. If nothing else, he thought with a smile, it would provide him with some light relief and entertainment to while away his lonely off-duty hours.

Sergeant Fitzsimmons bade him good day and vanished back along the corridor beyond, and when he immediately burst into a jolly ditty concerning the buying of brooms and the sweeping of houses as he did so, it came as no surprise to Evan Piper.

60

CHAPTER 6

"Ho'way and aw'll sing thee a tune"

Constable Ramsay was slipping his duty band over his wrist when Piper came back to the day room of the police station, having just devoured a plateful of pickled herring and rye bread, washed down with weak beer, at The Wheatsheaf a half hour previously. The pub was across the town, overlooking the Cloth Market, but had been mentioned as having music-hall connections, so in his idle hour before speaking to Ramsay, Piper had sauntered over to take a look at it. The public performance rooms were downstairs, in what had once been an old skittle alley, but were closed during the day. Piper was intrigued by the shabby grandeur and evident popularity of the establishment, but the stern jug-man at the bar didn't seem the type who would gossip idly about such matters, or any matters at all in fact, so Piper had ordered food and drink and studied the early afternoon customers as they came and went. They were mostly traders and market people, with one or two in river-worker's clothes. He'd sensed an understandable wariness aimed in his direction by each and every one of them as they'd entered, so he'd eaten his fill and left.

Now the constable greeted him almost with conviviality, in contrast to their last meeting, and Piper assumed that the duty sergeant had put a good word his way. Another constable who was there was soon dressed and left them to their own company, so Piper pulled up a

61

chair by the window and Ramsay did the same, brushing the pile of his hat while they chatted.

"You're not goin' to ask me to recite me verse about Mister Turnbull I hope," Ramsay said with a chuckle.

Piper laughed. "Well, maybe this isn't the time or place, but I'd be pleased to hear it at some point." He relaxed a little and took in the man. Ramsay was older than him, about forty or slightly more, and was missing a forefinger on his left hand. The mouse-brown hair was still thick upon his head, but his side-whiskers were greying, and his skin was mottled across his chin and forehead. He also had blue scars on the backs of both hands, and on his right temple, suggesting time spent underground at the coal face in days past. The wheeze of his breath confirmed as much.

"How long have you been on the force then?" Piper asked.

"These last four years," he said. He hesitated, then went on. "I started on the river like they all do, like me father did, and then the family came along, and there was more money in the pits, so down I went, at the Leazes on the Town Moor. Almost the end of me, that was!" He chuckled dryly. "Fall of stones, killed two lads on the shift, three of us dug out by bare hands, thanks to a deputy and a little trap-lad. Left a finger behind! That was it for me. They were just startin' to recruit here, and the first batch o' lads they took on turned out to be wrong 'uns, so they jumped at me when I walked in that door. And I'm happy enough, just bein' in the fresh air." He patted his chest, and breathed noisily. "I have a bit o' bother comin' up the rise from the quayside now and then, but I manage."

"But you'd rather be treading the boards in the halls with your verses, from what I hear," Piper said with a wink.

Ramsay shook his head. "No, not really. I enjoy makin' up the daft songs and that, but I'd be better pleased if I could get one of the proper turns to pick up on them, give them an airin'." He looked wistfully around the room. "It would be a thrill to hear them delivered in the proper style, in front of a public. There's some of the lads around here, they're as good as anything ye'd get down London, I'd wager. And some of them'll get there eventually, I'd bet on that as well."

"This man Selkirk," Piper continued, "He was quite a good hand at it, the composing and writing, that's what I've heard."

Ramsay shrugged, almost dismissively. "Long before my time he was, but yes. I know his verses. 'Swalwell Hoppins', that's the best of them. The Bob Cranky songs are my favourites, though it's not certain he actually composed all of them. There's them that claim otherwise."

"This Bob Cranky," Piper interjected, "Who is he exactly?"

"Who is he? Well, he's nobody as far as I know. He's just an invention of Selkirk's. A prankster, a lad out on the town who knows everything and everybody, and knows more and better than most. A hero worth havin', if you will. And Selkirk was the one who invented him, and then there's others who picked him up and used him in their own verses."

"Can they do that?" Piper asked. "Just steal another man's idea and use it in their own way?"

Ramsay looked perplexed at the question. "Well, I suppose they can. They do it anyway. In fact some of the other folk's take on it was better than John Selkirk's to my ears. But as I say, I'm fond of old Cranky, whoever it was who held the pen."

"Did you realise who the man was, that they took from the river?"

He frowned, uneasy at the thought of it.

"I did. At least, I felt I did. I'd seen him at odd times, in recent years, worse for drink, down at the Groat Market in the middle part of the week. You couldn't miss him, with his wild hair, white as snow, thick as a besom. And his own father a hairdresser in days past." He shook his head in wonderment.

Piper looked at him. "So it must've been a shock for you, when you realised who it was, when they brought the body up."

Ramsay nodded, his eyes cast down. "It was. I was sorry to see it, knowin' what he'd once been. I sent for Doctor Rossiter, 'cause he knew him well. It felt right that he should come and examine him. To do the final pronouncin'."

"So this Doctor Rossiter, he also knew him from former times?"

Ramsay again looked perplexed at this. "Yes, but just by vague association, I would imagine," he said. "Well, Doctor Rossiter was just as well known for his verses as Selkirk was. More so, probably, because he was at it for a longer length of time. He was a man in business, and a medical man, and yet he had the gift of verse as well. So he was very sad to see the body when he got there. I mean, they hadn't been friends or anything, as far I know. Competitors more than likely, if it was anything like as cut-throat then as it is now."

Piper was leaning forward now. "So it's a very competitive patch is it? People keen to be the centre of attention and so on?"

"Most certainly," said Ramsay firmly. "Who can be first to write a verse about the latest occurrence. And once they've done so, who can be next to write a verse in answer to the first one." He chuckled. "It's all part of the entertainment of it. Ye can't turn about before somebody's putting pen to paper on it."

"And so, Doctor Rossiter," Piper said. "He was at it as well, at the same time as poor Selkirk. It might be worth my while to speak to him. For the family's sake. Is he here in town?"

Ramsay looked surprised at this. "Well, he was in Gateshead. He had shares in a newspaper down at Shields, but it has recently gone out of business, I hear. He's a wealthy man, regardless. But I'm not sure what he could tell to you that I haven't already."

Piper sensed an unease in the man, that perhaps he was wise to Piper's deeper intentions with this line of talk, even if he couldn't possibly know just how deep they were. Piper felt he had to divert such suspicion in some way.

"The truth be told," he said, "There's a knowledge in the family that Selkirk had been used to some shady dealings during his time in London. My friend the constable, his first cousin, said as much. Coupled with the dismal way the man's life ended, Constable Selkirk implored me to search for some happier, more reputable character behind what was already known to them. Perhaps the good doctor might vouch for such a thing in him, and then I may report back with a gladder tale. You see my point?"

Ramsay did not seem convinced but nodded in agreement. "Then perhaps the brother, James, is the one to speak to, rather than the doctor. They hadn't been close in recent times, but he spoke fondly of him at the inquest."

"Yes, I'd heard tell of the brother," Piper said. "The father, the hairdresser, long since dead, I assume?"

"Oh yes, I dare say. There's a nephew too, but I know nothing of him. His name was mentioned by the coroner."

Piper sat back, his mind distracted. The portrayal of John Selkirk as a poet, a songsmith, had flummoxed him somewhat, though on the surface it meant little. This entire culture of bards and writers seemed such a vital essence of this city, with doctors, policemen, working men, all plying an alternative trade with pen in their hand and songs in their hearts. He again recalled the early morning labourers when he had first arrived in town, bursting into chorus at their very toil. And, in fact, it jolted him to remember, it was of this very Bob Cranky character that they had been singing! The whole thing struck him as being extraordinary, a curious coincidence, now that the hero of their song was revealed to him to have been begotten by the very man whose death had enticed him up here in the first place.

Ramsay had looked more uneasy, or at best more self-conscious, as their conversation had developed. Piper had taken well to the man, but his curiosity was pricked by him, by his measured responses, his stoicism in the face of what had seemingly been a life blighted by hardship, and his attitude of calmness and consideration, a rare attribute amongst the constables that Piper encountered in his own district. The whole effect was underlined by his way of speaking. The lazy clip of the local accent was evident, but not to the usual extent. There was an elevated flavour to his words, suggesting a man who, if not well-educated, was certainly well-read. Piper could see signs of the poet in him, he told himself, even from this brief encounter.

Ramsay had barely taken his leave when, as Piper sat gathering his thoughts at the window of the day-room, Superintendent Turnbull's unexpected footsteps were on the stairs, and he came through the door, a flat leather file case under his arm and his hat in his hand. He raised his eyebrows at Piper and wished him good day. Piper responded in kind.

Turnbull slowed his pace somewhat and looked at Piper warily.

"Have you made progress?" he asked, "Or is it too early to tell?"

Piper chuckled and shook his head. "Oh, much too early to tell!" he said. "I've nothing but a dead man, a gipsy landlady and a town where everyone is a poet or a songster! I've never seen the like before. It's quite remarkable."

Turnbull looked puzzled. "Poets and songsters?" he said. "You mean as tricksters and braggarts? They try to beguile you in some way?"

"No," Piper replied, "I mean truly, song-makers, The Bards of the Tyne! Even John Selkirk, the man himself. He was a poet of some renown in his youth, and part of a coterie of wordsmiths who seem to have the town gripped in a fever, even to this day. Everywhere I turn, there's talk of new songs, music halls and poets. Even here in your own police house, there are verses being written, did you know that? Little to do with my business, I would hazard to say, but a strange twist on it, I think you'll agree."

For the first time since he had set eyes on him, Piper saw Turnbull break into a genuine smile. He shook his head and then looked across at Piper.

"What I suggest," he said, "is for you to go to the music-hall, enjoy the songs that you seem so interested in, drink the health of your gipsy landlady, and then catch the next steamer back to your own river. There's nothing of interest for you here, not in terms of what you're after. This is a simple town, with simple, hard-working people. For the most part at any rate. Such subterfuge that occupies your superiors' thoughts is a London pastime. Here we laugh and smile at the follies of politicians and statesmen, we don't aim guns at them. We sing of their foolishness, and write verses that show we are cleverer and brighter than they will ever be. That is the fever of which you speak."

Evan Piper wished he could believe that to be true. For a moment the words had gladdened his heart, but he knew he had much more yet to do.

"Yes," he said, "You're right. The music hall is a better choice than the dead house and the police station. And the poems and songs and tall tales might deliver more information than a hundred witnesses would. It's a more inviting option anyhow."

Turnbull smiled again, and then raised his hand as a thought struck him.

"Actually," he said, "There's a man I know who has knowledge of such things. An upright man in my experience, though not one who is naturally helpful with people in our chosen profession, if you take my meaning. But he's an honest soul, and he had dealings with some of these entertainers and songsmiths many years ago, and had certainly maintained connections with them, on a casual footing at least, when last I spoke with him."

"Is he another one of these bards? They're thick on the ground, by the sound of it."

"No, his connection came by way of other matters. He helped a woman, a young girl from the Sandgate quays, in a matter over her sweetheart, who was accused in some military difficulties. She had involvement with singers and pub fiddlers and the like. This was many years ago, when uncontrolled Irish brigades were stationed here in the town. He also helped me in a municipal case when I was starting out in the Town Clerk's office. To be truthful, neither matter was handled within the law as it stood in those days, but certainly with discretion and good will in equal measure. He may be able to shed a light on your situation, if he was willing to talk to you."

Piper's interest was obvious. "He has no love for authority then?" he said, flatly.

"None," came the reply at once, "But a deep sense of justice and truth."

"Could you really persuade him to talk to me?"

"I could get a message to him, I believe, if he is still living that is. He is near to sixty years old by now, I would say, and has no love for English ways of government. He's a Scot, though he's lived in this district for more of his life than he ever did in his native land. If you channel your enquiries in the right way, he may be persuaded to assist you."

Piper was sceptical. "If he lacks such sympathy with the English, he would probably be more likely to rejoice at the thought of Mr Peel at the end of a gun barrel, rather than prevent it."

"Well, that is indeed likely to be the case," said Turnbull, "But as I say, he might be able to point you in some direction with regard to Selkirk and his former associates. How much longer will you be here in Newcastle, have you decided?"

"I can stretch my stay to the end of the week, after which my lodging is unpaid, and I'd need to return to other duties in London."

Turnbull nodded. "And are there enquiries you have yet to make?" he asked.

"I dare say," Piper said, without much enthusiasm. "There's Selkirk's brother, and the doctor who was at the scene when his body was recovered from the river."

Turnbull looked more than a little puzzled by that. "The Doctor?" he said. "Doctor Rossiter? Why him, for pity's sake?"

"Selkirk was known to him of old," Piper said. "He was a poet as well, on top of being a medical man, so there's a long association. I don't for a moment suggest there's any other involvement on the part of the good doctor."

Turnbull had lost his smile. "As you see fit then," he said.

"And the other man, the Scot? Will you try to arrange a meeting of some sort?"

"I'll get a message to him," said Turnbull, "Though whether it can be dealt with in the time allowed by what's left of your stay is doubtful. I'll try." He turned to leave.

"Thank you," Piper said. "And what's the man's name?"

Turnbull hesitated at the doorway. He looked back over his shoulder, without catching Piper's eye.

"His name is Parrish," he said, "Alec Parrish."

CHAPTER 7

"Off te the yell-hoose"

At three o'clock in the afternoon, Evan Piper stood at the door of a stone built, wide-fronted house that stood proudly on a steep rise, overlooking the busy road that ran south from the furthest boundaries of Gateshead. He'd learned the address of Doctor Rossiter from Sergeant Fitzsimmons before he'd left the Pilgrim Street police station, and had made his meandering way to the quayside, along the crowded river's edge and on to the stone bridge across the Tyne. It was busy with traffic, and horse-led carts laden with crates, with coal, and with rope coils, competed with handcarts piled with lesser wares, wood slats, white beets, tar-barrels and more homely, everyday goods. Their wheels had either slid perilously down the rise that led onto the bridge from one side, or were being aligned to be pushed up the other. The stench of a midden cart, splashing its way through a throng of declamatory cries, was barely enough to cover the smell from the river itself. The water was running low, and Piper watched a group of ragged youngsters, mudlarks, scavenging precariously in the filth of the bank that slid westwards towards the dingy, narrow lanes of nearby Pipewell Gate.

The climb up through Bottle Bank into the old town of Gateshead was steep and tiring. As he reached the corner of a long wall that framed an impressive, soot-stained church, perched half-way up the steep hill, the cold wind

73

howled menacingly at him from between two grey terraces. A group of men smoking pipes in the shelter of a gable-end watched him wordlessly as he passed. Beyond them, a fluttering-skirted clutch of bare-headed women turned in his direction, staring in silence until he was out of sight. He thought uneasily to himself that it would pay him to make the return walk before the daylight deserted him.

It took him some time, however, to find the house he was looking for. Over the brow of the hill, he passed a row of grand dwellings, punctuated by shrubs and bare bushes, and each set back from the roadway, with gated entries into raised gardens in front them. These were the houses of merchants and important townsfolk, many of them bearing particular names, usually feminine, in a similar tradition to the prettified names of coal-mines in nearby Durham. A vanity exercise, honouring their daughters and wives, elevating them to positions in society that would stand them in good stead for drawing-room gatherings, marriage prospects and the like. So it was in this most privileged of streets. Piper noted a Dorothea, a Rosalinda, a Clarisse, each name chiselled in stone on gateposts at their entrances, before finally and tellingly being confronted by a blunt "seven", cut in block letters, announcing a slightly less grand, and tired-looking abode, situated at the point where the town threatened to give way to the countryside beyond. The small slatted gate was open and he strode up the stepped path to the door.

Within seconds of his knock, a lad of about sixteen years, with tousled hair and a high-buttoned blue shirt stained from kitchen-work, opened the door and peered out. Before Piper had even spoken, the youth blurted out, "The doctor is retired. He doesn't see people. We can't help you."

Piper held up his hand, knowing that the door would be closed almost once in his face.

"Police business," he exclaimed. "From Pilgrim Street. A question or two, that's all."

The lad stared back in silence, eyeing him up and down. He obviously didn't look like a constable, dressed as he was in plain, though less than shabby, street clothes, topped by the somewhat extravagant headwear, hence the uncertainty. Then the door was pulled back from behind the boy, and an elderly man in a tweed waistcoat over a collarless shirt, a long-stemmed liquor glass in his hand, stepped out from the gloom within. He squinted at the visitor with a look of displeasure plainly etched across his face.

"I don't know you," he said, in a sharp, impatient tone. "From the police house you say?"

Piper took off his hat. "Yes, my name is Piper, Inspector Evan Piper. I'm currently on loaned assistance to the local constabulary while conducting investigations initiated by my own force, the Metropolitan Division in Aldersgate, London. If I could just take a moment of your time to ask a few questions about a recent accident at which you were noted as the attending physician."

"Accident? Who? When was this?"

Piper smiled benignly. "It was two Sundays since. John Selkirk. A tragic drowning."

There was no response from the doctor. He stared blankly at Piper for a moment, then turned on his heel.

After a few steps into the dark passage Piper heard his voice say, "Yes, come in, come in." He did so.

He followed the doctor into a sitting room on the right. The old man was putting on his jacket as Piper entered. The place was silent except for the deep tick of a large clock in the corner. The only window in the room was heavily curtained, and a dim lamp provided the only relief. The doctor drained off the last of the liquid from his glass and stood with his back to the lifeless fireplace.

"Yes, I was expecting this," he said at last. "Though not the appearance of someone who has travelled so far. I can't pretend to understand your interest in the matter, given that your work is in... Where is it you say you have come from?"

"From Aldersgate, in the east of the City of London," Piper replied after a moment's hesitation. The doctor's previous remark, that his visit was somehow expected, had come as something of a surprise to him, and he suddenly felt ill-positioned to pose the questions that he had prepared. A blur of other, very different questions had suddenly reared up in his mind.

He continued, "You say you were expecting this. You mean a visit by someone from the police, concerning Selkirk?"

"Well, can I say that I am not surprised that there's interest in him. But explain to me first your own concern. It's a long stretch from the Tyne to the City of London, for news of such a local occurrence to have reached so far."

Piper hesitated, then said, "My actual presence here is centred around another, quite different matter. My interest in John Selkirk however, is more of a personal nature, due to the entreaties of a friend of mine, who happens to be a relative of the deceased man. The tragedy has befuddled the family in London, being so far removed from the detail of it."

"Befuddled you say?" Doctor Rossiter let out a sharp, humourless laugh. "Befuddled indeed they should be, as should the man's near-relatives in his own home town, who despite my consultation with them, have shown no interest in probing the tragedy any deeper."

Piper stared at him. "Well," he said, "Perhaps if you could familiarise me with a summary of that consultation, then something deeper may come of it."

Another mirthless laugh came forth. "Well, it's too late now, surely. Poor Selkirk lies buried at the Ballast Banks, and has taken the knowledge of his demise to his grave with him. And truthfully, if he'd been a faceless, nameless corpse dredged from the Tyne, I would likely be tempted to ignore my own concerns. But alas, that's not the case. Whatever the man had become of late, my memory of him involves quick-witted discussions and late-night debates in salons and meeting rooms, with like-minded men of imagination and enthusiasm. The slang and coarse parlance of his written work belied a deep thinker with the skill and penmanship of a poet. A true Bard, make no mistake."

As he spoke, he approached a small table by the hearth, where an ornate decanter stood next to the glass he had just drained and put down. His hands reached towards it, and then caressed its length to the narrow neck. Piper noted this with interest. The process of pouring from it also involved a delicate use of fingers on glass, and a close peering from a lowered face.

With the glass filled, Doctor Rossiter sat heavily in the armchair behind him. He turned towards Piper once more. "Forgive my lack of hospitality in not sharing this brandy with you. There are undoubtedly other glasses somewhere in the sprawling house, but my lack of clear vision means I wouldn't be able to lay a hand to them with any certainty. And the lad there is clumsy in the extreme."

He took a sip from the glass and continued.

"My old age has brought with it many infirmities, but this encroaching blindness is the hardest to bear. I cope better in the dimness in which you find me now, and passably in near darkness. Broad daylight makes it painfully impossible for me to function. All of which, as you no doubt realise, is the reason why I wasn't keen to alert the coroner to my suspicions as to the true cause of death of John Selkirk. Who would trust the judgement of a blind man in circumstances such as these? My reputation rests on the achievements of my younger days. I daren't expose it to be ridiculed in my dotage."

"And these suspicions," said Piper. "I ask again. Would you care to share them with me now? It is, as you say, too late to have much of a bearing on the situation, yet it might cast a different light on the tragedy for the people who I represent."

Rossiter stared into his dim emptiness for a moment or two, then closed his eyes as he spoke.

"That morning, the constable sent word to me at around six o'clock, not long after the body was brought from the water. I was already awake and dressed, as is my habit.

Lawrence, the young man who answered the door, is the grandson of my late sister. He tends to my needs most days, and it was he who led me down to the bridge end. It was still dark, though the sky was lighter by the time we got there. The constable, who seemed quite familiar to me, probably from other such episodes, informed me of the identity of the victim. I personally hadn't set eyes on him for some years, but I did recognise him, even in the meagre light. A waterman had arrived with a lantern by that time. I soon made the assertion that the man was dead, but I was perturbed by the texture of his skin, and by the lack of water that came from his mouth and nostrils when he was turned and lifted. I pulled back the edge of his reefer, and asked the lantern to be brought closer. There were clear marks at his throat and also at the left hand side of his neck; bruising, and scuffed, broken skin. He wore no collar, certainly no neckwear. There was nothing present that could have caused those marks. My conclusion, in the suddenness of that moment, was that he had been done to death by strangulation. His body was already lifeless when it entered the water, which is why little or none of it had been imbibed while he was in the river."

"Can you be sure that this is what you saw?" Piper said steadily, despite his disquiet at hearing this version of events.

The doctor opened his eyes and turned to Piper. "Frankly, no, I cannot be sure," he said. "You have seen the struggle I have with everyday things due to my lack of vision. But I alerted the boy Lawrence to the marks on the neck, and bade him rub them as if to make them clean. He

79

was reluctant, understandably, but he did so, and they were still visible as before."

"Did you also alert the constable as to this?" said Piper.

"I did not. He was already occupied by a sizeable crowd that had gathered from the garths beyond St Mary's, eager to share in the spectacle. Within minutes, he had summoned a cart that arrived to take the body away."

"And at the inquest? You made no mention of your suspicions?"

Rossiter hesitated. "I had intentions to do so, believe me, but the proceedings were handled strangely. The coroner, Colonel Tindale, did not call me. He spent much time in lamenting the tragedy and sympathising with the family, as is his duty, but little time in establishing the facts. I don't fault him for it. It was one of five summaries that he had to give that day, but…" He again halted his words. "It almost struck me that if his intention was one of avoidance of the facts, and I'm not saying that that was so, then he certainly succeeded. The conclusion of accidental death by drowning was noted, and the body was taken away directly for burial."

"There was no service?" said Piper. "Even with living relatives present?"

"None, and there's the tragedy of it. If it was his lot to perish from the bad company he chose to keep, so be it. But the spark of a formidable man had been extinguished, and none cared to mark the passing of it." The doctor again sipped slowly at his brandy. Piper's mind raced.

Later, after he had left the doctor's company, and was walking back to cross over to the town on the opposite side of this troubled river, he knew there had been other questions he would have pressed upon him, had the true nature of his enquiry left him free to do so. But this was not his concern. It wasn't even his town. If there was a murder to be solved, it was up to others to do so. He himself still could not establish the political affiliations of John Selkirk, or those of his associates, if he'd had any. What matter if his death had been suspicious or even deliberately and maliciously inflicted? Such concerns played little part in the main thrust of Piper's own agenda.

Before he left the doctor, he had felt it polite to ask about the gentleman's own ballad-making success, and the old man had startled him by abruptly launching into what he assured Piper was his most famous song, 'The Road to Old Tynemouth'. A rather nostalgic verse, which he delivered in rather strained and uncertain tones, it had apparently remained a popular favourite until that present day, some thirty years after he'd written it. But ultimately, it had left a sour taste.

"In those more innocent days," he'd said, "Authorship was noted by one's initials on the manuscript. It was felt that it would suffice to do that. Imagine my consternation then, when another man stepped forward, and by way of the local press, claimed ownership of the ballad for himself. I objected, and in more recent times, the situation was clarified, and my authorship asserted. But once tainted, I sensed there was always a question in many minds as to the real truth of the matter. I wasn't the only one who experienced this. Others found themselves robbed of their achievements in a similar fashion. Robert Gilchrist, one of the most popular, washed his hands of it and limped back to his father's sail-sewing yard. He'd had his fill of the critics and cynics, and I don't blame him. What had been an enjoyable and rewarding pastime became a competition for public acclaim and personal glory. I lost the enthusiasm for it. I put down my quill and moved on to other things."

Had John Selkirk done the same, Piper wondered as he traipsed back to his lodging, and if so what alternative path had he chosen to take?

The river was high when he reached the bridge. Heavy November rain in the hills of Northumberland had made it swollen and bloated as it neared its North Sea liberation. He looked down into it from the shallow wall that ran the length of the bridge. How easily could he too swoon into its cold, muddy flow from where he now stood. Had John Selkirk done exactly that, his belly filled with gin and head swimming with schemes and plots? Piper moved on quickly and was glad to reach the other, already more familiar, quayside.

He guessed a rapid pathway through the meandering chares and alleys, higher and higher away from the sombre waters of the Tyne, and emerged with little trouble at the Cloth Market. As an afterthought, he had decided that tonight he would sample the delights of John Balmbra's Music Hall, in the deepest room of the Wheatsheaf Tavern. It was almost six o'clock and the evening's streets were quiet. He passed the opened doors of many ale houses and taverns, seemingly one such at every corner, and often another in the middle of a row as well. There was a peal of a woman's laughter from within one of them, as he walked by. At the door of another, two men were in earnest discussion, which ceased as he passed, and resumed once he was considered out of earshot. He glanced back to see money changing hands. A dog, its pale, bone-lined body grey with coal dust, barked ferociously at him from steps leading down to another.

Other doors on these streets were closed for the night. A butcher's, with bare white slabs outside, open to the weather, a printer's shop, festooned with papers telling of meetings, church services and theatre performances, many long since over and forgotten, and bakers, grocers and leather-workers, all lined up in silence until the new day. Street scavengers, reaping their rewards from the gutters and gullies that skirted the wide market street, were already creeping around in the dusk. The damp cold had taken a grip on Evan Piper, and he was glad to reach the sanctuary of the brighter, warmer taproom of The Wheatsheaf. The two men standing at the hatch stepped back in silence when he collected his pot of ale, and he sat in the farthest corner for a long while, collecting his many thoughts.

People soon began arriving to descend the wide steps that led from the centre of this room, down to the promises of mirth and joviality that awaited them in a lower place. Men in wide, stiff collars, and women in garish frocks and curious hats, all in varying degrees of excited anticipation, filed past Piper, in couples, and sometimes in groups, as from below the sound of waltzing melodies wafted around like invisible angels playing low harps and high horns in the heavens. Piper himself was immediately seized by the thrill of it, much to his surprise, and soon was descending the stairs, trying surreptitiously to blend in with a party of loud young men in low felt hats and short jackets still fastened against the cold. He followed their lead in paying a sixpence, which entitled him to stand at the rear of an already crowded room. He knew that this at one time had been a skittle ground, but now, scattered around at random, were tables and chairs, where customers had paid a higher price for the privilege of being closer to the entertainment. A narrow, raised platform stretched around three walls of this auditorium, with short benches arranged in staggered lines at each side. The central section of it was shielded by a large curtain of grey sailcloth, painted in bright colours, and bearing the legend "Balmbra's Saloon of Music", surrounded by freakish faces of minstrels and devils, all glaring greedily at the assembled audience.

A small band of musicians was crammed into the right corner, immediately in front of the stage, featuring a brace of fiddlers, a haut-bois blower, an accordionist and a zither player, plus a small buffoon-like character, beating a military-style side drum in the centre. They were busy with a piece played in a polska rhythm, something that Piper was familiar with from the Yiddish market musicians who played for farthings near St Paul's on Friday mornings. This style of music thoroughly reflected the strange un-English appearance of the troupe now in full flow.

The level of conversational noise increased as more and more people arrived. Piper allowed himself the occasional glance at the more dubious-looking characters, and then before he knew it, the curtain was pulled back at the sound of a bell, and three acrobats in tight, chequered outfits rolled on to the stage. They balanced and tumbled to the quickening pace of the music, much to the delight of the audience. The danger that one of them might be hurled sprawling into the midst of the crowd, so small was the stage compared to their ambitious antics, only sharpened the ecstasy of the spectacle.

Unscathed, the three acrobats soon yielded the floor to a coarse master of ceremonies, feigning drunkenness in a vain attempt at humour. The combination of the increased crowd noise and the man's strong local accent, meant that the attraction of this portion of the evening, and every time it was repeated as the night progressed, was lost on the Londoner.

Then a fragile-looking young woman was introduced, her first name announced triumphantly as Emily, but her surname buried by the baying reception that she was given. Her fair hair had been teased into an awkward ringlet arrangement, and she held herself stiffly and nervously. Piper was quite taken with her, almost at once. He was not alone. Her plaintive rendition of a ditty entitled The Waters of Tyne was obviously a favourite with the assembled mass, and she left the stage, her pale skin flushed in triumph, to wild applause after deftly catching a bunch of dry heather, thrown by a tall man, seemingly in tears, standing to the right of the musicians.

A heavily-bearded gent wearing a formal suit came next and sang two songs in succession in a pompous, flamboyant style, the first being a topical piece at a steady pace about a clock that seemed to be on fire, if Piper caught the correct meaning, and the second, to his surprise, a heartfelt rendition of The Road to Old Tynemouth, Doctor Rossiter's very own celebrated work, reeking even more of sentiment and nostalgia in this delivery, and a great success with the crowd. More acrobatics, an unintelligible monologue from the compère about a soldier missing his mother, and a lampoon of a police constable with a disobedient dog which brought roars of approval from everyone except Piper himself, brought the first act to an end.

A bewhiskered attendant with a tray of ale jugs held high, mingled with the crowd, and by the time Piper had caught his attention and had his pot refilled, the second part of the evening's entertainment was already beginning. To rapturous applause and raised glasses, a certain Master Billy Purvis was announced, and on to the platform emerged a small, round-shouldered, bald man dressed in an extraordinary costume of red and green striped knickerbockers, red stockings, a yellow ruff at his neck, and a pair of tiny green-glassed spectacles perched on his nose. The outfit was topped off by a tiny, round tam o' shanter cap of an Irish style. He called out a slew of grand speech to the company, in a cascading, slightly Scottish brogue, punctuated by the oft-repeated words "Aye, It's clivor, sae vorry clivor", which made the audience erupt in laughter every time he uttered them. Eventually he called the band to strike up, and he sang a weak-voiced ditty about a keelman's wife, followed by a similar but longer ballad concerning a ship's captain lost in a sea mist.

Despite the roaring approval of the entire house, Piper felt he had seen and heard enough, and eased himself gently through the crowd at the door, up the stairs and out into the street. The ale had left a salted thirst in his throat, and he welcomed the steady rainfall that greeted him. He gathered a tiny amount in his open palm and wet his lips with it. He was suddenly aware of the dark alleys that lay between him and his lodging, and made his way cautiously through the narrow passages. He passed not a single soul until he reached the Bigg Market and the sanctuary of The Unicorn. The tavern itself was quiet compared to the hostelry he had just left, and he slipped unnoticed through the side door and into the safety of his room. He stood at the window for a while, still wrapped against the cold that seeped through it. The words of Doctor Rossiter came back to him, as if declaimed upon a music hall stage, along with the hollow laughs, and the staring, non-seeing eyes. He knew the suspicions of the doctor were not his business, and that his own concerns were much bigger and more noteworthy. Yet he knew also that those suspicions would haunt him forever, if he did not take time to delve some way deeper into their origins.

CHAPTER 8

"T' Church we gat without 'im"

The next day dawned with bells across the city. Evan Piper had slept solidly, but awoke with a jolt. The sea of dreams in which he'd floundered, had overwhelmed him with a massive wave, the roar of which was still in his ears as he slowly drifted into consciousness and found himself at a twisted angle across the bed. The room was still again. He stared up at the stained plaster above him, and the dust-dipped cobwebs between the brown wood beams. The rain lashing across the window glass rattled angrily. That must've been the sound that woke him, he thought. The bells still sang mournfully, answering one another in the gloom of a November Sunday.

A thirst gripped his throat in a dry vice. He sat up in the bed, remembering that he was still wearing most of his clothes. He found his boots and coat, and was soon at the foot of the stairs. The room where he had eaten the day before was empty, its breakfast board bare. He poured water from a jug into a pot mug and gulped it down. The clock above the dead fireplace showed five minutes after nine. Its slow tap reminded him of another clock from deep in his past, but he could not remember where it had sounded. He walked to the door and unbolted it, as quietly as he could, and looked out across the deserted market-place, where a meagre rain was still falling. The sky was gathering a pale blueness to the west, but was still shrouded in black towards the sea. The morning air was chilled and heavy. Piper stepped out into it.

He was resigned to be spending his first ever northern Sunday alone. The streets of this strange town were eerily empty. With little hesitation, he went forth, and walked for a long time, away from where he sensed the river might be, through winding lanes and between close-leaning buildings, which soon petered out into grim streets with low rooves and smoking chimneys. He sometimes glimpsed people at a distance, most of them wandering with the same listlessness as he himself felt enveloped by. He avoided these folk wherever he could.

Suddenly, as he took a corner into a wide empty expanse, thick with black mud, he was confronted by something horrific, something that his mind took a long, desperate moment to comprehend. It was the tall, monstrous workings of a coal mine, pulsing like some devil's heart, and with a towering structure of stone leering down at him. Its wide eyes housed a massive wheel, still and squinting, and wrapped in thick ropes. A group of children were gathering black dust in cloth panniers at its feet. Upon seeing him, they let the baskets fall to the ground and ran off like a herd of wounded animals. The sight of it shocked him. He turned on his heel and tried to retrace his steps.

At the corner of a brick-walled yard, a twisted old woman had laid out some loaves on a canvas covering. She called him over with some cackling words. He walked to her, handed her two farthings, and she gave him a long side of bread, again coated in the same white grease that he'd eaten at his lodging the day before. She then offered him a slop of potatoes and green vegetable in a wrapping of burnt peel. She called it "neeps", as far as he could tell. He took it and nodded thanks. She then sat down in the dampness beneath her, took out a knotted string from inside her old black coat and started muttering what he took to be prayers. He thought of his mother in far-away London, and turned away from the old woman, almost embarrassed by her blatant display of devotion.

He ate as he walked. It was all salty and uneven. The potato mixture was curiously spiced, but he devoured it all the same. Then, weary for a moment, he sat by a lapping water-trough at the side of a long windowless building and tried to fight off the deep ache of loneliness that had gripped his insides. He felt cold. He could see the grey river snaking off, far to his right, and made his way to meet it, roughly in the direction from which he'd come. He reached it sooner than he thought he would. People were clearing away the remnants of a market on the quayside. He kept his distance again, but found their company oddly comforting. There were ships further down river, and looking back, up-stream, there were low-lying barges tethered to tall wooden frames, like jetties, their arms reaching out from the muddy banks.

This must be the day of rest for the people hereabouts, he thought. They were all hidden away from the dank November day, with loved ones gathered around them. If he hadn't been here, standing alone by the side of this strange water, he would have been in more familiar surroundings but with the same thoughts in his mind. And he would have been alone, struggling free from all his usual thoughts of lost love and regrets.

He walked again, searching for an escape from his loneliness, yet knowing none existed. There was a tavern, its doors being pulled open with a screech of warped, sodden wood. The street sign above it bore the word "Side" etched in dull characters. The rusted plate hanging above the door had an image of a fish, barely visible in the soot-stained metal, with 'The Dolphin' scratched below it in slanted script. He walked in before the landlord was even at his jugs, exchanged a curt greeting with him and paid four pence for a mug of ale. He was barely half-way down the drink when the landlord wordlessly filled another and slapped it in front of him. He drained the first, and felt in his pocket for more pennies, but the other man raised a hand.

"No lad," he said, "It's last night's barrel's end. Still champion, but it'd get swilled out if you don't take it."

"Thank you," Piper said, and was prepared to start an amiable conversation, but the landlord retreated to a scullery beyond, turned his back and busied himself with gutting fish. Piper watched his skill with the knife for a pleasant length of time. The strength of the draught of ale was also having a pleasing effect. He finished it off with a long swig, and shouted his goodbye, but no response came to it. He stood for a while outside, aware that the old stone bridge, where John Selkirk had met his untimely end, lay a mere fifty paces or so away. He felt himself sway slightly as he stared at it, and decided not to tempt fate by approaching it on this day.

He was back at his lodging, which was still as silent as the grave, within ten minutes, and thanks to the ale, was soon back in a tormented, storm-lashed sleep, which lasted, in fits and starts, for most of the rest of that day. Troubled thoughts of many Sundays, his mother's respect for them and his father's resentment of them, repeatedly clawed at his weary mind in spells of wakefulness, until the closing dark of evening brought atonement and relief.

It was quite a different city by the time Evan Piper was ready to face it the next morning. Despite the sleep, he did not feel at all refreshed, but at least the Monday had dawned with a purpose, and he strode forth into the swarming stew of streets to make a mark upon his mission.

A dingy, somewhat unkempt alleyway called Bell's Court lay almost hidden from view at the north end of Pilgrim Street. He had seen it mentioned in a police report of John Selkirk's demise, as being the workplace of the man's brother, James. Piper hesitated at the corner wall that led into it. As he peered along its length, he saw the crooked sign of a money-lender hanging motionless from the eaves, and a wooden board listed with official looking names, lawyers or some such, nailed at an angle to a wall-post beyond it. He moved slowly along, with what little morning light there was to be found, being smothered by shadows as he advanced.

The last door he came to was nameless, and open, and looking gingerly inside, he realised it was the back entrance to a workshop of some sort. A white haired man carrying a large ring of keys appeared, and looked up at the figure in the doorway.

"Can Ah help ye?" he called, wiping his brow with a free hand.

Piper raised his own hand in a pacifying gesture. "I'm looking for a Mr Selkirk, James Selkirk. I'm told he works here. I just need a word with him"

"Jimmy, aye," came the reply. "Is it a delivery you're askin' about? We've a loose horse on our hands, set us back a whole mornin'. He's tryin' to get it sorted out!

Piper shook his head. "No, no," he said, "It's a private matter, that's all. Is he close by?"

The man continued to look at him, and said, "Y'er not from round here are ye? Ye don't sound Tyneside as y'er talkin'"

Piper smiled. He was slowly getting a hold on this language. "No, I'm not." He forced a laugh. "Is Mr Selkirk inside?"

The man leaned his head back, his eyes still fixed on Piper, and called "Jimmy!" in a loud, braying voice. Almost at once a heavy-set man in a striped, collarless shirt and waistcoat, with a shock of thick grizzled hair parted in the centre, appeared with a sheaf of yellow papers in his hand. He looked at the visitor with narrow eyes and jerked his head questioningly.

"Mr Selkirk, my name is Piper, I'm a member of the police force of London. I'm an acquaintance of a relative of yours, also a constable in London, George Selkirk by name."

"That was me father's name," came the reply. "Ah know nothin' of any other."

Piper smiled. "No, he's never met you, but he was an acquaintance of your brother John, and as I had to visit Newcastle on other business, he asked if I could call on you and offer condolences on his behalf following your brother's death."

There was a cold look on James Selkirk's face. After a long moment, he said quietly, "Did he now? Well, that's very kind of him." All three men stood in awkward silence for a goodly spell.

Piper eventually broke it. "I can see you are busy," he said, "But I'll be at the alehouse, The Blue Posts, at the corner opposite, for the next hour or so. If you've time to join me, so I can pass on more of your cousin's wishes to you, I'd be grateful."

"Ah've a lot to do, mister," Selkirk replied turning away. "We've a calamity on our hands."

"Yes, I'm aware of it," said Piper, "But a drink awaits you if you find the time." He wished them good day and turned and left.

It was a good hour and a half before the door of the alehouse opened and James Selkirk entered, and spying Piper at a bench in the corner, approached him with a sour, impatient look on his face. Piper headed him off with the offer of a drink, and he nodded, pointing at a barrel perched on the counter.

When Piper re-joined him at the bench, Selkirk eyed him suspiciously, took a mouthful of the proffered ale and wiped his mouth with the back of his cuff.

"So this George Selkirk ye mentioned," he said. "A bobby, like yersel' is he?"

"He is. A good man for the job. I'm not sure of the nature of the family connection, but he spent convivial time with your brother when he was in London some years ago. He'd heard of the accident by way of the Newcastle Journal. The boatmen from hereabouts bring editions of it into London for the northern folk that have settled down there and who wish to have news of home. He was sad to read of it, so when he heard I was to be visiting the town, he urged me to make his feelings known to you."

Selkirk looked back at him. "And how does he know of me, when Ah've no knowledge of him?"

Piper shrugged. "Perhaps your brother mentioned your name. I only know what he told me." Piper took a sip at his own drink. "I hear from another local man, another constable who knows of such things, that your brother was a poet of some celebrity in his younger days. George made no mention of that."

The man nodded and lowered his eyes. "He was known for it. Ah'm only barely aware of it meself. Ah was just a lad when he went off to London. Ah didn't keep company with him then. He was a stranger to me when he came back." He paused and looked at Piper with a hint of regret. "Ah haven't been close to him these past years. He was a sorry sight, as Ah suppose you've heard. Ah don't know what ailed him, why he carried on so. People say it was the shame of comin' back here having failed in business in the South. My door was open for him, regardless of that, but he chose to ignore it."

"He didn't live with family here then?" Piper asked.

"Good Lord, no!" came the reply. "He spent the last months sleepin' in shavin's at Andrew Heslop's wood shop. He had a place with his own name to it over the river in Cannon Street, behind St. Mary's church, but he chose not to use it. Ah don't know why. He was always lookin' over his shoulder, suspicious of folk, yet he displayed no sense of dignity in his own self. Few in town would have placed him as the man who was thought of so grandly in years gone by. He himself had left that life behind, long since."

Piper leaned in towards him. "So he'd forsaken his poet's pen then, in later life? A shame, given his success of before."

"He wrote verses when he was in London, and sent them to my son Thomas, then urgin' me to get them printed here in the town. That was a dozen years ago. But we had no knowledge of such things, and no money to pay for such an undertakin'."

Piper's curiosity was pricked by this information.

"So what of these works, the poems? Do you have them still? I hear there's much interest nowadays in things of that kind. I've heard his work sung myself, here, in the very few days since my arrival. Surely there are people who would be keen to see them."

James Selkirk dismissed the notion with a curse, and snatched another gulp of his drink.

Piper continued regardless. "There may be value in them. A fine legacy perhaps."

Selkirk's eyes met his. He licked the froth from his lips. "I'd be surprised at that."

Piper sat back and feigned contemplation for a moment. "If they were something you could trust to be parted with, even temporarily, I'd happily pass them to the constable here in the Pilgrim Street police house who has connections in these writers' circles. Or I could arrange for him to meet with you, to discuss it further."

The other man shook his head, and then thought on. "Ah've no idea what Tom did with the package. Our John never mentioned them again. They could have been kindlin' for a fire years ago. We saw no worth in them for much else besides that."

Piper breathed heavily. "Well, if you can lay hands on them, bring them to your place of work and I'll ask Constable Ramsay to pay you a visit. You can discuss it with him. It seems a meagre effort in the face of such a tragedy, but maybe a suitable one."

Drinks were finished, and a few remarks more of casual condolence were shared, and then James Selkirk stood and left without another word being spoken.

Piper was in the police station within ten minutes, but the sergeant informed him that Constable Ramsay had already left for his second watch. Fitzsimmons himself then volunteered to pay James Selkirk a visit the next day, to collect the manuscripts. It was a single street away from where he lived, he said, and he was on good terms with another man in the same workshop. It would be an easy and sociable task.

Piper was on his way to the stairs down, when a voice called him back. He turned and saw Superintendent Turnbull, jacketless and drawn in the face, standing in the opposite doorway.

"How goes it with your enquiries?" he asked.

Piper hesitated, and smiled slightly. "I can't say for sure, but if you have a half hour to spare, perhaps tomorrow, I'd be glad to share what I have learned with you."

Turnbull stretched his neck back and grimaced with tiredness. "My time is somewhat over-used, I'm sorry to say, and I must tell you that tomorrow you also have a rendezvous to keep in the late morning. I sent a message to my friend Alec Parrish, the man I mentioned to you. He's agreed to meet you. He was surprisingly keen to do so, in fact, so can I impress upon you that it might be advantageous not to miss the appointment."

Evan Piper looked back at him with some degree of surprise at this news.

"He was keen, you say? What reason did you give him for such a meeting?"

Turnbull smiled thinly. "I merely turned the situation on its head somewhat. I admitted that you were being less than candid with the true nature of your investigations, but suggested that the real reason for your presence here was to lay to rest certain suspicions as to the nature of John Selkirk's death. That seems to have teased Mister Parish's interest."

Piper laughed. "You have yet to see the irony in such a ruse," he said, "But thank you for making the arrangement. Where do I see him?"

Turnbull was clearly taken aback by this remark, but chose to ignore it, and addressed the question. "He lives at Tynemouth, a good morning's journey from here. I can spare you a wagon, if a driver is willing to accompany you. Sergeant Fitzsimmons here thinks that one of the young lads from the firehouse below will be happy to do so, but you'd need to spend a sixpence on it. The lad knows the town. He'll get you to the door. An early start though, perhaps before seven."

"That's no problem for me. Maybe I can report on my progress to you when I get back?"

99

"I'll make time for it," he replied. "My own interest is somewhat pricked by what you say, I don't mind admitting." He turned away but Piper stopped him.

"One more question," he said. "Where do I find the Customs House? I need to visit a premises nearby."

"It's at the quayside, a step or two beyond the Guildhall. Follow the river downstream from the stone bridge and you'll be almost upon it." Turnbull looked searchingly at him. "May I ask exactly what premises you are looking for? The area is notorious. Care must be taken around that district."

"It's a sail-makers workshop, owned by a Mister Gilchrist," Piper replied airily. "Another poet, I'm afraid. As I said, the ground hereabouts is thick with them." He raised his hand as he left and disappeared down the stairway.

Once again the strong ale that he'd quaffed earlier had left him heady and ponderous. He fought against it, walking briskly up through the wider streets that sloped gently to the quieter, more residential part of the town. But the call of the crowded, chaotic narrow lanes with their noises and smells and senseless, twisting directions, pulled him back. He knew that they weren't Aldersgate, but there was yet comfort to be had in their bustling strangeness.

CHAPTER 9

"Thou's myed to my fancy"

It was mid-afternoon when he found himself once again trudging down the hill towards the Tyne. Halfway down, he veered off to the left, past a group of black bonneted women selling old boots and work clogs, lined up in their pairs along a walkway. Children nearby were poking sticks into a smouldering brazier that perched against the steps of a wooden hut, and jabbering nonsense rhymes in unison. Evan Piper found himself slowing to watch them, and to listen to the bold rhythm of their tiny voices. There was a charm to this place, an inner familiarity, that reminded him of his own childhood inside the old city walls of London, from where, he was starting to think, all the charm had long since been chiselled away into dust. He moved on, unseeing, his thoughts elsewhere, and suddenly emerged at the Sandgate water pant. A few women knelt around it, rinsing their linens and bedding, shivering in the cold wind drifting up from the riverside beyond. Piper followed the cobbled way towards the quayside, and was at the Guildhall in a trice. He skirted its rounded walls, and immediately saw a long building, on the near-end of which was hung a wooden board with the name Gilchrist scrolled upon it in tall, old-style lettering.

Sailcloth and canvasses were hanging from large hooks along the side of the building, and the tall doors were pulled wide open. Half a dozen men sat, pipes in mouth, stitching and sewing with long, fierce-looking bone needles, and gossiping in low voices. A lad in oilskins was helping a young woman fold a roped sheet into a quarter-size. She was bare-headed, wearing a man's reefer jacket, and Piper recognised her at once. She looked over at him, abandoned her task, and walked in his direction, wiping her hands against the sides of her coat as she did so.

"Are ye from the pilot's office?" she asked.

"No, I'm not," Piper replied, "I'm from the police house, up at Pilgrim Street. I was looking for Mister Robert Gilchrist."

"From the Peelers?" she said. "What do ye want with him? Does he know yer?" Her voice was as clear as it had been when Piper had heard her sing at The Wheatsheaf, two nights before, and echoed like musket balls across the cobbles to the river and beyond. The men across from them had set down their needles and were watching and listening keenly.

"No, he does not," said Piper, "But I've business to speak of with him, if he's about."

"If it's sail-cloth that's your business, ye can deal with me right enough. If it's not, I'm too busy to be standin' here passin' the time of day with ye, Peeler or not."

"My business concerns a man called John Selkirk," Piper replied in a quieter tone. He turned and pointed back at the bridge behind him. "He died at the foot of that bridge a fortnight past, and there are people who have concerns about it. I'm talking to those who might have known him at a better time of his life, and I believe Mister Gilchrist is amongst them."

She stared past Piper, at the bridge to which he'd just pointed. Eventually she looked directly at him and pulled her jacket in tighter.

"It's perishin' out here, ye'd best come in," she said and beckoned him to follow. They passed the observers without a word, and Piper followed her into a high warehouse lined with canvas strips and ragged nets nailed to joists high above. There was a rusting stove with a crooked chimney-pipe sticking out of it, reaching to the roof. Smoke belched from cracks at its every joint. She bent over and pushed a thick piece of wood into its metal mouth.

"Is Mister Gilchrist here?" Piper asked after a minute or so.

She turned and looked at him with defiance in her blue eyes. She was slim, slight and straight-backed. He brow showed a crease of sternness that work amongst men had etched there. Her fair hair was unkempt, her face was smudged with tar, and her hands were red and rough, yet she still possessed the unmistakeable grace that had filled the stage and wooed that audience, two evenings past.

She took a deep breath. "Ah'm his daughter. He's not here. Indeed, he's rarely here these days. He's a sick man, a severe weakness took hold of him this past year, so Ah try to keep him at home, especially on a day like this."

Piper nodded. "I'm sorry to hear that," he said. "Is there not a doctor that can help him, or..." He let the words hang loose.

The girl shrugged. "He's seen the doctor, but it's something eatin' him away from the inside. His own father was taken by it, he says, so he knows what's in store for him. We try to keep the business healthy, even if he can't be so himself, but it's a struggle. A lot of the custom that we've had for years is already driftin' off to other suppliers. They're used to dealin' with him, and frown on a woman takin' his place. And anyway, with the steam boats takin' over, sailcloth isn't the valuable commodity it once was." She sat on a chair behind her. "Ye were wantin' to talk about Johnny Selkirk, ye said."

"Did you know him?" Piper asked, somewhat surprised at how casually she dropped his name.

She laughed to herself. "Ah've known him since Ah was a bairn. He'd be in here most days, sittin' about, watchin' me father, chattin' a bit, starin' at nowt. And then he'd be off, gallopin' away up the quay to God knows where. He had some demons in him, did poor old Johnny."

"So he'd been a friend of your father's for a long time? They were both poets in their youth, I hear, and famous for it. Were they associates, competitors, or just acquaintances?"

She shrugged again. "All of those Ah reckon. Strange to think of it now. They used to recite their verses at a tavern called The Three Indian Kings, me father told me. It's where all the writers used to go, to try out their new songs and that. It was then that they got to know each other." Her eyes suddenly narrowed, and she stared at him. "But what's your concern in all this? Ye say y'er from the police. Is it because of how Johnny died? Because they said it was an accident, when he was drunk."

"Well," said Piper, "That's probably the truth of it. But some of his relatives have asked me to look deeper into it, for their own consolation, and understandably so."

She stood up suddenly. "Ah *knew* there was more to it," she exclaimed. "And me father did too, when Ah told him, though he didn't say as much. But Ah could tell he was shocked, more shocked than he should've been if it had just been a drunken man fallin' into the Tyne."

Piper tried to defuse the tone of conversation. He sensed that conclusions were being drawn that had no foundation. It was the sort of talk that gossip finds fertile and insidious.

"It was probably exactly what they said it was," he said, calmly. "He'd taken a bottle, a cup or something, to fill with water, slipped and fallen in. It must happen frequently enough, I'm sorry to say."

She stared back at him, as if he was an imbecile, and pointed towards the nearby Tyne. "Y'er tellin' me he was goin' to drink from that river, next to that bridge over there? He might've been a drunk, but he wasn't a fool. It's like a midden under there. Half the town chucks their waste off that bridge. And anyway, there's a burn from Pandon that runs open at the top of the Haymarket. That's only the same distance, and it's a damn sight cleaner than what's runnin' past here!"

Truth be told, Piper had considered this himself from the outset. It did not make sense to him that someone would drink river water from the centre of a town like this. And he himself had seen a water trough and a pant at a corner not a minute's walk from where Selkirk had perished.

"And you think your father felt the same about this? That he questioned the facts of it?"

She had calmed a little, and paused for a moment. "Ah've always thought that there was some reason why me father stopped his writin' when he did. He was celebrated and spoken of so very highly, and then he just quit it. And Ah know there was no money to be made in it, and that he had a new wife and family, and that his own father was tuggin' at him to take over this business. All of those things. But he's never picked up a pen again, unless it was to do reckonin' and ledgers. And neither did Johnny Selkirk. The same thing. He just stopped. And there were others, if ye ask about, there's names from twenty years ago that just fizzled out, just disappeared off the street. And the public was still there, hungry for it. The printers were still turnin' out the papers and the collections."

Piper looked at her for a moment. "Maybe their poetic flow simply ran dry," he said, knowing how lame that sounded.

She moved closer to him, and he sensed anger and frustration in her voice. "My father is sharp as a pin, brimmin' with knowledge and words and opinions, and even as he lies dyin', he's spinning yarns and crackin' jokes like a jester. There's nowt dry about him, and Ah'll not let any man say there is."

Her cheeks were flushed again, much as they had been when she had left the stage of Balmbra's, to a surge of cheers and applause. Her stern defence of her ailing father was delivered in such a way as to warrant a similar reaction, but there was no audience there to hear it. Even so, Piper felt stirred and moved by her passion. How he had thought of her as timid and plain when he'd first seen her, he now could not imagine. He watched her as she turned away, flustered perhaps by her own outspokenness, and even wrapped up as she was in a

106

man's work-clothes, he could recognise her true beauty and grace.

She busied herself with the stove and then, perhaps by way of contrition for her outburst, surprised him by offering him tea, "a tonic for a cold day", as she put it, and he accepted the offer with thanks. She went over to a hand-pump in the corner and swilled out the pair of tin mugs that she gathered up from the bench next to it. Piper felt his breath tight within his chest. The singer on the stage he had found entertaining enough, but the woman before him had enchanted him in a matter of moments.

His reverie was broken by the coarse voice of one of the workhands.

"Emily! That Stephenson from the pilot's office is here. Ye'll have to see to him."

She turned towards Piper, her face apologetic, but unsmiling.

"Ah'll need to speak to him," she said. "Ah'll be back presently."

Piper nodded, then sat for a long while, waiting for her to return. The kettle hadn't made it as far as the stove, and the day was ebbing away. His thoughts were many, and eventually he steered them towards the job in hand, and away from the image of a strong-willed young woman with an allure he had swooned for and a smile he had yet to see.

When he finally went outside, she was across the street in deep conversation with a waterman who was earnestly scribbling notes into a black ledger. She was dealing with him efficiently, and with an authority that he obviously found easy to recognise. She caught sight of Piper, and he raised his hat in a gesture that he hoped was both formal and familiar.

He left her to her chores. He had wanted to tell her how much he had enjoyed her song the night before, but there really hadn't been a right moment to do so. He ambled back up the hill towards the town. His mind was still turning over many things. The sky was darkening for evening, and he had a long day ahead of him in the new day's brightness.

CHAPTER 10

"Ho'way to the toon"

The slow, wide main street of Tynemouth was a disarming change from the tight back alleys of Sandgate and the crowded thoroughfares of busy Newcastle. The wind that blew along it came directly off the sea, and was a vivid, even welcome relief from city smells and the lazy stink of the river. The young lad, Robson by name, who had manhandled the juddering black cart along the road from Newcastle, had said little, and seemed determined to show Piper, and anyone else they passed, what a carefree but skilled driver he was. The poor animal that he had strapped into the shafts in front of them that morning, arrived foaming and snorting after almost two hours of unsteady buffeting of its human cargo, along muddy tracks and stone-spattered roads, high above the sea-bound Tyne in the valley below.

Upon arrival, horse and driver had repaired to a coaching inn at the head of a steep lane down to the fish quay, leaving Piper to make his way alone, along this central street, towards a stall selling crabs and headless mackerel, laid out on a slate table running with blood, in the middle of the market place. He was looking for Hotspur Street, and at once he saw it, cutting away from Front Street almost immediately ahead of him. It was ten o'clock, and Piper crossed to the corner where the two streets met, and stood there. The pummelling his backside had taken on the journey to this place had left him bruised and aching. He stretched his back for some relief. To his right, along the main street, people were passing to and fro, none with any obvious purpose to their meandering, as far he could see. To his left, the view was dominated by the shell of an ancient stone structure, a cliff-top fortification of some kind, spread randomly out across a narrow promontory, with high and holy walls, and capped by a broken castle-keep that looked ready to topple into the waters below at any moment. Not impressive as such, it still ached from the wounds that history had inflicted upon it. It was hard to match the ordinariness of these people on the street around him, with the noble majesty that those walls must once have represented.

An elderly man, wearing a long, shabby brown overcoat and with a blue river cap on his white head, limped across the road towards him, and poured blood from the loose paper of fish he was carrying, into the gutter almost at Piper's feet. Piper watched him do it, and then saw the man raise his head in his direction. He came a step closer.

"Are you the London Bobby?" the man asked, his gruff voice forming a slow Scots drawl.

Piper nodded. "Yes I am. Mister Parrish is it? Mister Turnbull said to meet you here. I thank you for being so prompt."

Alec Parrish cocked his head in the direction of a nearby doorway that soon led them into the bar-room of The Turk's Head. The ceiling was low, and the room was empty. A stout man appeared behind a row of barrels to the left. He glanced at them but made no remark, and disappeared once more. Parrish sat with his back to the opposite wall and stared wordlessly as Piper scraped a chair up to face him. The Scotsman's face was lined and blue veined around the eyes, his white whiskers were yellowed by tobacco, and his nose dripped from the cold November sea-air. He wiped it with a thin yellow rag that he pulled from inside his coat.

"That's a cold wind off the water this morning," Piper said, to no response from the other man. He continued. "How long have you been settled here?"

Parrish shrugged his shoulders slightly. "A good few years," he replied at last. "Yonder town held no claim on me. I'm used to the tides and the coast."

"A sea-going man then?" Piper said, a smile on his face.

"Never," came the gruff reply. "But I know ships, and I know the men that know them. There's plenty of that sort hereabouts."

Silence fell between them. Piper searched for a way to edge the conversation along. Eventually he gestured with an open hand. "I'm obviously very much a stranger in these parts," he said. "The main reason I'm here, the official reason, is not a concern that should bother you and me today. It's with this other matter, in which my involvement is by way only as a favour to a friend, that I hope you might be of some assistance. The tragedy of this man John Selkirk. Are you familiar with it?"

Parrish sighed heavily and sat back. "I saw in the town news-sheets that the man had died," he said. "Drowned it said. There seemed to be little mystery to it."

Piper nodded. "Yes, that's very probably the case. And as such, I'm merely acting as an envoy between his relatives in London, who knew him quite well during his time down there, and the close family here in Newcastle, who they've never met. I've spoken to his brother, and to a few of those who knew him hereabouts, either in former times or more recently, just so a more complete picture can be constructed." Piper hesitated. "He seems to have been a singularly unhappy man at the end of his life, in contrast to how he was in his youth."

Parrish shrugged again. "Is that not the way of life?" he said. His whole being spoke loudly of his belief in that very maxim, thought Piper, as he looked at the sallow-skinned, limp frame crouched in front of him.

He continued. "Can I ask you," he said, "Did you know him, this John Selkirk?"

Parish stared back, and shook his head. "Know him? Not at all," he said. "I remember him though. He was one of many that were prominent at one time, writers, poets, so-called, strutting the streets of the town like conquerors. Arrogant men most of them, full of self-importance, mealy-mouthed, acting like they knew better than most. But not Selkirk so much. He evidently had a skill with words, and a love for them. He tried his best to keep up with the rest, in showmanship and swagger, but he didn't have it in him. He wasn't like them, but they saw his value and allowed him to tag along. That's how I saw it anyway."

"So when was this?" Piper asked.

Parrish sighed and looked vaguely across to the high window across the room. "Oh, twenty five years ago. Even more perhaps, since I first saw him."

"So were you part of their company, these so-called Bards of the Tyne?"

"No, not I", he said, emphatically. "Never that. But as a younger man, I had some involvement with the singers

112

and fiddlers and the rest, who were heard around the taverns and alehouses in those days." He looked down at his feet, thoughtfully. "It was at the behest of a girl whose man I had once known. He found himself in trouble with the military that were stationed in the town at that time. She called on me for help in that. It was she who belonged to that world of ballads and rhymes and suchlike."

Piper nodded. "Turnbull spoke of it. She was a poet herself? I've heard only of men as part of that profession."

"No, she was a singer of songs, nothing more," he replied. "And her songs were of a simpler time, not the wordy gushings that they became later with John Selkirk and his like. Songs that had grown out of the hillsides and the cobbles of the street, and the waters of the Tyne. And believe me, she sang them well."

His mouth was dry and he ran his hand across it. "After she had left these parts, I drifted still amongst these people for the pure pleasure of their music and company. Gradually the freer, wilder voices of the olden times were pushed aside by scholars and technicals, those that strove to imitate them, to improve upon them, if you can believe it. The songs were claimed by men with a pen instead of a fiddle. The singers I knew had no time for them. And neither did I. I left them to it. And you're right, it was all men who drove it. Maybe the odd woman amongst them, as I recall, proud and haughty wenches, the daughters of rich benefactors or some such, I suspect, none of any consequence. It took a male arrogance to purloin the craft, and to suck all the goodness out of it."

Piper watched the man closely as he spoke. He seemed unused to conversation of this sort, with a desolate air about him, and a tired lilt to his words. His eyes blinked tightly and often, and never looked directly at the one he addressed. His sixty and more years had taken their toll, and there seemed little of interest left in him to pull him through many more.

Piper leaned in a little, though there were no other ears to hear him.

"All this talk of singers and fiddlers is beyond my usual realm," he said. "I came here with a much more dull purpose. I had no knowledge of John Selkirk's past, or his talent, or of the society in which he mingled. Maybe it's no wonder, despite my instincts, that something drives me to delve more deeply into it all than I had previously planned. I begin to ask myself who were the man's acquaintances, what were his habits other than the drink, and what soured his life so, to spoil all the ambition and skill that he obviously showed at one time."

"As I say," Parrish replied, somewhat cautiously, "I see no mystery to it. Do you?"

Piper laughed. "It could be that I'm merely intoxicated by the strangeness of it. These songs and tales and poems. I've never come across anything quite like it. I visited a music hall in town the other night. It was rare stuff. The comedy of it, the high melodies, and the emotion of it. If such a thing exists in my own town, as undoubtedly it does, I've had no dealings with it."

"I'm sure it does," said Parrish, softening somewhat at Piper's words. "It's easy to be consumed by it, and feel the need for it. It takes us away from our troubles of the day, and yet it reflects the heartbreak of it, all at the same time."

These words came as a surprise to Evan Piper, coming as they did wrapped in a tired Scots brogue that up to that point had shown nothing but bitterness. He thought of similar, long forgotten words, spoken with a Welsh slant, by his father, long ago. His mind shook away the thought.

"That would be it," he said. "Laughter and tears, no barrier in between. There was a song of tragedy sung the other night, about the waters of the Tyne, that reminded me of nothing more than the tale we discuss now, the death of this man Selkirk. Strange to say, perhaps that's the very cause of my deepening interest in the matter, to hear how his own song really ended."

Parrish lowered his head. "Yes, I'm familiar with that one," he said. After a moment he looked sharply back at Piper. "But that can't be all of it, surely," he said. "There must be a deeper reason why you chase this particular ballad. It seems to me that you have suspicions of a more tangible kind."

Piper thought for a moment. It had come to a point where matters would have to be laid out plainly, if Parrish was to be of any value to him. He was still muted by the secrecy concerning the official beginnings of his mission, but he saw no reason not to share as much as was necessary of the rest with this man.

"It's a tangled web, is it not?" he said. "This man John Selkirk was active enough in his younger days within the ranks of these poets and songsters, so that his work was accepted and well thought of, popular among the masses, published in collections, pamphlets and the like. Then at some point, still as a young man, he brought a halt to it, and very suddenly took it upon himself to leave this

115

region. He thought to make a go of it in business in London, we're told, where he remained, unchecked and anonymous for ten years or so. During that time he continued to produce verse, and indeed sent much of it back to Newcastle to be printed. The public hunger for such things had continued, increased even, in his absence, and perhaps he felt he still had a contribution to make."

Parrish looked at him. "And what was this contribution, these verses written in London? And who was the sponsor for it?"

Piper shook his head. "They've never emerged. His contacts here by then were only his family, still working as merchants on Pilgrim Street, with no time or money to do anything with wanton poems and songs."

"So what happened to them?" asked Parrish, suddenly very interested.

Piper hesitated, then admitted, "The pages may still be in the hands of his brother's household. There's a slim chance that I might be able to lay hands on them myself very soon, though what advantage that will be to me, I honestly can't tell." Parrish nodded, but made no response.

Piper went on. "So then, a dozen years ago, Selkirk returned to his hometown, ruined, destitute, embarrassed by failure, and from then on kept no company but his own. I know nothing of his whereabouts after that, until this year, when he was sleeping each night in a woodworker's shop in town, and it was from there he wandered off a fortnight since and ended his days face-down in the river."

He sat back, pensively, and then decided to continue.

"Two elements of his demise stand out, as I've learned them yesterday. Firstly, it's said that the death took place accidentally, as he took water from the river in a tin cup. I am not the only one to view that as a curious thing, to take water from the filth of a river fed by gutters and middens in the centre of a town!" Parrish grunted in agreement at that.

"Secondly, the doctor who attended the scene, while not prepared to swear to it, claims that the victim may have perished by other means, and was likely dead when his body went into the water."

Parrish twisted round suddenly. "On what evidence?" he snapped. "And why was this not mentioned?"

Piper held up a calming hand. "On sincere opinion, that's all, and one which he was prepared to share at the inquest, but was not given the opportunity."

A derisive laugh sprang from Parrish. "And this you are happy to ignore? And this drink from the river. You say a tin cup? Knowledge of that means it must've have been seen by someone. How so? I'd have thought it would have sunk beneath him, if he was holding it as he fell. That's a curious detail, even if you yourself are not aware of it."

Piper shook his head. "No, I ignore none of it," he said. "Yet equally, I see nothing that's not explained by a wicked but common enough attack by an unruly hand, upon a man who was too drunk to resist or to save himself. A mere grudge over money, or drink, or a thousand things could have sparked the incident. To consider more sinister reasons behind it, assumes a close or even intimate relationship between victim and assailant. And how can that be, when by all accounts, Selkirk had no recent involvement with anyone."

Alec Parrish made no reply to any of this. He trailed the toe of his boot in the sawdust on the floor beneath him, making a smart pile of it, as if gathering his own thoughts.

Piper stood and faced him. "I've told you what I know," he said. "Now, perhaps you have other strands to add to this that I am unaware of. If so, I'd be glad if you shared them."

Parrish stared back at him for a long while, then spoke.

"These poets," he said, a taste of contempt in his voice, "These writers. I watched them parade their notoriety in public until it sickened me. I avoided their company as I did their pompous verses. But there was one I had cause to meet up with some time after this. A slight character in the scheme of it, I have to say, named Jack Dent. I'd seen him swilling ale and puffing his cheeks with the rest of them in the Indian Kings and the Black House, though I've no recollection of ever hearing his work, if indeed it ever existed. Then about five years ago, I saw him again, by chance, here in this very street outside. I caught a glimpse of him as he walked through the market. I recognised him immediately. It was busier than you see it today, and he pushed through a gaggle of folk around a grocery, and slid out with a stolen shank of ham in his coat. He was skilled at such things, I could tell, and when he caught my eye he was much troubled. He came over and faced me. I let him know it was not my concern what risks he took for his meat, and dismissed it. My curiosity as to his situation got the better of me, and I let the conversation continue. I asked him what had brought him to that point in his life, acknowledging that I'd been aware of him in past times, better times for him, I suspected."

Parrish stood and walked to the high window, as if to refresh himself of the narrative by looking at the place where he'd heard it. He shook his head dismissively.

"There was much to it," he continued, "A rambling tale of bad choices and worse luck. He was a troubled soul, erratic and self-pitying. Much of it meant nothing to me. What comes to mind now though, is how similar the change in his life appears to be, to that of John Selkirk. The fall from on high, from the society of privileged individuals toasted by the town, to being in desperate exile in far reaches from it."

Piper listened closely to this. "What had caused this," he asked, "Other than the man's own flawed character?"

Parrish ran his palm across his brow in thought. "Many things, as I say. But more to the point was the impression he gave of being in hiding. His exile from Newcastle had been a necessity. He had come into conflict with people of influence, he said, and they had been the cause of his downfall. Such was their position of power that he had feared for his life, and he was here anonymous, nameless, lest they trace him and exerted some kind of revenge."

"Physical revenge, you mean? He was threatened?"

"As he told it, yes, beyond doubt."

Piper was perplexed. "But what had he done, other than insult the wrong person at the wrong time?"

Parrish shrugged. "It's hard to say. He mentioned something about how they had purloined his work, that others had claimed authorship of verses and prose that he himself had written. When he had questioned it, severe threats had been made."

119

Piper looked incredulous. "That's surely not enough to render him so fearful and to force him to flee in such a way!"

"Well now, that I can believe," Parrish replied. "The rivalry runs deep and ruthless among these people. There was much in the press about such arguments in those days. The origins of this verse-writing began casually and sportingly, then took a turn far more cut-throat and wilful as fame became such a heady commodity amongst them."

"Yes, I'd heard as much from elsewhere," Piper acknowledged.

"Whether this was true in Dent's case, I don't know," Parrish continued. "He claimed to have been wronged in this case by a woman who had betrayed him. He was very bitter about it."

"A woman?" Piper said. "One of those that you mentioned perhaps, the benefactor's daughter or a similar type?"

"Perhaps. Her fine name suggests that could be so. He referred to her as Rosalinda. She had plainly beguiled him, and it had left its mark."

Piper looked away in thought. The name, Rosalinda, struck a distant echo in his mind. He could not place it. He turned back to Parrish.

"This is a slender thread," he said. "Again, it all sounds so commonplace on the face of it. A deranged, impetuous individual, fuelled with resentment and regret. How many poets have ended their days in a similar state, I wonder? And where's this Jack Dent now, still here in the town?"

Parrish shook his head. "I saw him a handful of times after that. He never acknowledged me. He seemed more

120

wary and troubled each time I saw him. Then he was gone. It must be near to four years since I saw or heard of him."

A silence settled between them. "So what do you make of it all, Mr Parrish?" Piper said at last. "Am I to pull together the links of this vast chain and see if they connect, or let it dangle freely and go about my own proper business? What's the best course, I ask you?"

Parish looked sideways at him, and spoke quietly. "What indeed," he said. "I have no desire to involve myself with the rules of law, but it interests me that we have both smelled the wolf that may lie at the heart of this. My suspicion though, is that we do not know how big a wolf this might be, how long in the tooth it is, and how respectable is its disguise."

Piper chuckled at this. "This wolf," he said, "You seem previously acquainted with it."

Parrish turned away. "It's an elusive beast. I can sense its presence, its influence, and certainly the effect of its actions. They're all plain to see. But I've never seen its face. I'm reluctant to do so." He turned and stared Piper in the eye. "Can you even understand what it is I speak of?"

Piper hesitated. "I don't know," he said. "This is a strange land to me. My world is one of thieves and violence, even murder sometimes, and ultimately, one of justice. Wolves are scarce on the streets of my city."

"And what of corruption?" Parrish asked, sharply, suddenly rising to his feet. "Of scheming and plotting, lying for personal gain, at the ultimate expense of others. How scarce are they in your proud city?"

He walked a few paces into the centre of the room, deep in thought.

121

"Didn't Turnbull tell you how he and I met?" he said at last. "It was he, as a young clerk familiar with high places in the town, who came to me, asking for assistance to weed out the rotting roots of greed and avarice that were choking Newcastle at the start of a new century. He was an honest man, and I saw that plainly. He righted a wrong, with barely enough help from me, yet it made nought but a scratch upon the polished surface in the grand scheme of things. I dare say that he continues to scratch away in the position that he now holds, though I have no dealings with him now. But he knows a wolf when he sees one. As I can see that you do too, despite your mockery."

He walked to the window once more, and peered out, as if searching the sky. Piper watched him for a long moment. Yet again he found himself confronted by bigger things than he'd been prepared for, just as he had when talking to Doctor Rossiter, to James Selkirk, and to Emily Gilchrist. The scope of his own commission, related as it was to the attempt upon the life of a Prime Minister, rendered these concerns insignificant, laughable even, and yet if there was some sinister work behind them, surely he was under an obligation to seek them out, in case they were somehow linked to his main investigation.

Standing in this cold empty bar-room in a wind-swept sea-town, with the clipped, suspicious voice of this unkempt Scot still echoing around the bare walls, Evan Piper felt isolated. That brief, surprising tinge of affinity that he'd felt with Parrish, was slowly dissolving into a broth of old grudges and local intrigue, of which he knew nothing. The way ahead that was on offer to him was shrouded in doubt and uncertainty. The way back too offered little more than that. The old city walls of London suddenly seemed inviting, comforting even, a place to hide, a place to cherish, but a long, long way from where he now stood.

CHAPTER 11

"Spoil'd aw my fine jacket"

Superintendent Turnbull looked up from his cluttered desk when Evan Piper tapped on his half-open door. He felt the stab of stiffness in his neck. It was nearly seven o'clock, and darkness had crept in unnoticed as he'd sat with pen in hand, pages from the report of the railway tragedy at Shields scattered before him, since early afternoon. They had made grim reading.

Piper too seemed sore and weary as he entered. Turnbull suddenly realised he was pleased to see him. He laughed out loud at the sight.

"Look at us," he said. "We've both become old men since you got off that damn boat last weekend!"

Evan Piper laughed with him, and was equally surprised at the familiarity between them.

"The loan of the baker's cart for my trip to the coast was much appreciated," he said, mockingly, "But it's left me somewhat pained and stiff."

"Have you eaten?" Turnbull asked.

"I have," he answered. "I'd had nothing all day, so I sampled the pleasures of Ball's Scullery near the Cloth Market. A cabbage and bacon concoction, with ample bread to go with it. It had been waiting all day for someone to claim it, and I was glad to oblige. And you, you haven't?"

"I did, in fact, but three hours since. I'll wait until I'm back in my own home now I think." Turnbull raised his brows. "And today? Was Parrish helpful? He can be obtuse, I know, but I did warn you."

Piper nodded his head. "Yes, I can see how he might be," he said, "But in fact he was obliging today. He talked freely enough, though I confess, quite where his contribution leaves me is still unclear. The more information I get, the more confused and exasperated I seem to be."

The Superintendent looked down at his report, still a long way from complete. He sighed and threw down his pen. He snapped closed the lid of his ink pot, and nodded to the vacant chair that stood nearby. Piper fell heavily into it. The very presence of an extra chair in this room struck Piper as being pleasingly significant.

"So, tell me," Turnbull said, "What have you gathered up so far?"

Evan Piper took a deep breath and slowly recounted as much as he could recall of his comings and goings of the previous three days. Turnbull fingered the chain of the watch in his waistcoat pocket and looked at him with heavily lidded eyes, occasionally nodding with interest, but mainly just absorbing it all in stillness.

After he'd recounted the gist of his conversation with Alec Parrish, Piper sat back with a heavy sigh. Turnbull looked at him for a while longer, than spoke at last.

"So how did you leave it with him?" he asked. "You've opened a door on this matter with Parrish, and I know the man. I doubt if he'll watch you walk away now and not act upon things himself in his own way."

Piper shrugged. "I hope he does exactly that," he said. "I encouraged him to do so in my own way too, I think. I told him I'd be in Newcastle until Monday next, and that he could contact me here. I've no idea how he might do that, and his aversion to this town persuades me that he'd never venture so much as a fleeting visit, but you never know. He seems a determined man, a renegade in many ways, but with a keen sense of social justice, borne I suppose from his ill-starred life thus far." Piper stood up slowly, and allowed himself a groan of discomfort as he did so.

"I must return to my very handsome lodgings and rest these aching bones," he said. "I'll see you tomorrow perhaps?"

"I'll still be here, more than likely," said Turnbull, then suddenly he remembered something of importance. "Oh yes," he said, "There is a package for you, with the sergeant. He brought it for you an hour or so ago." He called loudly for Fitzsimmons, who appeared almost immediately at the door, holding a wide roll of ragged paper, a good four inches in diameter and the length of a loaf of bread, fastened tightly with cheap string.

"Yours sir, I believe," he said, holding it forth. Piper took it and Turnbull pushed an open pen knife across the desk towards him. Grabbing it, he cut cleanly through the binding, and placed the package on the desk. It rolled open upon the flat surface, its edges curled and loose. Piper spread it wide. He knew immediately what it was.

He was looking at John Selkirk's lost manuscripts.

With the sergeant and Turnbull at his shoulders, he pulled aside the brown-edged, yellowing sheets one by one, staring intently and silently at the wayward scrawls of dark green ink that spidered across the pages. The paper

127

was cheap and began to tear at his touch. Some of the writing was already beginning to fade. Much of it was indecipherable, amply scrawled with thick crossings-out and dotted with smudges of ink-blots and stains of varying colours and sizes. Each page, of which Piper counted seventeen, bore a tidy title at the top, sometimes little else, but others meandered downwards in meaningless lines of disconnected phrases. The titles themselves included "Bob Cranky's Gazette" and "Bob Cranky's Foot Race", "The Sandgate Goose" and "Captain Robinson's Bad Luck". Noted under that last, there was a list of foodstuffs, flour, apples, mutton, pork rind and lastly, tobacco. Turnbull's own finger pointed to a page headed "The Ale-drinker's Prayer at Dawn".

"What madness is all this?" he said. "The ravings of a sotted soul, surely. I'd be surprised if you learn anything at all from such gibberish."

As he spoke, Piper noticed another page, torn to half the size of the rest, and almost hidden between two others. He slid it free, and stared at it.

"I wouldn't be so sure," he said. He stepped back and held the paper nearer to the candle on the nearby shelf, for closer examination. There were a mere two short verses, in ink blacker than the rest, with the title "Corly Croons" written extravagantly at the head. He read them out, softly, to the room.

> "Yon Corly Croons, they cannot kna,
> What Rosalinda has in store
> Plucked from mither, rent from toon,
> To Frenchy wars to meet thy doom".

He cast a questioning glance at Turnbull, then continued to the end.

> *"Young Andy gan to lands o' plenty,*
> *Say fareweel to the Four and Twenty"*

He raised his brows and stared back at Turnbull once more.

"I think I grasp the gist of it, despite the strange cut of the language," he said. "It's meant to reflect the local pronunciation, I suppose. I didn't realise that verse was actually written down like that, rather than simply spoken that way."

"It's the idiom," Turnbull replied. "It's meant to raise the local way of speaking to a level of acceptance, of poetry even. A daft and clumsy effect, in my eyes. Do you find any significance in these lines?"

Piper nodded slowly. "I do. Though the nature of it is beyond my grasp at present, I admit. What is that, "Corly Croons"? That is one thing that escapes me."

Turnbull shrugged and looked at the sergeant. He shook his head as if also mystified.

"A place perhaps?" he suggested. "It's almost Scots in style, so maybe a border-country expression? Their tongue is quite different from ours, even though we're but thirty miles distance from them. I'm not familiar with it anyway."

Piper sat down, the page still held up in front of him.

"There is another thing," he said. "The name, Rosalinda. I've heard of it before. Your friend Parrish spoke of someone bearing it, a woman who had some involvement with the writers' circle that Selkirk was part of before he left Newcastle."

"Then a sweetheart perhaps?" Turnbull suggested.

"Perhaps," Piper agreed. "But I'd come across it even before Parrish mentioned it, a day or so ago, and now it escapes me where or when that was. Someone else spoke the name in my presence. Maybe not directly to me, but it's an unusual one. I'm sure I know it."

"And the name, Andy," said the sergeant. "A Scots name, that, Ah reckon. Ah knew an Andy who worked on the chaldrons. He was from Glasgow, and a mean man in drink."

"It all seems the work of a mind befuddled by the drink," said Turnbull. "I suggest we bind these papers again and examine them more thoroughly in better light. It's growing dim in here. Sergeant, can you collect them, if you please?"

Fitzsimmons began to gather them up. Piper sat, his mind distracted, the half-page still in his hand. He searched his mind for some clarity, but tiredness prevailed. He stood at last, as the sergeant knotted the string delicately around the roll of paper. He realised the half page had been left loose, so folding it once, he slipped it into the pocket of his coat.

"I'll take the bundle with me, I think," he said, "And look closer at them at my lodging later tonight. Though perhaps you could loan me your pen-knife to cut the wick of my lamp. My landlady Mrs Dixon is somewhat frugal in the lighting of her establishment."

Turnbull shrugged and handed him the knife. "I think you will need more than strong light to puzzle through these papers," he said. "Though Constable Ramsay was quite excited when he heard that Sergeant Fitzsimmons had brought them in. He seemed to consider them as some kind of lost treasure, as far as he and his fellow poets were concerned. This man Selkirk seems to be still held in some high regard on the strength of his early work, despite his pitiable end."

Piper laughed. "I'll try to see that Ramsay gets them for his own amusement when I'm done with them. You can tell him so tomorrow."

The sky had been clear when Piper had entered the police house, but a thin drizzle matched by a sharp chill greeted him when he left it. It was nine o'clock and the streets were almost empty. The blunted clap of horse shoes on cobbles echoed up from somewhere to his left, a crippled man muttered softly to himself as he made his slow way down the opposite side of the road, and a young couple huddled into each other lovingly, as they hurried around the corner towards New Bridge Street. Piper hunched his shoulders against the weather, and clutched the roll of papers tightly to his body, hoping to keep them dry. Pale light from a handful of high windows signalled his way across the road to the entry of High Bridge, the lane that would lead him up and along to the Bigg Market, but instead he slipped through into a narrower lane he had used the day before. He was still deep in thought. The name Rosalinda resounded in his memory, but it only came to him in the Scots twang of Alec Parrish. However it had first appeared to him was not forthcoming.

As he walked, he hugged the side of the pathway nearest the wall, most cautiously at the point where the alley sloped carelessly sideways halfway along. As he did so, he became aware of movement in the shadows beneath a set of steps, leading up to a stilted wooden structure that jutted from the second storey of a dwelling to his left. He glanced quickly over to it, and saw that two dark figures had already emerged and were advancing up towards him. He quickened his step, but within a dozen paces he knew that the figures had purpose, and that they were on his trail. A narrow siding was suddenly on his right, and he dodged into it, his pace quickening. He turned sharp left into another entry, breaking into a trot as he did so. He heard from behind that his assailants had done the same. He was running blindly now, the thick darkness of the passage overwhelming him. It suddenly opened into another wider alley, veering in a slope to one side. He slipped on a kerb, but regained his footing at once and ran on, his breath coming quick and hard from his chest. He grasped the brim of his hat and pulled it off for fear of losing it, while his other hand gripped the roll of papers tightly. The rise of the street was more than he had bargained for, and he felt himself slowing. The feet behind him sounded closer, pounding heavily on the stones. Another corner, and Piper swerved to his left again, choosing a more level pathway, but he slipped again on a loose kerbstone, and staggered violently. His hat fell from his grasp and rolled clumsily off across the stones. He abandoned it.

His pursuers were almost upon him. He looked frantically for a safe harbour. A young woman coming towards him stepped back against the wall in fear as he passed, and then an old man strode out from a doorway, and was in front of him. Piper pushed him aside and was cursed for it. To his right now, the shape of any buildings was gone, and he soon saw that there was open ground. He crossed towards it, and stepped into a sea of thick mud, wet and slimy. He felt his feet slide from underneath him. As he hit the ground, there were breathless men on top of him at once, and he felt a fist in his face, a sharp kick to his thigh and another to his ribs. Another punch to the side of his head made the cold mud beneath him feel almost soothing, and there was an instant when he knew nothing, until the feeling of the manuscripts being snatched from his hand caused him to rise up slightly. Fingers were at his throat, the stench of breath was close to his face. His own hand went to his pocket, and he grasped the pen-knife that lay inside it. He pulled it out and stabbed wildly with it, at the hand clutching at his neck. A sudden cry of pain, and the loosening of the grip around his throat told him that the weapon had found a mark, then a fist into his midriff winded him and he curled up in pain. His face was wet, with mud or with blood, he couldn't tell. He heard a gruff voice call out "Haway!" and he lay back in the hideous mud and breathed heavily, painfully, believing that his assailants had fled. Almost at once he recoiled, as he sensed that they had returned for more. He looked up, his eyes stinging from grit and water, and at once made out a softer, less threatening shape, looming above him.

"Are ye all right?" a woman's voice said, and he could hear the tremble in it. "Are ye badly hurt?" it said.

He tried to answer but his lips felt like they were on fire, and the sour taste of blood choked him at once. He coughed and winced with pain. He heard a loud groaning

133

sound that he realised was coming from him. He tried to sit up, his eyes closed tight with the effort of it. The woman spoke again, but his pain blotted out any meaning.

"Try and stand up," he heard her say. His breath was slowing. He grunted and put his hand down into the thick wetness. He slowly raised himself up on one side, then on to his knees. Then somehow, he got himself to his feet.

"There's water yonder, in the trough," the woman said. "Just wipe yersel' off a bit, ye'll feel better."

She stood a pace or two away from him, and then followed him as he staggered forward to where she was pointing. The lane led to a small open yard, with a squat trough in its centre. He slowly limped to it, leaned over the stone side and swung a handful of water across his face. He filled his mouth with a second handful, and spat it out on the ground beneath him. He was suddenly cold, his wet garments clinging to his bruised skin. His lower lip was heavy and smarting, and his ribs ached. His head pounded. Moreover, he was angry, both for the beating he'd taken and for the loss of the manuscripts. He was also aware that the whole incident had been for the sake of obtaining them, and this troubled him deeply.

"Are ye better?" the woman asked. He turned to her, and only then realised who she was.

"Miss Gilchrist," he said. "I thank you. Excuse the state you find me in. I wasn't expecting to be manhandled so in the streets of this town."

She took a step closer to him. "Ah saw you clearly as you ran past me," she said. "Ah could see you were in danger. Ah'm only glad you seem to have survived it as you did." She moved closer still, staring at what she could see of his face. "This can be a rough place. No doubt London is a safer, civilised place, but here you have to be on your guard."

Piper laughed at this naïve remark, and paid for it with a sharp stab across his chest.

"You have no fear of it yourself, then?" he asked. "To be wandering these streets in darkness alone?"

"No. Ah know my way about. Ah was on my way to the Wheatsheaf," she said, "For the music-hall. Ah wasn't due to sing tonight, but Ah know them that will be performin'. There's much to be learned in watchin' them."

"I very much enjoyed your performance earlier in the week, when I called in briefly myself," he replied. "I'm not used to such scenes. I was quite taken with it."

She sounded surprised. "What, they do not have music-hall in London?"

"I am sure they do," he said, "But I haven't seen it, and I suspect it isn't as popular in my part of the city as it seems to be here." The conversation was taking its toll on him. He slowly straightened himself. "Anyway, don't let me keep you. I feel I can manage to walk to my lodging." He looked about him, bewildered. "That is, if I can find my way to it from here."

"Ah can walk that way with you," she said, and again pointed the direction.

Their progress was slow, and he felt the need to converse politely as they moved.

"How is your father today?" he said.

"The same," she said. After a moment's hesitation, she continued. "Ah spoke with him a bit, about John Selkirk.

135

He obviously finds it unpleasant to talk about. Ah told him about your questions. He offered nothing much back."

"I've learned a lot myself since then," he said. "In fact this incident you've just witnessed, I'm sure it bore some relation to the matter, though I'm not sure in what respect."

"Ah thought as much," she said. There was a silence as they walked, then she spoke up again.

"You mentioned his family, here in the town. His brother is it, and his sons? Did you know that John himself had a son?"

Piper was surprised by this. "No, I did not. And does he still live in Newcastle?"

"No, sadly, Ah believe that he's long dead. He was listed in the militia, some twenty years ago, and was sent to fight in France soon after. Ah can recall him, Ah think, as a young boy of fifteen or so, tall and with thick hair and swarthy even then, much like John his father. My own father believes that his loss was what drove John to drink so. Who can tell?"

"And what of his mother?" he asked. "Is she known to you? I've heard nothing of any of this."

She hesitated, and said, "Ah really know nothing much of it meself. Ah'm reluctant to ask my father about it, but if you wish it, Ah'll do that. If nothing else, he might know a name of the mother, but many years have passed. Andrew would be forty years old now, more perhaps, if he had lived."

"Andrew?" Piper said. "The son's name was Andrew?"

"Yes, Andrew Selkirk. I can recall him plainly," she said.

Piper took a deep breath. "His mother may have had the name Rosalinda. Does that mean anything to you?"

"Rosalinda? That's a grand name," she said. "Ah would've remembered anybody called that, Ah'm certain. Ah'll ask me father though. As Ah say, it might sound a bell with him."

When they reached the door of the Unicorn, she said a swift goodnight, and continued on her way to the music-hall. Piper watched her go, then hoisted himself carefully up the stairs to his room and gingerly peeled away his sodden, stained clothes. The water in the shallow bowl on the table was brown with filth almost immediately, and he eased himself back in his bed, still caked in much of the mud that he had brought with him. He drifted once again into a sleep, his body sore, his head pounding, and his mind churning with names, rhymes, and dark, faceless shapes.

CHAPTER 12

"A' wor consarn"

"I'm to blame for this," Constable Ramsay said, his hands sullenly stuffed into his pockets, as he watched Evan Piper sip with painful care from a cup of strong tea at the table in the middle room of the police house the next morning. "I should've kept me mouth shut. I just didn't consider it a police matter, a few old songs and verses, lyin' around for twenty years with nobody takin' any notice of them. Who would've thought folks would go to such extremes to get their hands on them?"

Piper smiled up at him. "Well, at least you found my hat," he said. "Unmistakeable I suppose, though I'm surprised someone hadn't made off with the thing, before you chanced upon it."

"I beat a young mudlark to it by the skin of my teeth, if truth be told," said Ramsay. "There were very few other folk about at that time of the mornin'." He looked at Piper squarely and added, "Mind you, I was fully expectin' to find you lyin' somewhere nearby, to be honest. That alley is not the sort of place I'd recommend you visitin' out of daylight."

"It wasn't by choice, believe me," replied Piper, his features screwed in defiance of a mouthful of hot tea.

He was dressed in a pair of white constable's trousers, the sort usual for wearing in warmer seasons, and a flannel shirt of poisoned grey. Of his own apparel, only his boots were still part of his attire, the rest hanging on a thin rope stretched across the black hearth, where a fire had been lit in celebration of his survival. He'd spent a painful and somewhat chilly half-hour in the yard of the firehouse below, washing off the grime still clinging to his limbs, and soothing the bruises and swellings that the morning had revealed. His hat had been returned to him by the bemused constable, and stood proudly on the table in front of them.

Ramsay was probably right. His enthusiastic reporting of the discovery of the Selkirk manuscripts at the previous evening's meeting of his Poets Society, had likely led, directly or otherwise, to news of them reaching the ears of those who had attacked Piper, or at least to those who had sanctioned the incident. That was not to say that the ruffians necessarily had a firm link to Ramsay's group, but there was surely an efficient enough connection for the whole enterprise to have been thought of, set up and carried out in a matter of a couple of hours. Whatever the truth behind it, it was a matter of fact that they were now in possession of the pages in question. All that is, except for the folded half page that Piper had fortunately placed out of sight in an inner pocket, before leaving the police house the night before.

That page lay at that moment on the table in front of them. Ramsay had looked at it for a long moment, but had seemed to draw no more conclusion from it than Piper.

"It is not in the style of Selkirk's other works," he'd said, "Not the ones I'm familiar with anyway. Yet you say the stolen sheets contained new songs on Bob Cranky? Those were more than likely his work, and give credence to the thought that the entire set of them were by his own hand."

140

Earlier, Sergeant Fitzsimmons had taken it upon himself to search a police map of the northern counties and lower Border region that he had kept in the central office, but after an hour's searching had found no trace of any place named "Corly Croon". There were no charts available to him showing the country any further north, so he was at a loss as to what else they could do without wading through reams of land-lists and gazetteers.

As Piper and Ramsay occupied a long silence, Superintendent Turnbull appeared at the doorway at the head of the stairs. It was an understatement to say that he was surprised to see Piper sitting there, half-clad, his lower lip and right eye the colour of coal, and a rough bandage of white rag-cloth tied to his temple.

"What in God's name has happened to you?" he said, his eyes wide.

Piper ran through a tidy version of the events since the two men had last seen each other, dismissing the inevitable apology from Ramsay at the crucial point, and trying to maintain both a sense of humour and a sense of dignity as the tale unfolded.

Turnbull sat in silence for a moment at the end of his account, and then leaned back against the wall where he'd been standing throughout.

"You realise this is now a police matter," he said. "Discounting your connection to the force, as a citizen of the town, albeit a visiting one, you're entitled to the protection and the attention of this office. And given the complexity and clandestine nature of your own investigation, this makes things somewhat complicated."

Ramsay raised his eyebrows in puzzled surprise at these words. Turnbull noticed this and added, "We should discuss this further in my office perhaps." He walked through, with Piper following him at a slow, painful pace.

With the door closed, and the two men facing each other across his desk, Turnbull spoke.

"There's something deep and dangerous going on here," he said, "Something that I would frankly not have anticipated, given what you have told me of your business so far. I can't believe this revolves simply around over-zealous enthusiasm for poetry and songs. Whatever was contained in the writings on those papers was obviously very significant, and very important to somebody. And that somebody thought nothing of going to extremes to obtain those papers. Would you agree?"

Piper nodded. "It would seem so," he said, "Though I'm perhaps not so surprised as you, given what I've learned in the past couple of days. The strands were too connected, too interwoven, not to be part of a wider and more complex picture." He paused for a moment, then continued. "The girl, Gilchrist's daughter, Emily. She mentioned something to me last night that I've omitted so far. That Selkirk had a son. It might be nothing to do with this, and it wasn't mentioned when I spoke about him to his own brother. But she claims to remember the son well enough, and that his name was Andrew. Andy, in the childish shortening of it. The same name that's mentioned in that curious verse."

Turnbull stared back, unmoved. "Then surely, if anything, that renders the significance of that verse to be meagre. It's merely an ode to his child, is it not? Is the boy alive? A man now if so."

"He was in the militia," said Piper, "And ended up in the French war, again, as mentioned in the poem, and she believes he was lost in battle. But I don't understand how a member of the local militia ended up fighting in France. Were there volunteers from hereabouts, who ended up serving overseas?"

Turnbull leaned forward and spoke. His manner was suddenly cautious. "Not solely volunteers," he said. "Many of the young men were willing to serve in local militia groups, both here in Newcastle and in other towns nearby. The militia was a defence force, nothing more. We had professional dragoons stationed here who were destined for the wars overseas, and were paid for that purpose. But when the French Wars began, and more troops were needed, there were local landowners, men who had sponsored and initiated those local militia groups, who realised that money could be made by hiring the local volunteers out to the King, to be distributed as his generals saw fit. Thus many of these keen volunteers suddenly found themselves being transported to foreign battlefields, never to return. It was a piteous, treacherous thing that happened. The noblemen responsible, Lord Beaumont, Lumley and the rest, their families still thrive, while the families of the fallen can only mourn."

"So in effect," Piper said, "The local men joined the small militia groups to ensure that they could actively serve, without having to leave their homes and families behind, yet in the end, the opposite happened. They were betrayed, and sent off to war, as simply as that."

"Exactly so," Turnbull agreed.

"The Four and Twenty, also mentioned in the song. A regiment, do you think?"

Turnbull frowned. "Well, the term is almost familiar to me, but I can't place it exactly. We could find that out from the commander of the Town Barracks easily enough. But if it is, or was, a regiment, does that make these matters clearer to you? It certainly doesn't to me."

Evan Piper leaned his head back in his chair, and put his fingers to his bruised lip. He sighed deeply.

"To be truthful," he said, "It's no longer even clear to me what crime it is that we are investigating. Possibly the suspicious death of John Selkirk, perhaps the theft of some unfinished poems penned by a madman, maybe the false claims of authorship of songs written in doggerel slang, by men who are long-since dead themselves, certainly the attack on an embarrassed and bruised policeman from three hundred miles off, and just possibly a wider plot, that includes the attempted assassination of the Prime Minister of this land." He smiled ruefully.

"Whatever your next step," said Turnbull, "I'm at liberty to allow a constable, Ramsay perhaps, to accompany you. Only if you wish it. He's amiable company, as you seem to have realised!" he added with a smile.

Piper shook his head. "I think not," he said, "And I've no idea yet as to what my next step should be. Perhaps another cordial visit to Miss Gilchrist."

Turnbull chuckled. "For nothing more than to offer her thanks for her assistance, I'm sure. But you're hardly dressed for paying a visit to a young lady. Ask Fitzsimmons, he's sure to have a coat and some more

144

suitable leggings to lend you until your own look more respectable."

Within the half-hour, Piper was on the street outside. The drizzle of the early morning when he had limped his winding way from his lodging to the police house on Pilgrim Street, had given way to a thick sleet, that was already gathering white against the highest cobbles and kerb stones. A smattering of people was passing by, looking grim and unprepared for this first real taste of winter. The coat and trousers he'd borrowed were ill-fitting, but thicker and warmer than his London garb. His own hat was none the worse for its overnight adventure.

He walked into the force of the weather and had gone about ten paces when Alec Parrish stepped out from a doorway as he passed. Piper was more than a little surprised to see him, while Parrish himself showed equal surprise at the condition of the other man's face.

"Quite a picture," he said, by way of greeting. "And the subject of our recent conversation played no little part in it, I'd bet."

"I'm surprised to see you in this place," said Piper. "That same subject has some bearing on that too, I'd say."

"Is there somewhere we can go to talk, other than in there?" asked Parrish gesturing towards the police house with a nod of his head.

Piper motioned for him to follow, and he led him back to the bakery where Turnbull had taken him at their first meeting. The place was empty, save for the same flour-dusted man as last time, who looked up sternly, then softened, presumably in recognition from the earlier visit.

Piper felt strangely flattered by this, and motioned to the side room. The baker nodded with a knowing smile.

The two men took their seats and the same repast was immediately brought to them, the scones and the weak tea. Parrish looked confused by this routine.

"Eat up," said Piper, and carefully nibbled at his scone. His bruises made for painful eating, and he soon gave up. Parrish devoured his own in a minute.

"What happened to you?" he asked when he'd finished. Piper told him. He showed little expression as he listened, but expressed disappointment when he heard that the manuscripts had been taken.

"Well, that is a setback," he said, "Though it does show you we are dealing with men of purpose here. It's a shame it took the loss of Selkirk's works to convince you of that."

Piper bristled somewhat at this, but didn't react.

"And you," he said, "What's brought you all this way on such a day as this? You have better news?"

He nodded. "The man, Jack Dent, that I told you about. He's emerged again. He is in North Shields, though keeping himself well-hidden."

"A strange coincidence. How did you trace him?"

"By way of the landlord of an alehouse on the fish-quay, The Anchor. I had spoken with him before of the old singers here in Newcastle, which is where he lived as a lad. His mother ran the kitchen at the Keelman's Hospital, so he wandered the streets around freely from a young age. He still remembered many of them that I saw in those days, Blind Willie the fiddler, Bella Roy and the rest. I spoke with him last evening, and by chance he mentioned that he had seen a man from that time right there on the quay, only a week before. He described him, and I was certain it was Dent, though the landlord knew no name for him. This morning, I made a point of watching the second catch come in, and there he was, hauling nets to the spillers on the middle ranking. A filthy job."

"Did you approach him?"

"I did not. He had a wild look in his eye. I'm too old to deal with that. I thought if you were to come with me, we'd stand a chance of getting a word or two out of him. You'd have to pay for his ale though, and it could amount to a tidy sum."

Piper considered this. It was a forbidding journey to make for a second time. His days here were running out, and this seemed like nothing so much as a distraction. Instead of answering, he pulled out the half-sheet from his pocket and held it towards Parrish.

"First of all, take a look at this. It's the one morsel that I saved from the loss of Selkirk's papers. And not an insignificant one, if my suspicions are correct."

Parrish took it and squinted at it for some time. He looked at Piper, and then read it again.

"If this is really in Selkirk's own hand, this is quite a prize," he said, "Though I'm not sure what to make of it. There are two names…"

"Rosalinda, a name that you mentioned to me," said Piper, "And then Andy, which I suspect is the fond name he used for his own son, who was called Andrew. He died in France, I am told, during the wars with Napoleon. Possibly in a regiment called the Four and Twenty."

"Possibly," agreed Parrish, though somewhat reluctantly, "But The Four and Twenty means something else to me, something a lot closer than the battlefields of France."

Piper looked at him, somewhat unsettled by this remark.

"And what is that?" he asked.

Parrish hesitated. "Well, when I first came here to Newcastle, local governing councils were only just being set up, and the regulators who had a fast hold on the city were almost totally at the bidding of wealthy types, the Merchants' Guilds, on one hand, and The Hostmen, who owned the rights to all matters concerning the river, on the other. That was on this side of the water, the Newcastle side. On the other side, the Gateshead side, there was a self-elected body of men, businessmen and lawyers and the like, who had a much stronger and deeper controlling interest, not only on the docks and quays over there, but also on the mills to the west and the smaller businesses to the south."

He leaned in closer, and continued in quieter tones.

"They were just as ruthless, just as corrupt, but possessed a higher degree of sophistication along with that. These were educated men, with a wider view of the world, and from long-established, wealthy families, who had carefully absorbed the influence of the new industries, and were adept at using those influences for their own gain, without the need to deal directly with the workers that they employed. They ruled Gateshead with a rod of iron and did so for many years. They were feared and despised because of it. They were twenty four in number at any given time, and that's how they were known, The Four and Twenty."

148

Piper tried to take this in. "And this body of men were in control, until when?" he said.

Parrish frowned and scratched his chin. "Perhaps until a dozen years ago. More recent than that perhaps. There was eventually a mayor elected, and a proper governing council set up, alongside him. But the old ways of it, and the power of the old Four and Twenty, they wouldn't have gone without a struggle. If indeed they are gone at all."

This was perilous stuff, thought Piper. He had no desire to be involved in local politics such as this. Nor could he see what bearing it could have on his own primary task. These people, if they still had any power, would hardly be radical or subversive in attitude. Surely the upholding of Tory values would be paramount to their own position of power. Parrish of course was oblivious to this line of thinking. It was only Turnbull who had been brought into his confidence since his arrival, and this fact alone was fast becoming an obstacle to the advancement of his investigations.

He looked at the man who sat before him, whose sense of right and justice, as well as his knowledge of local events, were formidable assets as far as Piper was concerned. A decision would have to be made.

"I have something to tell you," Piper said. "Something that may sway you towards abandoning all this, and to wash your hands of it. And of me! But I can't tell you here. You'll have to come to the police house with me. Turnbull is there. He's in my confidence."

"And evidently, I am not!" said Parrish.

"You might be glad of that, once you hear of it," replied Piper. "It's an honest request from me. I need an ally, a

149

companion if you will. Turnbull offered me the company of a constable earlier today. That would be more hindrance than help to me. But I feel there's a chance that you would suit that role, without much inconvenience to yourself." He hesitated, then added, "But it would be perhaps, an insult to your principles."

CHAPTER 13

"Yor scarters and clawers"

A now familiar look of surprise, if not astonishment, on Turnbull's face greeted Piper as he ushered Alec Parrish into the Superintendent's office ten minutes later. No word of greeting passed between them, merely a curt nod and an exchange of glances. Piper pulled a chair forward for the older man to sit down, stepped to one side and leaned against the wall, a troubled look upon his face.

He spoke up at last. "I've decided to bring Mister Parrish into my confidence, as to the reason behind my presence here in Newcastle, and I thought it prudent to do so with a witness who was already aware of it."

Turnbull said nothing, but looked from one man to the other. His gaze settled on Piper, and he nodded slightly.

Piper spent a moment gathering his thoughts, looking into the near distance, and then addressed Parrish. "Put simply," he said, "earlier this year, there was an attempted assassination of the Prime Minister, Robert Peel. No doubt you've heard tell of it. A culprit was named and charged, but it's thought possible that a wider network of people was involved. Extensive investigations, in various parts of the country, were undertaken, and a list containing many names was compiled, names that were thought to be of interest in the affair, for one reason or another. One of the names on that list, as you've probably surmised, was that of John Selkirk. There were various reasons for his inclusion, as I say, but regardless, the man himself was not traced, until, of course, when his body was found floating in the Tyne three weeks ago. I was sent here, by my superior officer in London, to establish the circumstances of his death, together with as much background to his life as might prove useful to the case. That's how this investigation began, and in spite of all the circumstantial facts that have emerged, and in spite of last night's unfortunate incident, that is how it's now struggling to proceed. There was only one other person in this town privy to this information, and that was Mister Turnbull here. You are the second."

After a moment, Parrish let out a hollow laugh. He avoided the gaze of the other two men, and then stared sullenly at the floor in front of him as he spoke up.

"You are telling me," he said, "That a drunken poet from Tyneside plotted against the so-called leader of this country, at a time when the poor bugger was drifting in a mindless stupor in a wood-shop on Sandgate Street? Might I ask, what brand of whiskey was your superior officer imbibing when he cooked up that little tale?"

Piper came closer to him and stared until their eyes met.

"Don't play the cynical Scot with me, if you please, Mister Parrish," he said wearily. "I'm sure you can see that the reasoning behind this tale, as you call it, was sound enough, and the potential ramifications of the entire affair are serious enough for every avenue to be explored. Selkirk's stay in London involved contact with radicals and subversives, including the man who now lies in Newgate Gaol, charged with the murder of the Prime Minister's Secretary. The writing of a few ballads and poems, regardless of their worth in a literary or musical sense, does not render a person exempt from suspicion when matters of so high an order are concerned."

Parrish stared back defiantly. "But those matters are of no concern to me," he replied testily.

"But the death of John Selkirk is, as shown by your very presence in this town today. Your concern was strong enough to drag you all the way here from Tynemouth, and for you to offer your assistance to get to the bottom of that matter. And just because our priorities differ, it shouldn't prevent both of us from pressing things forward. A need for justice is common on both counts."

There was a long, uneasy silence, as all three men delved into their own thoughts.

"Selkirk means nothing to me," Parrish said eventually. "Your Prime Minister means even less." He paused, and looked at both of the other men in turn. He smiled slightly. "But there might be some satisfaction for me to find out what lies behind all this, I suppose. To expose something of the bigger plot, and those who are responsible for it. That would amuse me. But my interest is purely a local one, a close one. The antics of lunatics in London hold no attraction to me, whichever end of the assassin's gun they may be lurking."

"And that's why I trust you," said Piper with a smile.

Turnbull had still not spoken. He sat, his elbows on his desk and his chin resting on his clenched fingers, still occupied with his own thoughts. Piper sensed a deep uneasiness in him and looked at him questioningly.

"This leaves you worried?" he asked.

Turnbull roused himself from his reverie. He opened his hands to them. "To the extent that I'm responsible for the upholding of the law hereabouts, and I have at my side a squad of men in uniform who are committed to do the same. You two gentlemen, for all your good intentions, do not fit into that scheme of things. I cannot have you cutting a swathe through the streets of this town in pursuit of your own ends without somehow holding you to account."

Piper nodded. "I understand that," he said, "But you forget I've sworn the same oath as you, and that I too am bound to operate within the confines of it. I have no authority here, and I accept that."

"Exactly," said Turnbull. "And I can't give you any such authority, no matter how much I might trust you." He paused and took in a heavy breath. "I can however give you the assistance of someone who does have authority, even though you dismissed such a notion earlier today."

"Ramsay?" Piper retorted. "A lumbering constable in a stove pipe hat is the last thing I need to be seen with, if I intend to make any progress in all this. Surely you can see that?"

"I do see that," Turnbull replied. "But he's a good man, with or without his stove pipe, or his uniform. And he knows the streets and people of this town better than most. He also knows these poets and writers, and even has the voice to deliver their songs with grace and resonance, or so I'm told."

"So in his everyday clothes? Is that what you mean?"

"His uniform and hat *are* his everyday clothes. It's only his duty-band that gives him any authority. But yes, we can find him some plainer stuff, and the three of you can march out together like colliers on a spree. A formidable team, I feel."

Parrish leaned forward. "And is this constable to be informed of the wider plot as well?"

Piper thought for a moment. "Yes, I can't see how we can co-operate without him being fully aware of the facts. What risk could there be?"

All three looked at each other in turn. Turnbull pulled out his watch.

"Decide soon," he said, "Ramsay reports for duty in five minutes."

Half an hour later, Piper, Parrish and Ramsay emerged from the station house onto Pilgrim Street. The constable was wearing a smart grey wrapper, reaching to his knees, with a low felt hat on his head. As luck would have it, that very morning he'd procured a pair of thick woollen gloves that only added to his newly-found dapperness. Even so, they were an uneasy trio, and went their separate ways almost at once, having made arrangements to meet again at four o'clock. A small tavern called The Crown at the far end of Pudding Chare was recommended by Ramsay as a suitable rendezvous. It was far enough away from the busier streets, he said by way of reassurance, and was only frequented by old men and infirm dogs.

In the meantime, Parrish knew of another alehouse where he might renew some old acquaintances and glean some background information from them without arousing too much interest. Ramsay had the intention of seemingly chance-meeting his fellow poet-circle regulars to discuss the merits of the old Bards of the Tyne, and moreover their associations and motivation. There had long been a radical flavour to local verse, and the origins of such thought might prove significant.

Piper resumed the journey towards the quay that he had started earlier that day, to pay a visit on Miss Emily Gilchrist.

She saw him coming, as she stood half-hidden in the shadows of the warehouse doorway. She emerged to meet him, having tied her hair back, smoothed down her grey bodice and straightened the pleats of her long skirt. He in turn, before setting out, had belted his oversized trousers with a length of twine, buttoned his borrowed coat almost to the neck, and dispensed with the head bandage. Even so, he still looked like he'd just been pulled through a thorn-bush on a stormy day.

Her smile hid her wariness of him. His own smile was more genuine by nature, though somewhat twisted by the swollen lip.

"Good day," he said, almost brightly. "I had to come by and thank you for your assistance last evening. I could well have spent the night lying in the cold mud on the builders flats if you hadn't roused me."

She shrugged, embarrassed. "Well, Ah'm glad to see you out and about. You were a sorry sight when Ah left you at your lodgin' house. Do you know yet who those men were?"

He shook his head. "No, they were likely just ruffians who seized their chance with a stranger. I should have been more careful, as you advised, though a little too late to save me from a hiding."

There was an awkward silence. Piper went on, "You mentioned that you were going to ask your father about John Selkirk's son, Andrew. Was that his name? I don't suppose you had a chance to do so, but time is running out for me. I'll need to return to London in a day or two and…"

She interrupted him. "Ah did ask him. Ah was right, Andrew was lost in the war. He'd be about twenty two years of age at the time. Johnny his father had already left Newcastle by then. And then when he came back here, he never spoke of Andrew, not with me father, at any rate."

"I see," Piper said. "That's understandable. And what of the boy's mother? Did your father know what became of her?"

"He said not. He couldn't recall her at all. She must have been away before all of this, Ah suspect."

"And Rosalinda? Remember that was a name I mentioned to you last night. Did your father have any knowledge of someone of that name?"

She looked uneasy at this. "Ah mentioned the name. He gave me a very strange look when Ah did so. It's bothered me ever since. Tell me," she said, turning to him, "Who was she, this Rosalinda? It affected my father to hear her name, yet then he denied knowin' it. He began talkin' of today's business, avoidin' any more conversation on the subject. So who was she?"

Piper shook his head. "I don't know who she was. Her name was mentioned to me, casually, a couple of times. Once so casually in fact, that I can't recall by whom or where it was that I heard it." He looked squarely at her. "Is there still not a chance that I could speak to your father myself? I know he's weak with illness and I wouldn't tax him with persistent questions, but just so as I feel I've done all I can on behalf of John Selkirk's relatives." He hated

157

lying to her, but he could sense that her own curiosity was now troubling her.

She was silent for a while, staring wistfully across the river to the long-walled buildings on the opposite bank, where a tall schooner was being unloaded by a gang of men shouting in a strange language, stranger even than the one spoken by Emily Gilchrist and the rest of these townsfolk, and which Evan Piper was rapidly becoming used to.

"He'll be here, at the yard, tonight," she said at last. "He often comes down for an hour or so, after most of the lads have gone home. Ah won't tell him you are comin', so when he sees you, he's likely to be angry. But if you wish to chance that, be here at six o'clock. He'll go on to evensong at St. Mary's at seven o'clock."

Piper nodded. "I'll be here," he said. Then she touched his arm, with a sharp, worried look on her face.

"Don't mention my singin' at the music-hall," she said, almost in a whisper. "He knows Ah do it, but he doesn't like that Ah do. Can Ah ask you that?"

He smiled and nodded.

"Charlie Ramsay, lookin' the dandy aren't yer!" the barmaid of The Blue Posts at the top end of Pilgrim Street called out, as the constable crept in, somewhat self-consciously, and made his way to the bar. The three men standing there wheeled round and grinned broadly at the sight of him. The Blue Posts was long-known as a ballad-singers tavern, and that's what drew Ramsay to it, but even at poets meetings he would always be in his police uniform, as was the accepted way with all constables. As it was, the coat that he'd borrowed was of a quality that he would not normally have been able to afford, and he seemed grandly affected at how worldly it made him feel.

"Somebody's been burglin' Alder Dunne's!" One of the men cawed mockingly. The outfitter's shop in the centre of the town was plainly beyond all of their pockets.

Ramsay smiled at their jibes. "I'm guidin' a London grandee about the town, and he demands a smart escort to suit a man of his station. I feel stiff as a board in this get-up, I tell 'yer! " He laughed, and thudded his gloved hands together. "Allow me a breather, if you will, and if it's too early for a song, join me in a drink if you feel the need of it."

The four of them joked and chatted for a good while as the drinks were enjoyed. All of them shared a common love and knowledge of the local ballads, including one man whose father had been a setter at one of the many printing shops on Dean Street, where several of the early bards had brought their verse to be copied out for broadsheets and pamphlets, and then to be sold for pennies in the alehouses and markets north of Sandgate, and out to Benwell and Blaydon to the west. The other men all had similar long attachments to the art of verse, with a wide appreciation of its history, and even an awkward tendency to emulate their betters with verses of their own. They suspected that Ramsay's own interest may have had a less deeply-founded origin, but his enthusiasm and knowledge could not be disputed, and he was accepted as part of their coterie. The weekly meetings in The Blue Posts attracted many such enthusiasts, and it had been here that Ramsay had perhaps caused John Piper's recent assault, and had admitted as much since then, when he had boasted to the company of the discovery of Selkirk's manuscripts. There had been too many people there that night to know who had misused the information later. It was not long, however, before the subject of their existence was raised.

"So have you had the chance to read the John Selkirk poems yet?" one of the men asked him.

"I have not," he sighed. "They're still in possession of the Inspector from London, the last I heard, and he'll likely deliver them to the writer's relatives there, when he goes back within the week."

This brought a groan of dismay from the others.

He continued. "I caught a brief glimpse of a page or two when the package was opened," he said. "Very few seemed to be complete sets, but there were a couple of Bob Cranky songs that I didn't recognise, and a sea ballad I think." He gulped down a mouthful of ale, then added, with a degree of circumspection, "And an ode to someone called Rosalinda, a sweetheart of his no doubt, though I hadn't heard mention of her before."

"No, no," one of the others exclaimed. "Rosalinda was a poetess, surely, at the end of the last century. She wrote the famous "Ode to Pandon Dene". It was widely sung a good few years ago."

"No," said another, "Surely that was Gilchrist's, I've seen it written with his name below it!"

The other man shot back, "It was attributed to him in a collection, but wrongly. It dates back to 1790 at least, long before his time. The woman was well known, though she wrote anonymously. A Miss Harvey, I believe that was the truth of who she was. Obviously poor Selkirk was smitten by her still, when he wrote the verse of which you're speakin'. Was it worth a closer look?"

Ramsay shrugged. "I couldn't tell, it was nothin' but a glimpse that I got. But I don't think so. It was a trivial thing, unfinished even. But it's good to know the provenance of the name, if that be the truth of it. I will say as much to the Inspector when I see him. "

He sat for a while longer, but he seemed distracted. There was more talk from the rest of them about Selkirk's other works, and that of other writers of the period, but Ramsay paid little attention to it. He was occupied enough by what had already been said.

A mere four streets away from the Blue Posts, Parrish slowly entered the main bar of a tavern called the Blue Bell. The landlady in days gone by, Mrs Cant, had been fond of his accent, having once been married to a Scot herself, so he had often paid her a visit in the past. She was long dead, but upon entering, he immediately recognised a couple of crusty, watery-eyed faces at either end of the bench by the long window. They both took a second look at him, one waving a weak hand, the other raising a half-empty pot. He ordered porter for both of them, and took a whiskey for himself. He sat between the two old men and exchanged mild greetings and idle chat for a minute or two, but then it was to the man on his right, known as Nibbler Wilson, that he pulled in closer, leaving the other man happy with his nose in his cup.

Nibbler had been a drayman, and had frequented every public house in town during his working life. In doing so, he had gathered a mountain of gossip and trivial detail, with which he was very discreet, at least when sober. At this time of day, he was perfect pickings for anyone who needed to know things.

Recent deaths of local characters, some known to Parrish and others not, were soon the main thrust of their conversation. Parrish took a cue from it.

"I heard there was a drowning a fortnight since," he said vaguely. "That man who had the medals for poetry and suchlike. John Selkirk was his name. Did you hear that?"

Nibbler assumed a serious tone. "Oh yes, Ah heard all about it. Very tragic," he said. "Just by the stone bridge. His brother is a clerk yonder, at Watson's Yard. Ah know him, the brother, but the dead man was a souse. Took badly to the drink some years ago. Still a sad end, no doubt about it."

"So he went into the river due to that, did he?" Parrish asked.

"Very likely, yes," Nibbler replied. Parrish paused as the other man took a deep draught, then resumed.

"Somebody said that ruffians had caused it, seeing him stagger about and raving on. But I see little truth in that, not if he was in as bad a state as they say."

Nibbler shook his head. "Now Ah hadn't heard that," he said. "There was talk of him bein' grudged against, but folks are suspicious enough when a tragedy comes out of the blue like that. Ah reckon he'd just had too much, and lost his footin' on the bridge. It's a disgrace, that bridge. There's talk of a mechanical one being built, did ye hear that?"

Parrish did not want to be distracted by that line of chat. He backtracked easily.

"I can't believe that," he said, "And I can't believe anyone would have a grudge against a man who was a well-known drunkard. That's a petty way of behaving."

"Oh, the grudge was said to be held over from years ago," said Nibbler. "Somethin' about a property in Gateshead, behind the old church there, on the hill. He'd been a man of means at one time, and had owned a property, so he'd had influence on that side of the water, even though he belonged to this side, by birth. Votin' rights and levies and all of that. It was hard to fathom, with him bein' in such a condition in recent times."

Parrish looked at the old man, and stood up. "Another small porter for yourself, before I'm on my way," he said.

When he came back to his seat, Nibbler's eyes were heavy and unfocused. Parrish tried to snatch back the conversation.

"Well, here's to him, John Selkirk," he said, raising his glass and encouraging the other to do the same. They drank, and Parrish continued.

"He had a lad, didn't he, a son?"

Nibbler looked vaguely at him. "Who?" he asked.

"The man Selkirk. I'm sure I remember a son, joined the militia down there at Westgate."

Nibbler raised his mug halfway to his mouth, and stopped, his mind turning over the question. Then he nodded.

"Yes, yes, Ah believe that's right, now ye mention it. He did have a young 'un. He might've ended up as a militiaman. Possibly. But Ah recall him as just a young

163

bairn, long-legged with a corly croon, just like his father. And dark-faced like him as well."

Parrish stared at the old man for a long, silent moment. A rush of realisation surged through him.

"A corly croon? You're saying 'a curly crown'? That he had curly hair, is that what you mean?" he said.

"Aye," Nibbler replied, "A thick corly croon, the same as his father had."

Parrish threw back the last half inch of whiskey in his glass and smiled to himself. He thought on for another few moments, and when he looked back at Nibbler, the old man's eyes were closed and the pot was empty in his gnarled old hand.

CHAPTER 14

"For nyen saw'd se weel"

"A curly crown!" exclaimed Piper, when Parrish recounted his conversation with Nibbler to him an hour later. "So that's all it means then, a headful of curly hair. My God, why can't people talk in proper English in this town? A corly croon indeed."

"That's what it means, but what does it signify?" Parrish responded. "It suggests to me that the verse is nothing but what you first took it to be. A lament for his fallen son."

"But what of Rosalinda?" Piper said, a note of desperation in his voice. "If there's still a mystery to be solved, then surely it lies there."

"No mystery," said Ramsay, hearing Piper's words as he swept into the taproom of the public house where the other two men were already sitting. "But firstly, here, see this!"

Ramsay slapped down the folded front page of the Newcastle Mercury that he had been holding in his hand. Piper took it, and a headline immediately caught his eye.

Newcastle Poet Linked to Prime
Minister's Attacker

it said, across a single column on the first page. Piper caught his breath and read the piece beneath it.

> *The name of once-celebrated poet John Selkirk from Gateshead, who died in tragic circumstances three*

weeks ago in a river accident, has been raised in connection with the attempted assassination at the start of this year upon the Prime Minister Sir Robert Peel. Currently Daniel McNaught of Glasgow is in custody charged with the crime, which resulted in the death by shooting of Edward Drummond, Private Secretary to Sir Robert. Monday's edition of the London Times has reported that further investigations have revealed a network of radical groups both in the capital and in other major towns in the nation, who are thought to be linked to a bigger, more wide-ranging plot to undermine the government, given the Tory Party policies concerning the Irish Question. Officers from London are already said to be in Newcastle making extensive inquiries.

There was more. Piper skimmed through it, lest his own name should be mentioned, but it was not. He dropped the paper on to the table and Parrish snatched it up.

Ramsay pulled off his hat and ran a smoothing hand over his hair. He seemed bewildered by it all.

"The whole town will know of this by now," he said. "It must have been reported in your London newspapers within a day of you leaving for the Tyne. I don't understand it, considering all the lengths that you have gone to, to maintain secrecy since your arrival."

"Nor do I," Piper said bitterly. "The buffoons probably don't even consider that Newcastle has such a thing as its own newspaper, and that word of this would be reported here. So it's either idiocy, or betrayal."

Parrish finished reading. "So where does that leave you?" he asked. "Everyone that you've spoken to so far will soon know that you did so under a falsehood, including Selkirk's own brother, and of course whoever it was who took your precious manuscripts last night."

A thought struck Piper. He was due to meet again with Emily Gilchrist and her father within the hour. His duplicity would be known to her, sooner or later, and would surely sour the meeting, if not prevent it happening at all.

Then Parrish spoke to Ramsay. "You mentioned the mystery of Rosalinda. Is it solved?"

"To a point," said Ramsay. "The name is known among the songsters that I spoke to. She was a poet herself, but some fifty years since. She was published, a well-known verse, too flowery and ornate for my tastes, but popular none the less. Her true name was thought to be Miss Harvey. From a well-off family hereabouts, if my friend is correct in his thinkin'. No real connection to a man like John Selkirk, I would venture."

Parrish raised a thoughtful hand at this.

"Harvey was her name? And well-to-do? There was a family of that name who were merchants years ago, connected to the mills on the south side of the river. A wealthy lot. They lived on the Durham Road, going south through Gateshead."

Piper slammed his fist upon the table in front of him. "Rosalinda!" he shouted. "Of course! That's where the name first appeared to me. It's carved into a gatepost there on that very road you mentioned, near to the house of Doctor Rossiter. I passed it when I visited him."

Parrish threw his head back in despair. "A name on a gatepost, you say? Another meaningless link in this ill-begotten chain." He thought for a moment. "And there's yet another," he said. "John Selkirk was in dispute over a property, also in Gateshead, but a common one, in Canon Street, I believe, behind St Mary's. He was in breach of payment on taxes for it, or some such."

Piper raised an eyebrow at this. "I passed that street, I'm sure, on the same walk to Dr Rossiter. It strikes me that if John Selkirk was making his way to that property on that fateful Saturday, he would have obviously crossed at the stone bridge to do so."

Parrish let out a chuckle. "That church, St Mary's. Another strange coincidence. It was the meeting place for the Four and Twenty, the governing committee, in times past." He paused. "It feels like we're twenty years too late in all this business, or at least looking for answers on the wrong side of the Tyne."

"It's to the Tyne I have to go, despite all that," said Piper. "I have to meet with Robert Gilchrist at his sailmaker's warehouse, though if he or his daughter have read this newspaper, I feel my reception will be colder even than the one I was promised."

The church clock tolled its six bells as Evan Piper turned into the quayside from Sandgate, and saw Emily Gilchrist standing by the line of carts across the street from him. He sensed an angry defiance in her even from that distance. There was no attempt at cordiality from her when he drew closer

"You said you were actin' on behalf of Johnny Selkirk's bereaved relatives!" she blurted out, the hurt in her voice not eluding him. "Now the newspaper is tellin' a very different story. This is beyond deceit. This is woundin' and merciless. And might Ah say also, that your idea that he's an assassin or a plotter or whatever it is you wish to call it, is beyond stupidity. It's a joke. And you are deservedly the victim of that joke, to have come all this way on such an errand."

Piper made no reply. He turned his gaze to the river, much as she had done earlier that same day, fully expecting her to walk away from him after this outburst. But she stood there, as if hoping he would deny everything. Of course, he couldn't do that.

"There has been deceit on my part, I don't deny it," he said, "But that report of my presence here, which you have undoubtedly read, is not the whole story. My secrecy was imposed upon me, acting as I am under the orders of the government, but as soon as I arrived in this town, the nature of my job changed completely. The people who sent me here under orders, had no understanding of the reality of the place, nor of the feelings and loyalties of the people I was to meet."

She stared at him, as if trying to see what truth there might be within him. She shook her head, still unconvinced. "But the whole thing is surely ridiculous! Plots of murder on Prime Ministers and kings are not concocted by the likes of Johnny Selkirk, a man who has wandered these streets for the last ten years in a daze of gin and bad ale. And you're so earnest in your talk. Can't you see what a fool you are in this?"

169

Deep down, Piper was beginning to see just that. The puzzle he had been sent to unravel was diminishing in his own mind. It was a new puzzle, a very palpable one, concerning events much closer to this river, which was now occupying his thoughts.

"Well," he said at last, "I may indeed be a fool, but this fool thinks he's uncovered something else, another crime perhaps, I don't know what it is, but the victim is clear to me. And that victim is John Selkirk. Regardless of his possible involvement in bigger schemes, he seems to have been the object of a scheme himself. And he has died for it. That's as equal a concern to me as are Prime Ministers and kings. And I still need your father's help in solving it, though I expect that will not be forthcoming now. And I understand why that might be, I have to say."

She turned her head from him. "He knows nothin' of any of this," she said, her face clouded with uncertainty. "If as you say, you think there are answers to be had as to Johnny's death, what use is my father in all this? How do Ah not know that he too will end up named in the Mercury as an assassin in the pay of the schemers and plotters that you seem to think are lurkin' behind every corner?"

Piper laughed at this. "Rest assured, that won't happen. I have small pieces of information scattered in front of me, that's all, and any chance I can find to pull them nearer to me, and in some sort of order, I would greatly appreciate. But truly, if you deny me your father's help in it, I can see why and I'll think nothing less of you for doing so. I'm content to walk away and look elsewhere, though I don't know in which direction at present."

170

She sighed in exasperation and made an extravagant gesture, half in submission, half in anger at herself, for him to follow.

Robert Gilchrist sat on a pile of wooden slats just inside the doorway of the warehouse which bore his name above its door. Even in the half-light of an orange lantern flame next to him, Piper could sense the physical weakness of the man. He was folding bills of sale and other papers in trembling hands when they entered and he looked up in surprise.

"Father," the girl said. "This is Mister Piper. He's up from London on business of his own, but he's the man Ah mentioned, askin' on behalf of Johnny Selkirk's relatives down there. You know, Ah asked you about Johnny's son?"

The old man stared at her, then turned his gaze to Piper. His right eye was cast badly, as if from birth, and his skin was a pale greyish-yellow. He was well wrapped against the winter chill in a shabby Chesterfield coat that had once been an expensive item. His head was bare and his face was gaunt and drawn.

"I know nothin' of him, I told yer," he said, his voice weak and thin. "Why has he come here? It's not our concern."

Piper stepped forward. "Forgive me for intruding upon you," he said. "It was only due to Selkirk's links with the poets and writers, and as you were so celebrated and renowned amongst them, naturally your name was mentioned. I haven't managed to trace many of your fellow-writers, but with you being so prominent in business in the town, you were easier to find of course."

171

Gilchrist looked at him steadily. "You have a way with a silver tongue in listin' my success and distinction Mister Piper. But none of it means that I can help you in any of these matters, I'm afraid."

"These matters?" Piper replied. "Oh, the question of the woman Rosalinda, you mean? I know your daughter mentioned that also."

Gilchrist stared back, but made no reply.

Piper continued, "In fact, I believe I've reached an answer to her identity, though what part she plays in the overall scheme of things is not yet clear. And whether or not she was the mother of John Selkirk's son is hard to fathom."

Gilchrist snorted a derisory laugh at this. "She considered herself much too grand a lady to ever be with John Selkirk, so you can forget that notion."

Piper was taken by surprise at this and scrambled for a response. "Her family were called Harvey, I believe."

Gilchrist looked sternly back at him. "No!" he said. "I know nothing of her family, but she wasn't one of the Harvey girls. They were gentle, well-bred women. She was often together with them at times, so people may have assumed as much, but she was not one of them." There was a certainty, an anger in his voice now. Piper was still fumbling for a way to steer the conversation onwards.

"Selkirk mentioned her in one of his later songs," he said. "He seemed to hold her in some way responsible for something, though I don't know what."

Gilchrist was growing more and more disturbed by all this. He turned away and put his hand to his mouth. At

Piper's side, his daughter was also bothered by it, but made no move to interject.

"In one of his songs?" Gilchrist said, dismissively, almost bitterly. "No man would have the right to condemn a woman in verse like that. No," he exclaimed, "I know nothing of it. I do not wish to speak of this stuff. It was all a long time ago, and it's of no matter. And there's nothing to connect it to Johnny Selkirk's death. He was a drunkard. I pity him for it, but I leave well alone, as you should also."

He lifted himself up, and at last his daughter went to his side, to help him.

"The song I mentioned," said Piper. "Would you have known it? The title is 'The Corly Croons', though it seems unfinished."

Gilchrist stopped and stared at Piper, his eyes wide, his mouth trembling slightly, as if searching for a reply that would not come. He breathed heavily, and eventually spoke.

"So it's a song that brings you here?" he said. "And not even a complete verse you say? A typical piece of doggerel, in the Border dialect by the sound of it. And you grace it with the distinction of a song? Well, look to those songs if you must, Mister Piper. Do that, by all means. The answers will be there if you know where to look, because that's how we spoke, both to the world and to each other. Through verses and songs. So look to them, they'll likely tell you all you need to know. Because they're full of ghosts. And it's the ghosts that are responsible. They bear the guilt, the regret, the betrayal. No, the ghosts aren't spirits, they're the hidden truth." He reached for his hat on the shelf behind

173

him. "Now if you please, I'll make my way to the church yonder, as is my custom."

CHAPTER 15

"Aw myed wour bairns cry"

"So much for secrecy!" said Turnbull, pointing to the newspaper lying on the table in the middle room of the police house. "My superiors round the corner in Grey Street are not impressed by this. Or with what they see as my part in it. Your presence in this city, officially or unofficially, is not something they are happy with at all, I'm afraid to say."

"So am I to leave then?" asked Piper, sitting wearily down in the chair by the window.

"That wasn't said explicitly, but they do feel that there's been a certain amount of guile involved in your presence here. I don't think they took your investigation seriously when I first alerted them to it. Now it's before them in writing, and before the public too, they've suddenly sat up and taken notice. You may need to speak to them yourself as to your progress."

Piper groaned. "I'd have little to tell them. And even less to tell my own superiors in London. The more I delve into this affair, the more I see it as a local concern, with no connection to the reasons for my being sent here." He pondered for a moment. "But no less worthy of deeper investigation, despite that." He looked at Constable Ramsay, sitting across the room looking somewhat morose. "Where's Parrish?" he asked him.

Ramsay shook his head. "He said he had other things to attend to and went his own way after you'd left us."

Turnbull laughed derisively. "He's likely already back in Tynemouth by now, and will have washed his hands of the whole affair. He said he had no love for the English government, and no doubt this," – he pointed at the newspaper again – "has brought those feelings to the fore, and he's made good his escape. Did he have lodgings here in the town?"

The other two men looked at each other and shrugged.

Piper's mind was too full of other things to care at this point. His meeting with Robert Gilchrist had unsettled him, and not least because of his daughter Emily's part in it. But at least, he had a sense that Superintendent Turnbull was developing something of an interest in the case, rather than just maintaining his role as a supportive bystander representing officialdom, as he had been until now.

There was a moment's silence before Turnbull turned to Ramsay.

"This man Gilchrist," he said. "You know of him through your poet friends?"

Ramsay nodded. "He had a grand reputation as a writer in his younger days, and is still seen as a significant figure in local circles, though he's produced nothing for many years."

Turnbull leaned in. "I feel we should know as much as we can about him, his business interests, as well as his literary standing, his life, his family. And the same too with any of these other people, his contemporaries. I have a list of them here that Fitzsimmons brought to me." He handed a piece of paper over. "One is a man called Watson, and there is a Leonard, a Cameron, all published writers. We should know about them, and any others that we come across, especially if they are still resident in town here. Perhaps you can sort through it, and quickly, and ask your cronies. Then present your findings to me tomorrow, as early as you can?"

"Certainly," Ramsay said, and stood to leave.

The mention of Gilchrist's family caused some concern to Piper, though he didn't know why, or at least did not admit to himself the reason for it. But he said nothing. Ramsay left and the two men sat in silence for a while. Rain upon the window glittered silver from the lamp in the room against the darkness outside.

"You spoke to Gilchrist yourself?" Turnbull said at last.

"I did," said Piper. "He's a sick man, and his conversation was confused, as well as being reluctantly delivered!" He related the gist of what had been said. The sour look on Turnbull's face as he listened did nothing to encourage Piper's account.

"Ramsay told me all about the other developments, the 'Curly Croons' and the woman Rosalinda," Turnbull said quietly, at the end of it. "It still makes little sense to me."

"Nor to me," said Piper. "But tell me, do you have jurisdiction across the river in Gateshead?"

"To an extent," he said. "There is no separate force stationed there at the moment, so we have a responsibility for the place. But they have a different, self-governing council. They've retained the system of watchmen, and of beadles for church land, of which there's much. It's a system we have mostly abandoned here. They have a somewhat antiquated approach over there, to many things, not just to law-keeping."

Piper nodded. "And what of this Four and Twenty committee that Parrish mentioned? Were you not aware of it?"

"Yes, I was indeed, but the reason it didn't come to my mind was that I knew it by a more official name. 'St Mary's Council', or some such, named after the church where they met. They felt that gave them an air of sanctity and authority that they would otherwise have lacked. They were a formidable body, with immense power and control. There was much self-interest involved, of that there's little doubt, but the members were well respected, and feared even. The task of getting them to relinquish their position and to hand over to an elected mayor was a long and difficult one. They resisted and fought back. There was much in the way of defamatory accusations and name-calling on both sides. Even now, they still may have some influence, despite being disbanded more than ten years ago. It's like a family concern you see. Those powerful and much-moneyed family businesses hold sway in so many ways. When one generation goes, there's always another to replace it. It goes on and on."

"So it may possibly still exist, this Four and Twenty, albeit surreptitiously?"

Turnbull's expression urged caution, but he agreed. "Indeed it could, but probably more in the guise of a merchants' guild or some such, the same as we have here in this town."

Piper frowned. "But the guilds here are well-known and sanctioned bodies, while there'd be no official seal on this one, if it does indeed exist. Is there a way to find the names of those who were involved in it, at the time it actually ceased? I'm curious, that's all. More and more of our paths seem to lead us over the river to Gateshead. The place seems so unlike Newcastle, despite its close proximity."

Turnbull nodded. "It would be easy to find out, if that's what you wish. The committee was still in existence when I was a young man in the borough office here in town. There are people who work there still who could advise me on it. I can pay them a visit in the morning on the way here."

Piper nodded and thanked him, and then fell back into his own thoughts yet again.

The next morning, Turnbull opened the door of his office to Ramsay and Piper at ten o'clock. They were somewhat surprised to see Alec Parrish already there, his back to the window. As ever, he offered no greeting as the others entered. Regardless, there was much to discuss. Ramsay, seeming curiously exalted by his new-found freedom of ordinary clothes and these inner-sanctum confidentialities, was brimming with the results of his allotted task. He took out his duty notebook and began to unfold the life-story of Robert Gilchrist.

He was a man of forty-six years, he told them, and had been in charge of what had been his father's sail-making business, situated near the Customs House on the quayside, for the last twenty years or so. Before that he had worked variously as a clerk and as a book-keeper's apprentice, but more notable had been known as a verse-writer, poet and songsmith, winning a silver medal for his efforts at the age of twenty one. He was a widower with one daughter, and had been exempted from balloted militia service due to his partial blindness in one eye. His business had been failing somewhat in recent years, partly due to his own illness, and partly to a recession in the sail-maker's trade caused by the shift towards steam-powered brigs on the river. His literary leanings had all-but ceased as soon as he took over his father's business, but he was still much respected and his works remained popular, despite never being published in a collection of their own.

Turnbull looked at Piper without comment, and then said, "And any others among those companions who would be of interest or relevance?"

Ramsay looked sheepishly back at him and shrugged. "There's none who live here still," he said, "Indeed many are dead. There was William Watson, a shoemaker by trade, but very adept at popular verse. He had a political career of sorts, followin' some time spent in London, but he's been dead these three years. His brother is a hairdresser in the town. Nathaniel Watson. I know of him."

Again Piper made no comment. Ramsay was quickly losing confidence. He continued.

"Jack Leonard. A fly-by-night. There's no trace of him, though his best song was Winlaton Hopping. Perhaps you know it. It's widely sung to this day."

Turnbull shook his head, a sardonic look across his face. Ramsay pressed on.

"George Cameron was mentioned to me. He was a hairdresser by trade, but also served as a sergeant in the volunteer regiment for a long time. He was well-known at the Three Indian Kings for his recitations. He seems to have written only one song of note, entitled 'The Pitman's Revenge'. He too is now dead."

At last Piper spoke up. "He was also a hairdresser, you say?"

Ramsay looked again at his duty book and then nodded.

"And the other man, Watson, his brother is a hairdresser also?"

Again, Ramsay confirmed it. Piper thought on for a moment.

"Our man Selkirk, his father was also a hairdresser, was he not? A curious coincidence. I suppose men are all forgoing the styles of wigs and plaits these days, so there are fewer and fewer hairdressers on the street fronts. It's strange that we come across three in this single enquiry. Or perhaps it isn't."

Turnbull looked puzzled by this observation. "Hairdressers? More interest to me is the man Leonard, if only that he is perhaps the only one on the list still living?"

Ramsay shook his head and was about to pass comment when Parrish spoke up.

"I recall Jack Leonard. A poet yes, but a brawler, a know-it-all, and as I remember, a radical too. He was a Gateshead man. His family were wealthy, but he squandered most of what he had. He landed in jail a few years ago, for attacking a man in Middle Street, near the Cloth Market."

Turnbull rose and began to scramble through a gathering of papers on his desk, pulled one out and almost immediately uttered a cry of success. "And Gateshead is indeed where he is," he said, "Or his family at least, I would swear to it. This is the list of members of the Four and Twenty Committee, wheedled out of my old office this very morning. It's dated March 1826, ten years before it

181

was disbanded and the first Mayor of Gateshead and his administrative council was set in its place. Two members bear the name Leonard. John Wilson Leonard and..." He stopped and stared more closely at the paper in front of him. He looked up at Piper with a dumfounded expression on his face.

"The other name," he said, "is that of a Miss Rosalinda Leonard, residing at the same address. But unmarried, presumably the sister of the other."

"And the address?" asked Piper, already up from his seat.

"It is Durham Road, Gateshead. The very house you passed, I would surmise."

This new information, as surprising as it was, left them in a quandary as to how to proceed. Ramsay once more took his leave. He knew of someone, he said, who might know more of Leonard. Parrish then also departed, though with no explanation. The other two sat for a long while in discussion. Around and around they went, as if circling a deep trough that neither of them could peer into with any clarity.

After almost an hour of this, Turnbull realised he had other business to attend to, and Piper left him to it. A steady rain had persisted since the night before, but regardless of that, Piper found himself walking the wynds and chares around the market streets to the west of Pilgrim Street, turning many things over in his mind. He was dressed in his own clothes once again, and mindful of his last venture in them, he kept an eye on every knave and vagabond that he encountered, lest he should recognise something of his attackers in them. None fitted the bill as far as he could see.

He found himself on the opposite side of the flat ground where he had ended up stretched out in the mud. He could see the entry to the yard where he had washed his face down with the aid of Emily Gilchrist. Work was progressing all around him on imposing new buildings that would eventually form an ornate square of offices and halls, so he was told, making an impressive centrepiece for this part of the town. Right here where slums and rat-infested dwellings had once stood, a new official grandeur was to be installed. The cholera epidemic had struck the town severely twenty years before, and any chance of eradicating it, both physically and mentally, was obviously a priority for the elders of the city.

He felt the presence of someone closing in on him from behind, and he jerked his head around in alarm.

"Broad daylight isn't the best time to have at ye!" Alec Parrish said with a laugh in his voice. "And I didn't want to interrupt a man from his dreams. Are you missing your home perhaps?"

Piper smiled back at him. "No, that wasn't it. And anyway, I'll see it soon enough. I'm due back by Tuesday next. I sail on Sunday morning. Two days to solve this blasted puzzle." There was a thoughtful silence between the two men. Piper continued. "So do you have anything that might help in the task? Only yesterday we thought you might have given up on it and gone back to Tynemouth."

"Indeed I did return to Tynemouth, but not out of desperation. I spent an interesting night with Jack Dent.

183

You were right not to return with me. God, that man can drink!" He put his hand to his head as if to pull back an ale-soaked curtain from in front of his eyes. "Anyway, he was talkative with it, if somewhat meandering. I learned things from amongst the dross, I think."

"Such as what, might I ask?"

Parrish came closer. "Well, I had for a long time seen the whole songster and poet concern as a pastime for the alehouse and the street corner. That's all it was when I first became aware of it, and even knowing that the academics and pretenders had taken hold of it, I never realised how far they had taken it. In fact, it progressed from barroom to drawing room in a very short time. It became a thing of fashion, and quaint gatherings of refined ladies and gentlemen took it for their own. Those who produced it, the common clerks and printers' jobbers with a skill for verse, suddenly became fêted and coveted. That is why men like Jack Dent were so keen to be part of it, and were willing to claim what was not theirs, in order to sidle their way into a brighter and better social standing. Equally, I assume it was why men like Selkirk and Gilchrist backed away from it. Their principles and true allegiances to their own class, from where they took their inspiration, forbade them from pandering to the niceties of wealthy benefactors. Dent laughed at them for spurning it, and resented them for throwing away a chance that he would have grasped with all his might, had he had the talent to be offered it."

Piper listened to this very closely. A fog was slowly beginning to clear from his thinking.

"So these writers fell under the ownership of sponsors and benefactors who saw them as their property," he said, "like performing lapdogs?"

Parrish nodded. "Exactly so, and those benefactors would go to any length to protect and promote their chosen pet. They had the money and the influence to do so, let's face it. And that's where Dent holds the most bitterness."

Parrish looked around him at the stretch of open ground where the cinders of the old city had been scraped away. He obviously saw something else in his memory. It distracted him momentarily. Then he pulled his coat tighter about him, and continued.

"There was at that time a ballot for duty in the local militia service. The threat of war was real enough for us then. So any man in this town was liable for service, for local defence if they were lucky, but as time went on, more and more of the militia troops were being sent overseas to fight. That's where influence and money came into it. You wouldn't find the son of a wealthy merchant having his name being drawn up in such a ballot. His father would see to that. And equally, why watch a talented poet be hauled away into oblivion, when you could have him recite and sing in your own comfortable drawing room to the envy and admiration of your rich friends?"

Piper stared at Parrish. "So you are telling me that there was a method by which those in favour could be held back from militia service? But only as long as money was paid on their behalf to those with the power to make it so?"

"Not just a few poets and songsters, you understand," said Parrish. "The practice was widespread, I'm certain of it, but usually only for the sons of rich and prominent families. But these poets were commoners, men from the streets and cottages here, right where we are standing. It must've taken considerable organisation and attention to achieve such favours for the likes of them."

"So Jack Dent presumably was not afforded such a helping hand, and had to serve?"

"He did indeed," said Parrish. "He ended up in France, serving under Wellington, without proper training or equipment. He was lucky to survive. He holds great bitterness towards those who sent him, and to those of his peers who managed to escape the same fate."

"But how was such a thing managed?" Piper asked. "A simple loss of relevant documents might work for one such case, but the same technique repeated over and over would arouse suspicion, surely?"

Parrish smiled knowingly. "And there we come to it," he said. "It was done by a system of substitutes. An officially sanctioned system, but open to abuse. Young men who had actually been spared by the ballot, suddenly found themselves being hauled away to take the place of others who had been fairly chosen, but who could somehow summon up the funds to escape conscription."

Piper shook his head in disbelief. "But if Dent told you this, how did he know so much of it? He surely had been balloted justly. Was he expecting to be spared and his place taken by somebody else?"

"He was expecting exactly that, but no-one thought enough of him as to pull the necessary strings. But he knew that the process existed. He actually served with some of those who had been falsely taken, more than a few of

186

whom fell in battle, or were captured and taken to ungodly prison camps in France." Parrish stopped and put a hand on Piper's arm. "And what is more, Jack Dent acknowledged the name, the secret name if you will, by which these substitutes were known."

The fog lifted now from Piper's eyes, and he smiled back at Parrish. "The Corly Croons?" he said.

Parrish nodded. "The Corly Croons. Why that, I don't know. They were simply the unlucky ones, the cheated, the betrayed."

Piper breathed out heavily at this. "Those were the words that Gilchrist used. The ghosts, he called them, the betrayed. He knew. He knew it all. And it torments him."

"And he is not the only one who knew, I would guess. There are undoubtedly others, both the betrayed and the betrayers. And I would bet that John Selkirk was somewhere amongst their number."

CHAPTER 16

"The flesh and breed day"

Gateshead, the dowdier, less confident sister to the loud and brash Newcastle – that was how Alec Parrish had described it as he and Evan Piper walked to the end of the old stone bridge together. They had gone their separate ways at that point, and now Piper found himself tackling Bottle Bank once again, and the road that would lead him to Doctor Rossiter, the man who had been on the spot when John Selkirk's body had been laid on the cold quayside on that fateful morning two weeks before, and whose credentials as a writer and poet gave him an even stronger connection to this sorry business.

Once he had cleared the bridge, Piper looked back again at the other town, spread lavishly on the opposite side. The castle after which it was named lay in direct line from where he stood. It was less than impressive to eyes used to a London horizon, one which was peppered with ancient buildings, littered with palaces and cathedrals, and habitually entertained by pomp and ceremony. Yet somehow the shabbiness of the tattered keep and the crumbling walls of this northern fortress stirred something within him, as indeed had the whole city, much against his own expectations, since he had arrived here a mere five days ago. He would be sorry to leave it, despite the incessant grim weather that had plagued his stay, and was continuing to do so as he stood there.

The climb ahead was made treacherous by rainfall. Piper paused for breath at St Mary's Church, where the old Four and Twenty Committee had met to tend to the welfare of this town's inhabitants, as long as it coincided with their own interests, if what he'd heard was indeed true. The church itself looked like a holy enough place, not as grand as some of its brethren on the other side of the Tyne, but suitably chaste and sombre, especially on this late November day. It certainly had a presence, being in such a dominant position overlooking the river below, where a tall barque seemed to be doffing its sails with respect to this house of God, as it claimed its mooring at the water's edge.

Sharply to its right, Piper eyed the stubbed, uneven terraces that clung to the stepped hillside, their chimneys smoking, their doors closed against the wind, and the streets between them empty and bereft. The first one bore the very name, Canon Street, that had been mentioned to him in connection with John Selkirk. Maybe this was where the man had been heading to, on the night he perished, though for what possible reason, Piper couldn't guess. There were a dozen dwellings in the street, and it would be a hazardous quest to knock on each door to find out which particular one was special to John Selkirk.

He trudged on for a mile or more. Once again, the journey had been a late decision for him, and he grew anxious at the fading light. He passed a group of men digging out a cess-pit by a stone factory building. The stench of it hit him from fifty paces away, yet the workers seemed unbothered by it. He imagined the sneers on their faces as he passed, they in their leather jerkins and thick leggings, their caps pulled down over their eyes, their bare hands covered with the contents of the foul hole. One held up a fistful towards him, and laughed hideously, in a stupid pretence of hurling it across the street at him. He stopped in his tracks and stared at the fool that faced him, still laughing and nodding, taunting and gesticulating like some wild ape with a new toy. Piper was angered, disgusted and even ashamed that such a man existed. He turned away, wondering why such antics affected him so, all the while expecting to feel the thud of the stuff upon his back. He kept walking, and when he eventually turned back to look, the men were at work once again at their sickening toil.

Within another few minutes, Piper was looking at the name on the gatepost which had eluded him for so long. 'Rosalinda', it said, repeated on both pillars at either side of a weak track, leading to a low stone house, spread across a sizeable plot of elevated land. It boasted four, perhaps five chimneys, none of them giving off smoke, and a set of brick outbuildings. There was no light in any window, and a lone white horse, thickly-maned and grey with grime, stood like a sentry in a paddock to one side. A black carriage was positioned near to it, shrouded in grey canvas, and apparently unused for some time. The surrounding grounds were well-tended, but the house looked closed up. Tempting though it was, and knowing that he had no authority in this district, Piper resisted the urge to walk up to take a closer look at the property. Quite what he could expect to learn from such an inspection, he could not imagine.

The sky was darkening. He quickened his pace and made for the end of the row of houses towards Doctor Rossiter's door. As he passed each one, he noticed that all the dwellings in this row looked equally stern and forbidding. It was a curiously unhappy place, he thought, for people rich enough to want for nothing.

He reached his goal and approached with hesitation, going over in his mind how he should confront the old man, without aggravating him from the outset. Indeed, he wondered if he would even be invited across the threshold a second time.

The thick gloom was unchanged in the doctor's dismal sitting room as Piper followed him into it once again. The lad who had answered the door on his last visit was nowhere to be seen, and it had been the old man himself who had eventually opened the door to his persistent knock. He'd squinted painfully at his visitor, shielding his eyes against the greying daylight, and had let him in with barely a word. It was almost, Piper felt, as if he had again been expected.

They sat opposite each other and Piper watched the old man wriggle a thick brown blanket around his shoulders before starting the conversation. He decided to speak out plainly from the start.

"Thank you for seeing me again doctor," he began, "But my enquiries about John Selkirk's death have taken a few unexpected turns over the last week."

The doctor smiled. "Firstly Mister Piper, I'm afraid I'm barely seeing you at all this evening," he said. "My eyes are particularly sensitive today, so I'm not sure how long I can sustain this meeting. But secondly, as to the unexpected turns you refer to, they come as no surprise to me."

"I thought they wouldn't," Piper replied in a level voice. He paused for a moment, then continued. "Tell me sir, and forgive my pronunciation of the words, but does the expression 'Corly Croons' mean anything to you?"

There was silence from the old man. He closed his eyes and put his head back, as if he'd drifted into a deep and sudden sleep. Piper watched him. Then the doctor sighed heavily and nodded his head slowly.

"Of course it does," he said, "Though it's one I haven't heard for a good few years. But I'm interested to know your interpretation of it, just to see if it tallies with mine."

"Well," Piper replied, choosing his words carefully, "I'm told that it was a term used to represent the young men who were used as substitutes for certain individuals who had been balloted to serve with the militia during the conflict with France, initially as a defence force, but subsequently as regular soldiers. They were to be dispatched to battlefronts by the commanding generals serving under Wellington. It was a deceit, a ruse, that meant that certain men who had been legally chosen to serve, by ballot, were saved from doing so, and others who would normally have been spared duty, were forced to go in their place. A very distasteful and cold-blooded scheme, enabled by illicit payments from those with interests in seeing the arrangement carried through." Piper paused. "Does that tally with your own interpretation, doctor?"

The old man bit at his lower lip and nodded again. "More or less," he said. "And I would agree with your judgement that it was distasteful, cowardly even. But with this qualification. When the arrangement was first set in place, there was no suggestion that the defence forces would be anything more than that. There was no indication at that time that they would be transported to foreign conflicts. The local militias were part-time squads, based in their own district. They lived in their own homes. It wasn't until later that some of them were unscrupulously hired out to serve with regular forces, and by that time the process of substitution was thoroughly entrenched. Then when the first platoon was shipped to Flanders, objections were raised by those involved. More money changed hands, and more still, until the whole thing was eventually halted."

"But by then, there had been casualties, I take it?"

"Oh indeed. They had had no training, you see. They were lambs to the slaughter, these men. Many were killed, or taken prisoner. Very few made it back."

Piper looked at the man, and marvelled at the casual, matter-of-fact tone in his voice, given the scale of what he was saying. He pressed him further.

"And the perpetrators of this deceit, you were aware of them? I mean the men with the immediate power to carry it through, once the payment was in their hands?"

The doctor hesitated, his hands gripping the wooden arms of his chair. "I would say again, it all began very innocently, and what money there was didn't necessarily remain in the hands of those who initiated the scheme. There were contributions to be made at many and various levels. It was only later, when war seemed imminent, that there was a rush to keep the thing in motion, as more and more well-to-do families saw that their sons' lives would soon be in peril if they did not act."

"But where did the poets and writers fit into it all? None of them were from rich families and suchlike."

"No, but it was with them that the process had started. One fine and celebrated writer, his star in the ascendancy, popular in every drawing room in the area, was balloted and was about to be sent off to the militia. A casual remark and a few quiet words ensured that this did not happen. Well, once that particular door was opened, everyone saw it as a way out of such a predicament. A man with a precocious daughter to keep content, who had a fondness for a particular songster, perhaps. He could ensure her happiness by saving her favourite bard from having to don the uniform and be taken off for service. It meant nothing, at first. The Corly Croons were paid as well, or at least their families were. It all had to be kept secret of course, but few had the connections or influence to create a fuss."

"But where did that come from, that expression, 'The Corly Croons'?" Piper asked.

Doctor Rossiter opened his eyes at last and looked across at him in a moment of what could have been remorse. "It came from the first one," he said. "The very first lad who was used in that way. I don't know who's place he took in the ranks, but it was a test, to see if it could indeed be achieved. And it was. And he himself, this poor young lad, had thick curly hair, and was referred to as 'The Corly Croon', not just as a secret byword, but also as a jest. A snide, sarcastic jest. So as the arrangement was set in place, so all the others who followed were referred to in the same manner, by that same name, whether or not they had the curly topping on their head. It was really only the first one that did."

Piper stared at him, his heart pounding. "John Selkirk's son? 'Young Andy?'" he said softly.

The doctor nodded. "Yes. John Selkirk's son. A cruel coincidence. Of course, he wasn't known to be so, at the time. He lived with his mother, in a house on Canon Street, on the hill there. Selkirk owned the property, but he lived over the bridge. They never lived together as a family. Nobody realised. It wasn't until the lad was shipped off overseas with the local defenders that a connection was made. Selkirk himself was working away in London, and eventually learned of it there. The word was that the boy was a prisoner, as many were, so his father went off to search for him, to bring him back."

"So that is why he spent time journeying in France."

"I would imagine so. Even when the French were defeated, many of the captives remained incarcerated, sometimes for years. But of course, the lad was never found. Eventually, John Selkirk came back here, a broken man, blaming himself, because he had been so involved with the poets and Bards and singers, the very people whose popularity had spawned the entire scheme in the first place."

"So how many young men were treated so?" Piper asked.

The doctor opened his hands expansively. "Scores, maybe a hundred or more. Once the channels had been opened, more and more money was laid on the table. A solid, almost casual routine was put in place, and people came from all over the region."

"And it was all dealt with from here? From right here in this town?"

"Undoubtedly in other places too, but it became a profitable business for those who started it, here in Gateshead. The management of it was straightforward. The risk was minimal, to all but the Corly Croons themselves of course."

"And for your own part, doctor, I have to ask. How involved were you in this?"

The old man straightened himself in his chair. "I was well aware of it, but I did not benefit personally, and yet I am as guilty as those who initiated it."

"How so?" said Piper.

Rossiter sighed and closed his weak old eyes.

"Because my own son was balloted," he said softly, "and I would have given anything to spare him from the fate that ultimately took him from me. I would have paid their price in an instant. And I tried. I offered all I could afford, but by then they were greedy. They were all greedy. All along this chain of deceit, more and more payments were being asked for, more and more silences had to be bought. And I pleaded, I promised much, but nothing I could offer was enough for them by then. And my son was sent off and never came back. And they showed no mercy, no remorse, nothing. Their greed had poisoned them."

"And who were they, these men?"

Doctor Rossiter looked at him, his dim old eyes blinking rapidly.

"Men? No, it wasn't men. It was a woman who was behind it. She began it all, and controlled it, and made a tidy fortune from the proceeds. She was single-minded, ruthless and cold-hearted. Her name was Rosalinda."

CHAPTER 17

"Thou'd best haud thee whist"

Piper couldn't help himself. It was late, past six o'clock, and he needed to get back to the police house to catch Superintendent Turnbull before he left at seven, to tell him of his conversation with Doctor Rossiter. But at the end of the stone bridge, instead of heading directly up Sandgate and on to Pilgrim Street, he followed the river down past the Customs House, on the off-chance that he might see Emily Gilchrist as she ended her working day at the sail-makers warehouse. Instead, much to his surprise, just as he crossed the quay, in sight of the open doors of the building, he saw Constable Ramsay coming towards him.

Ramsay lifted a gloved hand in greeting. "I was wondering where you were Mister Piper," he said, smiling.

"Oh, am I needed?" he replied. "Mister Turnbull knew where I was. I've been back to see Doctor Rossiter." He gestured back in the direction of where he'd come from. Ramsay looked surprised and then smiled again.

"My word, it's quite a climb up that hill," he said. "I hope it was worth the walk!"

Piper nodded. "It certainly was. The old man had plenty to say. He knew more than he was letting on at that first visit, as I suspected. But I could hardly stop him talking this time. He's told me almost everything we need to know. There's more, I reckon, but he was getting a bit agitated, the longer he went on. I'll go back tomorrow and speak with him again, once he's had a chance to calm himself, and gather his thoughts."

Ramsay was about to reply, when Piper caught sight of Emily Gilchrist. She was pulling the big doors closed and fumbling with a large set of keys. Piper walked over to her, followed by Ramsay, who kept a discreet distance as they approached. She turned at the sound of their feet on the cobbles. Piper tried to determine the look on her face, but the shadows of the evening prevented it.

"I was just passing, on the way to the police house," he said cautiously. "I just thought I'd ask how your father was, after we spoke last night."

"He was fine," she said, and turned back to locking the door.

"I'm glad," Piper said, rather lamely. "I know it wasn't easy for him to talk to me. Or for you in fact. But it was very helpful. Please tell him so."

She turned and faced him, casting a glance at Ramsay when she did so. "Ah'll tell him," she said.

Piper nodded, and continued. "And tell him he was right. What he said as I left, tell him he was correct in that, and that I've fathomed a lot of what I didn't previously understand. I thank him for that also."

She nodded, but again, the dark of the evening prevented him from knowing whether she understood what he meant. He raised his hat and said goodnight, and then both he and Ramsay turned away. She watched them go for a moment, but said nothing in reply. Piper was glad when Ramsay excused himself at the pant-square and went about his own business, as it gave him the chance to turn over his thoughts as he walked back to the police house. After so long a day, and so many twists and turns of information that had come his way, he felt a slight guilt that his major concern was a wispy but determined young woman with the voice of a lark who had wheedled her way into his heart. There was an ache too, that in two days he would leave this place, and likely never see her again.

It was the thought of this, of how time was pressing against him from every side, that jolted him back into a reality of sorts. He rushed back to the police house and looked questioningly at Sergeant Fitzsimmons as to whether Turnbull was still in his office. The sergeant nodded, and Piper made for his office door.

Turnbull already had his coat in his hand, and with the other he was at the lamp on his desk, ready to douse it for the night. He saw the look on Piper's face as he entered, and let the lamp burn on.

"I have much to tell you," Piper said.

"I can see you have," Turnbull replied, and moved the chair towards him with the edge of his boot.

Piper began with Alec Parrish's account of the substitution arrangements in the militia ballot. The whole idea of an exclusive, class-based favouritism at the expense of honest but impoverished young men immediately struck a chord with Turnbull. It was such injustices as these which had first connected him and Parrish thirty years before. For all their disparate attitude towards the law, here was one place where the two men met, their shared principles outweighing their differences.

The testimony of Doctor Rossiter flowed easily from this, and even as he spoke it, Piper himself saw the clarity of how the situation had developed. Turnbull shook his head in amazement, at the incessant greed and desperation which was manifest in the tale. But at the end of it, he sat back in his chair and grimaced with apparent frustration.

"But where does this leave us?" he asked. "Again, we are faced with an abundance of hidden indiscretions that we're told happened ten, perhaps twenty years ago, with no proof as to their criminal nature, save the word of a blind and broken old man. The one possible crime that has taken place on my watch is the death of a drunkard, which has already been ruled accidental and a line drawn beneath it. And what of your own investigation, the link with the assassination attempt? Where does that fit into the scheme of things?"

Piper shrugged. "It doesn't. I see no reason to think that such a link ever existed. Everything incriminating in John Selkirk's behaviour can be accounted for and ruled out with regard to my original investigation."

Turnbull laughed derisively. "And is that what you are going to tell your Superintendent Banks, when you return to London on Monday? After the expense and trouble of sending you all this way, he'll surely expect something more than that!"

"And yet there's nothing. I truly believe that. And that conclusion should be taken as valid as any other that Banks might have expected. But you're right, he'll be somewhat less than pleased."

Turnbull leaned towards him with a sigh. "Then in truth, Evan Piper, I have to tell you that your work here is done. That is the reality of it. Whatever more there may be to investigate, then I shall follow it through to the best of my abilities, but to be frank, I think we're too late. It pains me to say it, but I think that the guilty ones have long since escaped justice, and that there is insufficient evidence as to the cause of the death of John Selkirk to be investigated further."

Piper began to protest, but Turnbull held up his hand to silence him. "Think about it Evan!" he said. "Consider it all. You never had any authority here, though not through any choice of mine. I would gladly stand by you in any matter you might name. But you had a specific task, and you admit yourself, it's done with. Anything else that may have been uncovered along the way, that will be up to this office to deal with. And I'll look closely at what you have told me, but I can't see any meat on it, any reason why I should open a casebook on any aspect of it."

There was a silence in the room. Then Piper spoke up, softly.

"What about that fellow, Jack Leonard? The radical that Parrish mentioned. He would perhaps be a suspect, both in my case and in yours, would he not?"

"The man died in Carlisle jail, some eight years ago. Sergeant Fitzsimmons found a note of it in the dispatches from Grey Street. He could possibly be linked to your enquiry, but could not have been involved in the death of Selkirk." Piper made no reply. He turned and stared into the darkness outside the window, and sighed heavily.

Later, after he had left Turnbull, he walked as far as the Wheatsheaf, where a new sign had been erected, heralding "Balmbra's Music Saloon." He could hear music from within, but he turned and made his way back to his lodging. The rain was light on this night, but brought a chill wind with it. The oil lamp in his room was dry. His body still ached from his beating of two nights past, and his lip was still swollen. It seemed to him that these bruises would be the only thing that he would take back to London with him, when his ship sailed in two days' time.

As he turned from High Bridge into Pilgrim Street at around nine the next morning, Piper immediately sensed that something momentous had happened. Outside the police-house, a large black carriage, its sides and back closed in except for a barred slit on a rear door, was being manoeuvred into place behind two harnessed horses. Next to it, four, perhaps five constables, none of them familiar to him, were on the pavement outside the door, as if waiting for orders to be handed to them. Sergeant Fitzsimmons' head briefly appeared, and barked something curt and incomprehensible, just as Piper reached the entrance. As he mounted the stairs to the offices, another constable came rushing down and past him. Piper walked into the middle room, and immediately saw a young man at the side table, obviously in some distress, his head in his hands and a mug of black tea untouched in front of him. The lad looked up at him, and there was recognition from both of them.

"That's him!" the youngster shouted, pointing at Piper, "That's the fellow that came callin' for the Doctor the other day! That's him I tell yer!"

Fitzsimmons, in full uniform for a change, came rushing in from beyond, uttering soothing sounds and grabbing for the lad, who was already advancing towards Piper, his eyes wide, his throat seized with groans of determination. Turnbull was quick to appear at the doorway behind him.

"We know, we know!" Fitzsimmons was saying. "Sit down lad, we know who he is! That's Mister Piper. He's a policeman like us! Now, sit down with yer!" Another constable appeared, jacketless, took the boy by the arm, and led him back to the chair.

Bewildered by it all, Piper looked wide-eyed at Turnbull.

"What's happened? That's the lad from Doctor Rossiter's house, isn't it?"

Turnbull steered him about and marched him back to the stairs.

"The boy found Rossiter dead this morning at around half past six," he said gravely. "He seems to have been throttled, by what the lad describes. I've sent constables from Grey Street over there. Come, we'll take the black wagon." He turned to Fitzsimmons and called, "Sergeant, you're with us. Make haste!" The three of them trundled down the stairs, and were soon hoisting themselves onto the driving bench of the vehicle, with Fitzsimmons at the reins. The contraption bounced violently across the cobbles. Piper at one side, hanging on desperately to the frame-bar. The horses struggled on the slope down towards the quay, and then settled into a jerking trot as they approached the bridge. Turnbull raised himself up and swung a large wooden crake-rattle in an ear-splitting crackle, causing a bunch of tramping walkers to scatter in fright. He did the same again at the halfway point of the crossing, then sat back. He turned sternly to Piper with a withering look.

"You now have your reason for me to investigate a crime at last, though I dare say, not the crime you were expecting!"

Piper made no reply. Fitzsimmons deftly cracked a whip so the horses would pick up enough speed for the hill. As they passed St Mary's church, Piper looked across at it from the vantage point of the high wagon's seat. Its stone façade showed nothing but defiance to his eyes. He saw no holiness there. Moments later, they passed the house named Rosalinda. Nothing there had changed. The old white stallion was agitated by the sound of the hooves of the police horses, and was circling the small paddock. There was no other sign of life. Turnbull watched Piper's head turn towards it but made no comment.

They halted at the gate which Piper had walked through only the day before. Half a dozen people were gathered by it, local folk, poor and agitated, their old eyes watching their arrival keenly. A handful of children peered over the wall. Alighting, Turnbull led the way towards the weathered front door, where a constable stood waiting for them.

Inside, Doctor Rossiter was lying face-down, half-way into his own sitting room. The angle of his head and arms suggested that he'd been attacked from behind, as if he'd been leading someone into the room, as he'd done with Piper on both of his visits. It was a clumsy, hurried assault that smacked of anger and determination. Piper stood off to one side, nibbling the knuckle of his thumb thoughtfully as he watched Turnbull and his officers go through a routine that he himself was very familiar with. He looked about the room, and it looked like nothing had obviously been disturbed, but the lack of light made it hard to know for sure. After a few minutes, he withdrew and stood outside the front door. The crowd at the gate had grown, and all their eyes were on him. He avoided their gaze the best he could, while trying hard to feel some sort of sympathy for the dead man. He had certainly felt some the previous day, when Rossiter had told him of the loss of his son, but the tragic parent had now become a corpse, a victim, his house a scene of a crime, his death merely something to be investigated.

Turnbull and Sergeant Fitzsimmons came out after a short while and stood with him.

"A bad business," Turnbull said. "It has to be connected to your visit here yesterday, don't you think?"

Piper nodded. "I would say so. It's too much of a coincidence to be anything else."

"Someone must've seen you come here. Were you aware of anyone, somebody following you up the road there, or passing you going the other way?"

He shook his head. "There was no-one in sight, I'd swear to it. I remember turning to look as I opened the gate."

"Then did you tell anyone that you were coming here, or even that you'd been here?"

Piper was already ahead of him. He nodded slowly. "I did," he said. "When I met Ramsay at the quayside, we saw Robert Gilchrist's daughter. I told her that I'd seen Rossiter. I also said that I intended to come back today."

Turnbull breathed out deeply and raised his gaze heavenwards. "You think she is capable of this?" he said, looking Piper firmly in the eye.

Piper hesitated. "I don't know. I really don't. Would he have let a young woman into his house, unless she was known to him? Maybe she was. Her father is a sick man, and has seen doctors, but Rossiter was retired from practice, he told me. Or maybe she told someone else what I'd said, unwittingly perhaps, and it's them that's responsible."

"Her father?"

Piper grimaced and shook his head. "He's too ill. He would never be able to reach this house without being seen, in a carriage or some such. But he has men who work for him. Who knows what influence he has with them?"

Turnbull stared back at him. "My suspicion falls on the daughter. I'm sorry to say it, but she's determined to protect her father, as you said yourself. If she somehow felt that Doctor Rossiter's words would incriminate him in some way, she may have felt forced to act. There's no-one else I can think of who has reason and opportunity to do this."

Piper didn't respond.

Turnbull continued. "We should go to Gilchrist's warehouse on the quayside, and confront whoever is there. They all may have been elsewhere and can prove it, including the daughter. But the question has to be asked."

They left the constables at the scene of the murder, and with Fitzsimmons at the reins, took the carriage back towards the town. Again, no words could be exchanged over the sharp clattering of the hooves and the mad drumming of the wheels on the roadway. When they reached the Customs House, they could see the doors of Gilchrist's workshop were open, but no-one was in sight.

The three of them approached cautiously and went inside. Robert Gilchrist sat alone, in the same place as where Piper had last seen him. He stood up, painfully, when they entered, and blurted out his words before they'd even had a chance to speak.

"Where is she?" he said, his voice in an clear panic. "Don't tell me that something has happened to her!"

Piper stepped forward. "Emily? She's not here? Then where's she gone?"

Gilchrist steadied himself. "She didn't return last night, from the music hall. I assume that's where she went. She thinks I don't know it, but she's there almost every evenin', and she's always back before ten o'clock. She never came back last night. I sent one of my lads to ask at The Wheatsheaf, but he was told she wasn't there, that she'd left the place at the same time as she always does." He stopped, and looked enquiringly at the three men. "What are you doing here? Were you expecting to see her here?"

Turnbull looked at Piper and spoke up. "Mister Gilchrist, we have just come from the house of Doctor Rossiter. Do you know him?"

Gilchrist's expression intensified. "Is she there? Is that what you're saying? Is she hurt?"

"No, no," said Turnbull raising his hand, "That's not it. Doctor Rossiter has had an accident. He was found dead in his house this morning, and we are trying to find out what happened."

Gilchrist stared at them in confusion. He looked at Piper, then at the uniformed sergeant, and then looked again at Turnbull.

"Accident? What sort of accident has he had?" he said weakly.

Turnbull persisted. "Do you know Doctor Rossiter?"

"Yes, I know him. I knew him well at one time, but I haven't seen him for years. He's a blind man isn't he? Is that what's happened? He's fallen or something? I'm sorry for him, but I need to know what's happened to my daughter!"

Two men entered behind them, workers at the warehouse, and immediately went to Gilchrist's side. Sergeant Fitzsimmons stepped up and spoke to them, offering words of calm, and official assurances, as Turnbull nodded to Piper to join him outside.

"There are two options to this," he said, as they walked into the daylight. "Either she's done away with Rossiter and has taken flight, or else she herself is the victim of the same assailant. Neither is good. We need to find her."

Piper was agitated, deeply troubled. "No," he said, "There is something else here. I can't remember what I said to her exactly, but it wasn't enough to lead to her trudging over to Rossiter's house in the dead of night and choking him to death. I just can't believe that."

Sergeant Fitzsimmons came out, accompanied by one of the warehousemen.

"This is Daniel, sir," he said. "He was at Balmbra's last night and says he saw Emily Gilchrist there."

"You saw her?" Piper said. "She sang on the stage last night?"

The other man nodded his head. "Indeed she did. She went afterwards in the company of one of the other girls. The flame haired lass who does the saucy songs. They're chalk and cheese, the pair of them, but they're pals. They were at the back, watchin' the jugglers when Ah saw them."

"And 'til what time did she stay there?" Turnbull said. "Did you see her leave?"

"Ah don't know what time," he replied, "But half way through the performances. Ah went across to the side with me jug of porter and she was by the stair then."

"With the other girl?"

"No, with the Peeler. She was speakin' to him as they both went out. She did look concerned."

Piper moved up to the man, who stepped back instinctively, a fearful look on his face.

"With a Peeler? What Peeler?" he demanded urgently.

"Ah don't know his name," he stammered back, "But Ah know him. He's usually in the swallow-tail coat and the lum-hat, like they all wear, but he had on a quality wrapper last night. But it was him. He was holdin' a draught early on, and Ah saw his hand, with his finger missin'!"

Piper reeled back at this. He felt his head swim with confusion and disbelief. Turnbull lurched forward and grabbed the collar of the man's coat. He responded with an oath and raised hands.

"You're telling me that you recognised this man," Turnbull hissed, "that he was a constable, even though he wasn't wearing his police tunic? I have to say I think you are lying!"

The man Daniel snarled back at him, "Ah don't care what you think! Ah saw what Ah saw, and Ah'm tellin' you. We all saw it, Ah can bring you three others who remarked on it. We naturally thought that the old man was

211

taken bad, and he'd come to fetch her. What other reason would there be for a Peeler to come for her like that?"

Turnbull loosened his grip and let out a long breath. He looked at Piper. "What indeed?" he said.

CHAPTER 18

"Some conj'rer he maun be"

Outside The Wheatsheaf, in the damp gloom of the previous evening, Charlie Ramsay leaned back against the coarse sandstone wall, and felt himself tumbling, over and over, rolling away beyond the grip of his own body. He looked down and saw his fingers stretch open and wide, and felt the ache that remained in his grip where his recent surge of strength had taken its toll. Even the finger that he had left in a pile of jagged rocks, half a mile below the ground, fifteen years before, made its presence felt, as it often did in cold weather and under physical duress. The pit would make a man of him, she'd said, and feed them through desperate times. All it had done was to shred his lungs and maim him. He stared at the wrinkled stump that made a mockery of his clenched fist. The heel of his palm was tender, and his thumbs burned with a strange glow that felt almost like a luxury, a warmth of a kind that he had rarely experienced before. All the while, his coarse breath forced its way through his lungs like fingernails dragged down a wall, such as this very wall behind him. It was deafening in his ears, fighting for attention with the pumping of his heart, pounding and ringing in the bell-tower of his head. As it escaped, he saw how it made a dancing, swirling cloud in the cold night air. He tried to rein it in, to pull it back with those fingers, and to get a grip of this raging body. But it rolled away from him, reared its head back and laughed at him.

He closed his eyes, and saw the shape of a man at his feet, the twisted head, the back, bowed over with the indignity of death. He saw the quivering outline of his own hands, missing finger and all, held outstretched above it, as if pleading for forgiveness. He wondered at the power within them, that he could take away the functions of life from someone so completely, even with these deformed, spoiled tools at his disposal. It hadn't been such an unpleasant process, not like the time before, at the river's edge, when it had felt like taming a struggling runt, dirty, wet, spitting and wriggling like an Ouseburn eel, refusing to end, hanging on to its own misery. He had grown angry with it, and had felt his temper surge through his body and into his hands. That is what had left the tell-tale bruises. He should have thanked the blind old man for being unable to see them, in the early morning darkness, though he'd been suspicious, of that there was no doubt. And that was the start of the old doctor's downfall, the poor, pathetic meddler. It had become clear that he knew too much, and had lost all ability or even desire to keep it to himself. He had paid quite a price for that, a mere hour or so ago, and lay alone and still now, until the boy would discover the cold sack of skin when he arrived in the morning.

Now, he thought, once again the bitter bitch was a step nearer to the long sanctuary of anonymity that he had pledged to uphold for her. It was she who had led him down this path, and he hated her for it, yet he was quite resigned to the duty to which he stayed true, to protect her, to cosset her, to ensure her survival. For her survival was his own survival.

Rosalinda was her name but he had never used it, and certainly "Aunt" was far, far beyond the boundaries of familiarity to them. He could remember her pretty, when he was a boy. She would arrive, a fountain of exotic extravagance, at his father's house, and she would dominate the man, her own brother, treat him shabbily in his own house, and ignore his son. The two of them would talk secretly together, the brother and the sister, of money, of cities, of schemes involving strangers and untrustworthy visitors. The boy would hear them talk, but couldn't understand the meaning of it, yet it thrilled him, the secrecy, the deceit, and he was thrilled again, now, as he stood in this cold doorway, huddled in the dark with the hands of a murderer spread before him.

But the biggest thrill had been the mad men and debonair dandies who would come to the big front room in that house on the Durham Road, and laugh and talk and shout, and recite long, clever verses, and sing with chest-filled passion, of lovers and seas and rivers and wars, or act out hilarious antics in song, of stupid oafs and crafty clowns, who apparently thronged the streets of Newcastle in broad daylight. Rosalinda would bring them in, kiss them and applaud them, and he was allowed to sit in the corner and watch them all. This, he thought, was what the world outside must be like.

How wrong he had been. The world outside was cold and cruel, and he had been cast at its mercy, suddenly and harshly, when his father had been lured away forever by his misplaced ambitions and dubious associations. Their house on the hill was locked up, its windows shuttered, and he, still hardly more than a boy, was sent to live across the river, in the house that Rosalinda rarely used, with a filthy coal mine on its doorstep and a hangman's noose blown by callous gusts of northern wind outside its window.

She had never really lived there. She had skipped through the drawing rooms and ballrooms and bedrooms of well-off society names and had merely thrown her soiled remnants and discarded gifts into this bare cave of plunder like so much chaff. Then, when her mantle of high position and influence was stripped from her, and people stopped feeling the need to invite her into their lives, she had limped bitterly back to that squalid midden of unwanted belongings, to find him, a lonely and uncultured young man by now, wrapped up in her discarded waste, without any idea of what his life was meant to be. She couldn't look after herself, so he became her saviour, her guardian, her protector, seduced by the promise that there was wealth, that there were riches, and that one day they would be his.

But she'd kept them hidden from him, and whenever he asked about them, where they had come from, and asserted his right to deserve them, he soon realised how tainted they must be. These were ill-gotten gains. The scheming and underhand planning from which he had derived such childish pleasure, was founded upon very real lies and cold-blooded transactions. His choice was either to expose it all to justice, or to accept it and flow along in its current. He could reassure himself, now as he stood in these shadows, that he had taken the only sensible and obvious direction. He knew she was taunting him with her vague promises, but despite the hunger-driven years clouded by coal dust, and the humiliating charade of a policeman's uniform, and even when his dreams dripped with the blood that had lately stained his hands, he could not really regret his decision, to stand by her.

But now her biggest deceit of all had been uncovered. He had always clung to a whiff of admiration for her, in the knowledge that she too was a poet, a songster, with a youthful ditty, her "Ode to Pandon Dene", written by the wide-eyed girl that she'd once been. Or so she had claimed. Now, a charade of his own had revealed that this claim was a lie. That coy conversation with his cronies in The Blue Posts the day before had taunted him with it, and his own reckoning of years and ages had proved it. The song must have drifted anonymously for years before she pilfered it and falsely stamped her name across its fading page. A common enough ruse, perhaps, but unforgiveable in his eyes. Such was the poisoned platform of deception that he had climbed upon, at her behest. It towered far too high now for him to step off and walk away from it.

This fever of fear and guilt that cursed his thoughts at times like this, it would surely pass, as it always did, and his journey to salvation and financial reward would be a comfortable one, and a just one. He was sure of that. If only, *if only*, he could wash the image of the dead doctor out of his mind's eye.

"Charlie?" he heard a woman's voice say. "Are ye not speakin'? What are ye doin', standin' out in the rain all dressed up? Is it a sweetheart you're waitin' for, ye old devil?"

He slid easily into it, this character that he'd been playing, inhabiting even, for so many years now. What better guise for a deceiver of justice than an officer of the law?

"Hello there Ruby," he said, in a jolly-enough voice. "Dressed up you say? Me? Look at you, in your plumes and glossy beads!"

"Well, it's Friday night man, ye've got to show the town ye can turn out like the best o' them," the woman replied in a gleeful giggle. "Ah'm away inside, are ye comin'?"

"In a minute," he said. "I'm waitin' on me pals comin'."

She left him with a cheery wave and another giggle, and waltzed off across the road and into The Wheatsheaf. Ramsay watched her go. This wasn't the woman he was hoping to see in Balmbra's that night. The one that he was interested in was already inside.

As he walked down the steps from the bar-room and into the music saloon, no-one even noticed him. All eyes were on the stage, where she was standing demurely, her hair pulled back from her face, a blotch of crude red dust on either cheek, and a blue frock and matching bonnet catching the flicker from the line of spirit lights along the edge of the platform. The accordion and the fiddle were coaxing her pure, high voice through a song that Ramsay knew well, called "On Ropery Banks". He stood at the foot of the steps and watched her glide through the melody, and close it with a sighing, descending coda of plaintive regret. As the bow sounded the last note, the crowd erupted into wild applause and a stirring mish-mash of cheers and calls of delight. Emily Gilchrist took a timid half step back, and then broke into a generous smile. With a hint of a curtsey she was gone.

The music struck up raucously, and a painted-faced clown tumbled from the other side of the stage with a wooden peg fixed on his nose and a pair of rather unconvincing blue fishes held, one in either hand. He began to wave them frantically at no-one in particular, and Ramsay chose the moment to ease himself back towards the jugs of ale, newly filled and displayed upon the bar at the back of the hall. Now, more than a few people noticed him, and one or two even called him by name, but no-one approached him. He called for a pot of beer, and when it came, he sidled into the remotest corner and looked around the room. He'd only been in this place once before, and then it had been half full and dreary, but tonight it was teeming with all-comers, all braying loudly with high spirits and joviality. He resented every one of them with a cold intensity, and he surely knew why. His burning passion for the fabric of the repertoire that these people had usurped in such a crude fashion, to be regurgitated in places such as this, made him feel almost defiled. These were the songs he had grown up with, that he had learned by heart, even knowing that he would never have the gumption or the nerve to perform them himself. Moreover, he had imbibed their spirit to create new pieces in their image and likeness, that no-one was likely ever to hear. His mind drifted away yet again, to those warm and respectful scenes in the drawing room of the old house, and to what he had convinced himself to have been happier, more meaningful times. A shrill caw of laughter from across the room jolted him back into the present.

He looked over to the opposite corner of the room, where Emily Gilchrist had emerged from the side of the

219

stage, to warm embraces and open hands of congratulations. The men stared at her as if she were a china doll on display, the women did the same but with harsher, somewhat envious glints in their eyes. The girl was gracious but unsullied by it all, and linked arms with another lass to cross through the crowd, to an empty space at the other side of the stairs.

A man called Jepson who Ramsay knew from the balladeers gatherings at the Indian Kings public house, approached him with a look of surprise on his face.

"Now then, Charlie," he said, "Ah've not seen ye in here that often before? And no swallow-tails either! The bobbies haven't given yer the push have they?"

Ramsay forced a laugh. "No, just a few days on special duty. Age and experience still has a place in this world, I'm glad to say!"

"Yon lass was good, mind" the man went on. "It's Robbie Gilchrist's daughter, though ye'd never know it. She must be bonny after her mother! And she never sings his songs, always sticks to the old ones. I know they're out of favour these days, but when they're done well, ye can't beat them, I don't care what folks say."

"She'll find her footin'" Ramsay replied. "There's plenty songs out there that she can lay claim on as hers, once she gets a bit more certainty and style about her."

Jepson nodded with a sagacity that such men believe they have in abundance, even when they know no more than anyone else. "Ye should have a word with her on that," he said. "She needs takin' under a wing."

Ramsay looked over at the young woman, by now chatting and smiling with a bunch of others, her moment of glory behind her. "Aye," he said. "Ah might do just that."

Jepson backed away with a nod, as the deep thud of a loose-skinned drum filled the room, and another act was announced. This time it was a smiling, garishly suited young lad of about sixteen, who confidently waved up the speed of the musicians behind him, before soaring his way into 'The Fiery Clock Face', displaying none of the skill that the song needed. His voice was harsh and shrill, never quite reaching the notes, but with an edge that made it plainly audible above the noise of the audience. Even Ramsay could acknowledge that such a voice had a distinct advantage in this environment. But on every other level, he found the performance coarse and shallow. At least, he also acknowledged with a sudden skip of a heart-beat, the surroundings were moving him beyond the desperate melee of dark thoughts with which he'd battled over the last hour or so.

But there were still pressing matters to attend to. He looked again at the Gilchrist girl across the room, all carefree smile and tossing hair. He had seen the look on her face, earlier that day, when Inspector Piper had mentioned his conversation with Doctor Rossiter. It was plain to him that there were matters of significance that had been discussed in her presence, when Piper had spoken with her father. Ramsay had turned it all over in his mind as he'd walked back along the Durham Road towards the Tyne an hour before. Old Gilchrist was a liability, certainly, but there was no time to consider that now. The girl, on the other hand, could be easily dealt with, and freely too, as there was nothing to outwardly connect him with her.

Ramsay's challenge now, was to be seen all-too clearly here tonight, in Balmbra's, then to depart unobtrusively in order to attend to the girl quickly as she made her way home, and to be back here in plain view for the remainder of the evening. It was a mere ten minute journey to the place that he had in mind. She would soon be leaving, as he knew from Piper's account of her habits. He would anticipate that by leaving before her with a ready excuse, and would be waiting for her outside.

His watch showed twenty minutes after ten o'clock. He walked to the man Jepson, and patted his back. He leaned into his ear.

"I have to check at the police-house, that the night-watch is in place," he said. "Is it worth me while to come back to catch more of this?"

Jepson nodded. "Oh aye, there'll be a fine baritone, next to last. We'll likely be here until quarter to midnight!"

Ramsay smiled and nodded back, then made for the stairs, his head low. But just as his foot reached the first step, he was aware of a woman's voice. It was the Gilchrist girl, there was no doubt, and she was calling to him. He felt his face redden and burn with the shock of it. He pretended not to hear and quickened his pace up the stairs, but then he felt her tug at his sleeve, and knew that others had certainly heard her. "Constable!" she had repeated. "A moment please!"

He halted and swung around, staring back at her in some confusion.

"Ah'm sorry," she said, haltingly. She drew closer to him. He pulled back instinctively.

She continued. "Ah saw you with Mister Piper earlier today. Can you pass a message to him, that me father wishes to speak to him tomorrow, if it's convenient." She stepped closer still. "We've talked together, my father and me, and we agreed that there are matters to discuss with Mister Piper. Can ye tell him so?"

Ramsay felt dazed and breathless. He nodded slowly and deeply at her, but found no words of reply. He turned and stretched his legs up the stairs, two at a time, and strode at a pace, across the bar-room, through the door to the night outside.

By the time that Emily Gilchrist herself emerged from the same door, Ramsay's mind was clear as to what he had to do, even though his original plan was now crushed under the weight of necessity.

CHAPTER 19

"And cross ower the buckle"

Piper and Turnbull were still at the Police House at three o'clock that next afternoon, an hour after Charlie Ramsay should have turned up for his shift. Fitzsimmons strode in purposefully with a duty roster in his hand, having bolted up the stairs like a man half his age.

"He's not reported for work," he said, his voice steady, but his eyes blazing with anger.

"It could mean anything," said Piper. "It could all be just circumstances coming together to paint a black picture. He could be at home. He's got a wife and children to tend to, hasn't he? Anything could have happened."

Fitzsimmons shook his head. "Ramsay has no family," he said, dismissively. "Wherever he is, he's likely got the girl with him, either willingly or not."

Piper stared back at him. "You're wrong, surely," he said. "About him having no family. He spoke to me about a wife and children, on the first day we met! Here in this very room, not a week ago!"

"He's a single man," Fitzsimmons said flatly.

Turnbull slammed his hat down onto the table, and stamped across the room, shaking his head in disbelief. "Where does the bugger live?" he exclaimed. "Do we at least know that for certain? We must go there immediately!"

Fitzsimmons nodded. "At Spital Tongues, somewhere, by the Town Moor. I heard him say his room overlooks the old gibbet." He looked at the front of the duty book, and thumbed his way through a few pages. "There's no address by his name here, just 'Town Moor'."

"Overlooking the gibbet!" cried Turnbull. "He'll be closer to it than he bargained for, when I get my hands on him!"

"What's to be done?" asked Piper, sounding agitated. "Do we just spread men across the moor and the surrounding streets, asking from door to door? The army camp is nearby, isn't it? Can we ask them for assistance?"

Turnbull raised his hands at that. "No, we can't get the military involved, no matter the urgency. There'd be uproar on the streets, and I'd be out of a job if I even suggested it. But nor have we the numbers to conduct a thorough search, even with assistance from the men from the section stations in Walker and Arthur's Hill. And if the man takes fright, who knows what threat that would be to the girl if she's being held. We're going to have to handle this ourselves, the best we can. Sergeant, are there any men here not yet on their watch we can take with us?"

Sergeant Fitzsimmons pointed to the shelf, where three hats remained to be collected.

"One of those is Ramsay's, but there are two men downstairs who are just off their watch. They can be brought into use."

As he spoke, a figure appeared at the door. It was Alec Parrish. He looked around the room with a puzzled, anxious look on his face. He nodded a greeting.

"The bobby downstairs told me about Rossiter," he said. "Do you know the culprit?"

No-one replied. Turnbull sat down heavily and ran his hands through his hair. Fitzsimmons slunk back to his office. It was Piper who eventually spoke.

"Constable Ramsay is missing, unaccounted for. He was seen last night taking Gilchrist's daughter from the music-hall. She never returned home last night and is missing as well."

Parrish looked back at him, his face twisted in disbelief. "Ramsay? You really suspect him? Of what? The murder of Rossiter? The abduction of the lassie? But what is his connection to it? Could he himself not have come to some harm? That would account for it!"

Piper sighed deeply. "I realise now that he was the only one who knew I had spoken to Rossiter again. I told him so, and I told him as well that the old man had given me vital information. He knew also that I intended to go back to him this morning to hear more."

Piper circled the floor, staring down at it, as if collecting his own thoughts as he spoke. "It was also Ramsay who was on hand at Selkirk's death, as you'll recall. He was the one too who let it be known that we had possession of Selkirk's lost papers. And his hand!" – he held out his own as he said it – "I remember drawing blood from the hand of one of the men that attacked me on Monday night. Have you noticed? Ramsay has worn those coarse gloves ever since, on the premise of him being out of uniform."

"But as you say, there were two of them who came at you," Parrish pointed out. "Who was his accomplice in that escapade?"

Turnbull spoke up. "He could have paid a shilling to any one of a hundred quayside rascals to shadow him in

227

that. Ramsay knows them all. He was also very reticent with what he knew about Jack Leonard, do you remember? It must have cooled him somewhat when I linked him with Rosalinda Leonard. Perhaps that's what forced his hand in all this." He banged his fist on his knee in rage. "This so-called police force. My God, is there no end to the scum that it attracts. People hungry for any chance they can get of having an advantage over their townsfolk, and for misusing the trust that is allotted to them."

Piper sighed deeply. "I fear this won't sit well with the ordinary decent folk of this town, when the news gets out. If it's anything like my own district, there is already distrust in Robert Peel's setting up of this force, and at every level. The ordinary folk mistrust us for the power that they feel we have, the criminals think we are blood-thirsty bullies, and the rich folk think we are corrupt. And in the newspapers we are portrayed as fools. What chance do we have? And now one amongst us is exposed as a murderer, if what we suspect is true."

Turnbull looked suddenly serious. "Ah yes, the newspapers. There's another point that I forgot to mention in light of this morning's events. I spoke with Lavery, the editor at the Mercury. That story they published that revealed your presence here in town. It didn't come to them from the London Times. In fact, they were only *told* that it had been reported there, but no-one has actually seen the piece as printed. Someone merely spoke about it to one of the writers on the Mercury when they met in the street on Tuesday morning, just in time for it to be written up for the Wednesday edition. He had no knowledge of who the informant was, but I surmise we can now guess as to his identity."

Piper grimaced. "Damn!" he said. "That will stand badly against me with my superiors. It was the one piece of ammunition that I had to hurl back at them, when I'm pilloried upon my return, thinking that they had blundered by announcing my presence here. Ah well. A stove pipe hat and a swallow-tail coat for me, come next Wednesday!"

Fitzsimmons came back into the room, a large book open in his hands.

"I looked at the last census for addresses near to the Town Moor, from the Leazes to the edge of Pandon. There are some large houses on the eastern side, beyond the barracks. And see here, the name of one of the families that live there." He leaned in towards Turnbull, offering him the book. He looked at where the sergeant was pointing.

"Leonard!" he said. "On Barrack Road."

Parrish moved closer into the room, still looking puzzled. "You say there's a link between Jack Leonard and this Rosalinda. But I ask again, what is the link between those two and Ramsay? Why has he acted so, if indeed he has? He has worked amongst you for, what, six years? And now he suddenly turns to the bad and slaughters an old man, abducts a young woman and goes out on the run. This doesn't make sense to me."

"Who knows what that link might be," said Piper, "But this whole business has lain sleeping for exactly that same period, those six years. The Corley Croons and the Four and Twenty, all of it was pushed away at precisely the time that Ramsay became a constable. And then suddenly, with

229

some kind of action or involvement from John Selkirk, the affair was threatened with exposure. And it's for that reason, I believe, that we're witnessing these current events. Someone has dire need to keep things hidden at all costs, and somehow Ramsay is involved and is acting as their agent."

Standing in the doorway, Fitzsimmons spoke.

"There's a song high in popularity at the music-halls these days. A tragedy, in fact, about the death of Jean Jamieson. D'ye know it?"

Parrish looked round at him, in puzzled surprise. "'The Ghost at Sandgate Pant'?" he said. "That was too much of a tragedy for me to find a verse about it entertaining. It leaves a bitter taste for me."

"Ah can understand that," said Fitzsimmons. "I too remember the details of the event only too well. Jeanie was convicted and condemned for the murder of her own mother, d'ye recall? A fit of drunken anger, it was said, though she denied doin' it from the start. Her one witness, a man called Billy Elli, and he's still about the town to this day, was late in coming forward to help her, and his account was garbled and meaningless at the court. Many of us suspected that he was involved, that he was purposely muddled and confused. At any rate, Jeanie's journey to the Town Moor was her last. She still claimed her innocence, to the very end. Ah spoke with her meself, more than once. She told me that her mother had made a curious discovery, that Jeanie's father had been tricked into service with the dragoons. That there'd been money, paid by another man, so that he himself escaped his duty, and that her father was taken and transported to France in his stead. The father perished at the hands of the French. Is that not the same as what we're talking about here?"

"It is," said Turnbull, "And it surely shows that others had wind of it before us."

"More than that," said Fitzsimmons. "Jeanie claimed that her mother was in the habit of proclaimin' this scandal to all and sundry, and that it was due to her loose tongue that she met her end. But she couldn't explain how or why. Fanciful, we all thought. Well, perhaps. But look here." He proffered the open case-book to the room. "It reads here that the arrest of Jeanie Jamieson was made by Constable Charles Ramsay. He was first at the scene of the murder, and it was his testimony that condemned the girl."

They reached the wide, bleak Town Moor as darkness was falling – Turnbull, Piper, two constables and, despite a frown or two from Turnbull, Alec Parrish. A bitter, taunting wind whipped across them. Leaving the black carriage in the mill yard, they made their way cautiously to a clump of bare bushes by the cross-track. Far over on their left lay the barracks, a tattered flag flapping piteously above it. Behind them, the Leazes coal pit growled menacingly, its tubs and trucks moving like weary penitents, slowly, desperately awaiting their burden. Piper found it just as hideous and threatening as he had on that Sunday morning walk when he had first clapped eyes on it, like some sly monster lurking at the edge of the city, waiting to overpower its populace. He was glad that their suspect's lair was away from it, a tumbling row of houses skirting the edge of the pale, wind-lashed grassland.

Turnbull looked at a flimsy paper chart that Fitzsimmons had handed to him as they'd left the police house. The wind tore at it as he held it in his hands, and he fought to crease it over to a manageable size. He looked down at it, then raised his head towards the houses. He nodded in the direction of the largest, standing off to one side, perhaps three hundred yards away from them. It had once been grand, but even from this distance, it was clear that it was in a state of disrepair. The windows were all shuttered, except for the large ground-floor bay, at which pale cloths of sun-bleached green were pulled roughly across. The door stood high on four steps, and a knot of hawthorn bush to the right of it masked a lower cellar window. There was smoke rising languidly from one of the three chimneys.

Turnbull turned to the two uniformed men, and pointed to a roofless out-house halfway down the neighbouring terrace.

"Make your way there, but from behind the row," he said. "If you go back past the mill and on down the track at the back, you can cut along without being seen." The pair of them moved off. He then turned to Parrish. "Alec, I have to bid you stay here. I'm risking a reprimand by allowing Piper here to come with me to the door. I can't invite you to do the same."

Parrish smiled broadly. "I'm content where I am. I've got a fine view from here."

Turnbull nodded to Piper, and the pair of them walked slowly but directly towards the house. Neither spoke. The building looked even more dilapidated from the closer vantage. Piles of rubble filled the well of the cellar entrance, and rats scurried over the stones and back towards the building as the men pushed back a single iron-barred gate. They climbed the steps and Turnbull thumped on the door. Piper looked keenly around, and thought he saw a movement at the curtain in the window next to them. Turnbull knocked again, even more heavily. Piper backed down the steps to look up at the windows above. The smoke from the chimney had dwindled into barely a wisp. Then the sound of a bolt being drawn back echoed from within. Then silence. Then the door was wrenched open, and a tiny figure, her white hair wrapped in a shawl of dark mauve, and beneath it a loose, oversized, open-necked gown of green and black brocade, silk perhaps, or something that had once been equally grand, but barely reaching to her knees. Her ankles were dipped like fingers into a pair of ancient leather boots. Her skin had slipped into deep wrinkles down her face, but her black eyes shone, and showed a defiance that only riches and privilege can instil in a person, man or woman. Her whole appearance was extremely affecting, in a tragic, but nonetheless shocking way.

"Miss Leonard?" Turnbull said, his voice raised against the wind. "Miss Rosalinda Leonard?"

She snorted a response. Her eyes became even colder.

"Are you Miss Leonard?" he asked again, in a firmer voice.

"Yes, yes, what do you want?" Her voice was deep, clear, and belied the body from whence it came.

"I'm from the local Police Constabulary. My name is Superintendent Turnbull. My colleague and I need to come in and speak with you urgently."

She glanced quickly at Piper, then snarled back. "You can't come in here. Speak to me if you will, but you cannot come in!"

Turnbull took a step nearer. "No, we must come inside. I have the authority to do so, given the matter we wish to discuss. Now please, pull back the door and let us enter." He edged forward even more. She gave a soft whimper and shook her head, muttering something to herself, but then tugged on the door to edge it further open. Piper heard Turnbull take a deep breath, and advance inside. He followed.

They walked into a hallway with a high ceiling, its walls powdered with damp and black with mildew. The smell was thick and heavy, the darkness at the far end utter and complete. The old woman had scurried off like one of the rats outside, and could be heard pushing drawers closed, moving chairs, and coughing with an alarming retch. Smoke and soot hung in the air from a hearth somewhere beyond. A staircase to the right led up into a high black void. Turnbull cautiously moved towards the open door and followed the woman into the room.

When Piper entered, Turnbull was halfway across the floor, watching the woman as she was throwing a grey blanket across a bed piled high with clothes and assorted rags and coats. At every turn there was stuff, piled in corners to the ceiling, on chairs, on shelves: crockery, books, tins of various shapes and sizes, boxes with foreign words and exotic pictures on them, hats, tobacco pipes of various lengths, chains, glass, plumes of feathers, piles of newspapers, glazed figurines, all coated in dust and soot, all relics of a past steeped in some sort of opulence, now lost forever. Piper had never seen so many belongings in one place. The two men looked at each other. The woman busied herself, moving things, covering things, hiding things, and ignored the men in the doorway.

Turnbull raised his voice against the rattle of glass and china.

"Miss Leonard, are you alone in the house?" There was no reply. He tried again. "Who else is in the house apart from you?" When she didn't respond, he walked over to her and took her by the arm. She snarled at him and struggled, but he held on.

"Stop it!" he snapped at her. "Behaving like a petulant child does not convince me and will not achieve anything. If you don't answer my questions here, I'll take you with me to a place where you'll be *made* to answer them, do you understand me?"

She ceased her struggle and looked at him with undisguised hatred.

"Who else is in this house?" he asked again.

"No-one," she hissed. "There is only ever me."

"Where is Charles Ramsay?" Turnbull said, firmly. "We know he lives in this place. Where is he? Is he in this house?" He wrenched her closer to him. "What is he to you?"

"He's nothing to me!" the old woman hissed back. "I don't know where he is!"

Piper glanced towards the hearth, where the fire was now barely smouldering. Two dainty cups with ornate handles were on the mantle, both with the remains of something in them. There was a bottle half full of what could have been gin on the floor by a pile of cloth slippers and leather shoes.

"Do you know what Charles Ramsay has done, Miss Leonard?" Piper said. "Did he tell you? Or perhaps it was you who persuaded him to murder Doctor Rossiter."

She made no reply, but the change in the look in her eyes betrayed her. The remark had unsettled her. Piper continued. "And was it you who suggested abducting the girl? Or has he done away with her also? It is a deep pool of trouble that he's pulled you into. And if he has made his escape, it's you and you alone who will answer to his crimes. Your very silence here and now will ensure that."

Turnbull twisted her to face him again. "We know of your schemes, of the militia lotteries, of your part in the substitutions! The so-called Corly Croons, swindled out of their young lives by you and your high-society set of gluttonous, greedy parasites. And even now, you are still trying to wield your power and to cover your slimy tracks. Is that why you told Ramsay to silence those who had words to use against you?"

She stared up at him, her eyes bursting with hatred. "I didn't tell him to do anything!" she barked suddenly. "He only ever tries to protect me."

"Protect you from what?" said Turnbull, wheeling her around to face him.

"From you!" she snapped bitterly, "And from the likes of you. Sanctimonious do-gooders in your fancy jackets and polished hats, happy to sit back and let us work our fingers to the bone for your benefit, and then all too ready to pick the meat off our bones when we don't measure up

236

to your high and mighty civic standards. You are a pathetic lot in a god-forsaken place. You deserve all you get!"

"And what did you get?" Piper asked sternly. "A pretty penny, I have no doubt, from selling the souls and bodies of honest men, to save the privileged sons of high society from having to do their duty when they were called to do it."

"Privileged?" she spat out. "Not privileged! Gifted, blessed by God, with a talent, that would have been wasted in a barrack room or a whore house, and then squandered on a foreign battlefield, where we had no cause to be in the first place. They were common men, straight from the street, destined to end up on the Tyne or in that coal pit yonder. And we nourished them, displayed them, encouraged them, only to see them plucked from us by a stupid ballot."

Turnbull stared at her. "You talk of them as if they were Elizabethan poets, bards, the likes of Milton, or holy monks! They were jokers, guttersnipes, scrawling slang and ill-matched rhymes for the drinkers in quayside alehouses. They didn't ask for your patronage and coddling! And if you thought so much of them, why did one of them end up floating in the Tyne at your hands? What did John Selkirk do to provoke that fate for himself?"

"Not at my hands!" she cried, trying in vain to pull free from him. "He was past caring for himself, and yet he dared threaten us, that he'd report the whole story to the city fathers. We summoned him to the church, to make him change his mind, but he laughed in our faces. He left us no choice but to cast him to the fate he deserved."

"To the church?" said Piper. "To St Mary's you mean? The Four and Twenty?"

She stared at him with a sneer across her mouth. "What could you know of that? It no longer even exists. That was snatched from us and snuffed out too, after all the good and dutiful things we'd achieved for the likes of you. So much for allegiance, so much for gratitude. Then to be held to ransom by a drunken sot who lamented a son that he had never acknowledged in his lifetime, as was always his way with his bastard progeny, no matter the heartbreak of the women who bore them."

At those words, Piper glanced over at Turnbull, who responded with a look of puzzlement and surprise at what he'd heard. But still Rosalinda pressed on, the snarl of contempt in her voice brimming over with hatred and resentment.

"And that young brute that he had left to be raised by a slop-trade doxy in a slum on Canon Street. He had meant nothing to him. And he dared to preach righteousness at me. If the boy had lived, he would have returned from Flanders a hero, a better man than his father ever was!"

"But he didn't return, did he?" Piper said. "Very few of your victims did return. They had no training, no deftness at arms, how were they supposed to survive?"

Turnbull held up his hand to stop him. He looked the woman in the face.

"So Selkirk came to the church and refused to back down, is that it?" he said. "And he was returning, back across the river when he was cut down?"

"I don't know where he was going!" she said, a laugh in her voice. "But I do know that he was to go to the town

238

clerk the next day, to hand him a list of all our names, and all that he accused us of. He stood there and dared to threaten us with that. We were the cream of the town. And what was he? A stinking drunken wretch, not worth the rags he was standing in. Blame him for it all, and for old Rossiter, not me. That blind old fool knew everything, and had managed to keep it to himself all these years, but we knew he'd blurt it out once the lid was off the jar."

"But I ask again, what is Ramsay to you?" Turnbull said, "Why is he acting this way on your behalf?"

She stared up into his eyes, her half-open mouth trembling, as if fighting against the words it was about to speak.

"He is my brother's child," she said at last, "with at least the decency in him to defend me when he saw the peril I was in!"

Piper looked at her with contempt. "What he saw," he said, "was his inheritance being snatched away from him. That's all. He saw that if you were to be disgraced publicly, your ill-gotten wealth would be lost to him, and he would be left with nothing but a constable's wage that he had no right to claim in the first place!"

Her mask of defiance was slipping. She stared back at him, but her well of abusive retorts had all but run dry. Her head shook, but whether with anger or with fear, Piper could not tell. He drew closer to her still.

"Where's the girl?" he hissed. "Tell me and that at least will stand in your favour. What did he do with the girl?"

The old woman shuddered and tried to turn her face away, her mind in a turmoil, her black eyes darting to and fro, her whole body trembling, torn as she was between

239

resistance and desperation. She mumbled, cursed breathlessly, and whined like a cornered beast. The two men stared down at her, a mixture of distaste and anger on both their faces.

At last, the whole of her being fell loose before their eyes, and with her free hand she suddenly jabbed a talon-like finger in the direction of a small door in the corner of the room, shaped to open beneath the hall stairs. Piper lunged towards it, and ripped it open, scattering paper and pots as he did so. Inside it was black as night. Turnbull pulled the woman with him to the fireplace and pushed her into the corner. He made a thick screw of newspaper and pushed it into the dying embers of the fire. It smouldered and flowered into flame. He leapt to Piper, who took it and held it into the dark recess. There were steps going down. He called the girl's name.

"Emily! Emily, are you there?"

He moved down slowly, coughing from the smoking paper. It was burned to blackness in seconds and he let it drop. Turnbull handed him another, firmer one from behind him. The flames lit a cellar strewn with canvas sheets, boxes, firewood. A large pile of small coals was heaped against one side of it, and next to it, stretched across the floor at a horrible angle, her bare legs and fair hair reflecting back the flame, was the shape of a woman.

"Emily!" he called again. He saw a movement, as she pulled back her leg, and then the light caught her eyes, blinking from the brightness of it, filled with fear, her mouth bound by a filthy rag, her face smeared with coal dust, her cheeks stained with dried tears. Turnbull appeared at the door above with yet another flaming bundle. Piper let his drop and began to ease the girl into his arms. Her felt the sobs within her as he did so. He lifted her to her feet, and he half carried, half pushed her back up the steps. He heard a groan from deep inside her, and a half-squeal of pain. They struggled to the top in a confused clump of limbs and skirts and coats, and at last Turnbull took her from him, half-dragging her across to a soft chair near the door. The old woman was keening, an inhuman high moan that seemed to show she was unable to weep with remorse or pity. Piper snapped at her to be quiet.

Even when her mouth was free of the rag, the girl said nothing. She looked at nothing, certainly not her rescuers, her gaze floating off upwards, her breath coming in stuttering tremors, her body shivering from the shock of it all.

At that moment, one of the constables burst through the door behind them.

"Ramsay's on the run, sir!" he shouted breathlessly. "We saw him scarperin' across towards the pit. Constable Allen has gone after him. And that man Parrish is on him as well!"

"Stay here with these two!" Turnbull cried. "The girl needs help. I'll send someone from the mill. Don't leave them!" He pointed to the old woman. "And be careful of that witch. Strike her if you have to!" The sound of the old woman's yelp of distress at these words filled the room. It was Turnbull who cut it short with a harsh snarl this time. Then he and Piper hurried out of the door.

CHAPTER 20

"Chock full o' spite"

It had been the song that had saved her. Charlie Ramsay's agenda had been torn ragged as he'd walked into Balmbra's that evening and heard Emily Gilchrist in full flight, living the song that wisped from her lips with a heart-felt tenderness that he had not heard, not felt, since those drawing-room performances in the old house on the Durham Road when he was a child. The entire audience tonight had been spellbound, but none could have felt it as deeply as he did. The thrill of experiencing a glorious melody, with every nuance and twist of it flowing easily and sincerely along, was like a warm breeze across his heart. He knew that when he tried to describe it to the old woman later, she would jeer and scoff at him. But why should she, a proven charlatan, have exclusive claim of such high-minded taste and appreciation? He had known the breathless beauty of these songs all his life, as if by instinct. He knew too when they were delivered with their artistry intact.

So the thought of spoiling the source of this, as he had planned, now filled him with revulsion. The girl had almost broken the spell when she approached him unexpectedly like that, as he'd tried to sidle out of the auditorium unnoticed, and her vulnerability in those moments of conversation hadn't impressed him. She had become just another obstacle in his path once again. But now as he stood in the cold night, his eyes fixed upon the door of the Wheatsheaf, from which he knew she was due to emerge within moments, the sharp memory of her voice and how it had made him feel, came flooding back to him. If only, he thought, he could cage her like a singing bird, a captured delight, to be covered and uncovered at his whim, and bade to sing for him so that he could relive the thrill of a pure song whenever he wished it.

The wide market-place was empty. The cobbles shone in the damp night air. A single voice, a man's angry rant, echoed up the wynd from somewhere distant. A bell clanged lazily on the river and the sound rolled up from beyond the castle-keep and sparkled across the stones. Ramsay became conscious of his breath again. It struggled from his chest and out through his nostrils. He drew it up like water from a deep well, and squandered it into the night air. He dragged his mind towards a decision, as to what he was to do next. The woman knew too many things. Her father must have brought her into his confidence by now. It was Gilchrist, after all, who had long ago allowed his stupid qualms and principles to rear up and throw everything into jeopardy, and it was this girl, his daughter, whom he had used as a lame, pathetic excuse for doing so. It was all well and good, he had said, to throw nameless, faceless young men, these anonymous Corly Croons, to be devoured by the dogs of war, but what if his child had been one of them, a wide-eyed, fearless son, instead of the fair-skinned, dewy-eyed daughter that fate had bequeathed upon him? No, he had said, he could not be part of such a scheme, and he had turned and walked away with a sanctimonious look of contempt upon his face. The old woman and the rest of the Four and Twenty had watched him go, knowing that one day his knowledge and his conscience would erupt and cause trouble and grief for them. And now it had.

The Four and Twenty had overstepped their mark on so many occasions that it was ironic that a much more trifling matter had been their downfall. Greed had soured their union, and it had been the ungainly snatching of money from the city purse which had exposed them and destroyed them. They had shrivelled like dead leaves and with barely a rustle when the end came, and only a few, including Rosalinda, had had the sense enough to stash away what they had taken, and feign poverty and ruin. It was that cache that Charlie Ramsay was now fighting for. She had promised it to him, if he would protect and defend her as she withered into old age. The time to collect on that promise had come, he felt, now that he had gone to such lengths to maintain that protection.

But now here he stood, deliberating over what should have been a straightforward next step towards his salvation. There was a rope store, a hole in a wall half-way down the Long Stairs, about the size of a pantry, with a sturdy door and a strong lock, a place where someone could be bound up and left without anyone knowing what was inside. A broken midden oozed by the path just there, and passers-by avoided it, or at worst hurried by it. No-one would think to look inside the store. And that had been his plan. The girl would walk past the foot of the steps as she made her way home. He could take her with the minimum of fuss and violence, and then leave her to her own luck and fortune. Perhaps she would eventually be found, but he would be long-gone by then. But now, his heart sank at the thought of silencing something so pure and precious. Did the lure of her voice outweigh the risk of the calamity that its words could expose, like some entrancing siren in the cold city night? His mind raced in a turmoil as he stood there.

Then all at once, the door across from him had opened, and she was there, pulling her shawl into place and wrapping it across one shoulder. She stepped out into the road to cross the market place towards Union Street. Before he knew it, he was walking towards her from where he had been waiting. The scuffle of his feet alerted her and she spun around with some alarm.

"Emily!" he said, and thought better of it. "Miss Gilchrist! It's me, Constable Ramsay."

She stared at him, taking a step back.

"Yes, what is it?" she said, her voice betraying a quiver of wariness.

"I'm sorry," he said, already easily drifting into the veil of deceit, however unformed it was in his mind. "It's yer father. He's been taken bad. He must've been on his way here, and was taken up by two lads, who found him breathless in an alley by Northumberland Street. They were on their way to the mill by the wagon way, so they've taken him to the old infirmary up there. You've to come!"

She was already advancing towards him, with a different sort of fear in her eyes, a fear arising from concern, perhaps of impending grief. For an instant it affected him, but he shook it off, and reached out a hand towards her.

"Is he very bad?" she gushed. "What brought him out? Had he been taken ill by himself? He surely wasn't comin' here to see me. He must've been all alone and felt bad, and Ah wasn't there to help. But it's such a long way, they shouldn't have taken him all that distance. He's so weak at night. Is he goin' to be all right?"

"Come," he said. "I'll take you to him. I only know what I have from the message."

"But who sent the message? Who's told you this?"

"It was at the Police House," he said. "They told me there, when I went to report just now. Come, let's be quick."

She stepped forward and he pointed in the direction of Newgate. Her pace was already rapid. They hurried along in silence. Ramsay's mind was forging ahead as well, and grasping its way into the next part of his scheme. They walked into the dip of Pandon, where a loud group of men and women was emerging from a public house called the Crown and Thistle. Ramsay twisted his face away from them, and quickened his step, but the rise towards the edge of the moor began to take its toll on his breath. He felt the coldness of sweat on his brow, and the stab of pain in his stomach muscles. The girl strode on regardless.

"Over there," he said at last. "The house at the end. He's there."

She looked around in confusion, trying to get her bearings in the darkness.

"But the infirmary is across there," she said, pointing vaguely to her left. "Ah can see the mill yonder. The hospital lies just beyond it."

"No," he replied. "It's closed after dark. The nurses' house is open for late comers and the like. That's where they'll have taken him."

He sensed her doubt and hesitation, but then she turned and walked on in the direction that he was pointing.

"Is it nowt but an old wife that runs the place at this time of night?" she said suddenly, a panic in her voice. "If it's not the real hospital, there surely can't be a doctor there!"

"He'll be looked after, don't fret," he said. "There are girls there to fetch a doctor from nearby." He gestured across the common. "And there's the barracks. There's always a doctor at the infirmary there."

Her pace quickened again. Ramsay was struggling to keep up with her. He felt his breath scratching madly in his chest. At last they reached their goal, the tall, solitary house which stood diffidently apart from the rest of the squat terrace. Even in the darkness, its ragged shabbiness was plain enough. Not a light showed in a single window. Emily Gilchrist stopped at the gate, suddenly confused, anxious.

"But the place is empty!" she said, turning to Ramsay. "It's derelict, surely. This can't be where they have taken me father!"

Ramsay tried to reassure her. "Come, it's near midnight. That's why it's in darkness. There's a lamp in that middle window, I'm certain. We'll enter by the back way. Go on, they know we're comin'. The path is clear, quickly!"

The girl was reluctant, that was plain enough, but she edged around the side of the building, egged on by his gentle encouragement as he walked behind her. There was indeed a crack of light, coming from a raised wooden door reached by three stone steps. She ascended cautiously. Ramsay leaned over her from behind and pushed the door open. Again he reassured her with a whisper, and she was soon inside a small scullery that smelled of boiled cabbage and bad eggs. Emily held her breath, as much out of confusion as from the foul odour.

"This can't be," she said, and immediately a door in front of them gaped open. An old woman was there, stooped and bent, with a lit candle in her hand, her black eyes squinting at them as if in a fury.

"What's this?" the woman exclaimed in a throaty croak. "Why have you brought her here, you damn fool?"

Emily heard the voice behind her snap "Shut up!", but in a strange, sharp tone, that made her catch her breath with fear. The old woman came towards her, her eyes burning with a flame of rage and hate, her dribbling, twisted mouth glinting like that of a mad dog in the candlelight, a low groan gurgling deep within her terrible, bone-bound chest. The ghastly jaws opened as if they were about to tear the flesh from the young girl's face, as a deformed hand reached across it from behind.

Emily Gilchrist felt her own senses falling away from her, drifting, tumbling, draining away. She swooned into a faint and barely felt the thump of the stone floor against her slender shoulder as she hit the ground. Her forehead cracked against it and a tight, low noise oozed from her open mouth.

Standing above her, Charlie Ramsay was still battling breathlessness. He heard the old woman snarl, "Pick her up!" as if she were chastising a dog. He slid his hands beneath the limp form and struggled to hoist her into his arms. He fought for a grip, and for balance. The old woman was already wrenching open another door in the corner of the room, that led down to the cellar beneath. He followed her, paying little heed to the bumping and scraping that the body in his arms was having to endure as he edged his way through the tiny door, down the roughly-hewn steps to the filthy floor at the bottom. The old woman pushed back a pile of sail-cloth with her foot and Ramsay leaned forward, letting his burden fall like a sack of loose coals on to the cleared space on the ground. Rosalinda flung a coil of tarred rope on top of the girl, and watched as Ramsay wordlessly clenched the wrists together and bound them as he would the feet of a rabbit before gutting it. She leaned over her. He saw her stretch a filthy rag across the girl's mouth, and tie it tightly and deftly behind her head. Then the pair of them turned and mounted the steps towards the scullery above.

She turned to chastise him again, the snarl of contempt and accusation already ripe for the plucking in her throat, but he pushed passed her, his mind wracked by torment, his body by exhaustion. He kicked his way through the debris that hindered his every step, and fell into the squalid sanctuary of his own room, bare and barren in comparison to the rest of the house, but the only oasis of seclusion he had known for too many years. He fell face down on the cold damp bedding by the shuttered window, and was immediately overwhelmed by tormented sleep.

It was dark again when he stirred. But it was always dark here. He had no idea how many hours he'd lain there. The realities of the previous day suddenly poured over him like poison. His limbs ached, and his chest burned. He pushed himself painfully to his feet.

Rosalinda was sitting on a filthy coverlet on the pile of bedding in the next room, like a serpent in waiting. A pathetic candle crookedly planted into a slab of uneven tallow on a stand next to her flickered in ghastly antics across her wrinkled face. He came in and made his way to a table in the corner where he poured a draught of tepid, watery beer from a tall jug into a mug. He gulped it down.

The hours waiting for him hadn't dimmed her sneer. She spoke to him with the anger still plain in her voice.

"Why did you bring her here? I thought you said you had a place on the quayside to leave her! Do you know what you've done, bringing her into my house, you fool?"

Ramsay knew. He sighed and cast a lame excuse back at her.

"I couldn't get her out of sight of people. I had to persuade her, to tell her that her father needed her, that he was at the infirmary up here next to the mill." He closed his eyes tightly in despair, and then barked angrily, "It wasn't an easy thing, do you know that?"

She scoffed at him with a throaty laugh, but then saw him turn towards her in anger, and so held her tongue. Then she spoke again, but more softly.

"What of the old doctor?"

Ramsay looked down at his feet. "I finished him," he said. "He's not a problem for you now. But I don't know how much he told the London Inspector. I got the idea that there'd been much said." He looked up suddenly. "In fact, the girl might be able to tell us how much is known. It seemed like he'd spoken to her and her father about it."

The old woman dismissed this with a cackle.

"They can't lay any of this at my door!" she said, "That is, not until now, now that you've brought the slut here! Now she's more of a liability than she ever was. You'll have to finish her and then get rid. And do it tonight! Get her over to the wagons yonder, and she'll be away down that tunnel and to the river by daylight. Then you'll have to see to Gilchrist. He's the only one left who can point the finger now."

Ramsay stared at her. He rose to his feet, the anger boiling up inside him.

"What are you talking about?" he said. "Piper has spoken to him already, I told you. They'll have found Doctor Rossiter this mornin', they'll realise the girl is missin', and they'll be all out to find a culprit. I'd have had a chance to bluff them if I'd stuck close with them and marked every word they said. That was my only chance, to keep ahead of them. But you pressed me on, scoldin' me to finish them, and I was seen talkin' to the girl last night. She was at me before I had a chance to get out. That Piper isn't a fool. He's goin' to look my way soon enough, I can guarantee it. I've got to get out now. I've got to take my chance while I can. The tunnel is a good idea. I reckon I can get through it when it's dark. I'll wait until the last set goes down and then follow it to the river. I'd wager they won't be sendin' another set down until mornin'."

The old woman's face was a mask of horror as he spoke. "What about me?" she screeched. "Am I supposed to sit here until they come knocking at my door, and then take the blame for it all?"

He was face to face with her now. "There's nothing to link me to this place," he said, almost believing it himself. "And nothing to link me to you! I've never used your name. They won't come here. Piper will be back off to London, and there's no-one else that has his gumption to

252

follow this through. And if they eventually do come here, you can tell them you knew none of it. It'll be easy enough to convince them how much you despise me, and that you had no involvement in any of it." He stepped towards her, his eyes blazing. "But you have to give me what I'm due. I can't leave here empty handed. You have to give me what is mine, what you've promised to me all this time!"

"There's only this hovel, and the old one on the Durham Road," she said, turning away. "That's all I've been left with!" She held her hand to her scrawny throat, as if fearful that Ramsay's own hands would reach for it. He looked at her with disgust. Her eyes flickered back and forth, first at him, then around the squalid room where they sat. The bones stuck out from her neck and chest, and he glared at the yellowing, wrinkled skin, the thickly veined hands, the long, filthy fingers gripping on to the garish glass baubles that she always wore, as if they could somehow temper the ugliness that had overcome her.

"I'm not talking about property!" he snapped. "I can't carry bricks and mortar around with me. It's the spoils from your schemin', from the Four and Twenty and all their wrong-doin's. That's what I want. That's what I'm due, after all this time. You've always told me you had it, and more than your own fair share of it. It was your contrivance, you were always the instigator, the spark behind the whole rotten swindle. And you were the only one who had spirit enough to grab what you could, before the door slammed shut behind you. You've told me that too many times to turn around now and say it all comes down to a pair of tumble-downs full of rats and rags!"

He was upon her now. He gripped her wasted wrist like it was a twig, and reached for her throat with his free hand.

"Get away from me! You'll snap my lovely beads!" she cried. "Get your hands off me!"

"Then tell me!" he shouted at her. "Then I'll be off. But I'm not goin' empty handed. Tell me where you've hidden it, or by God I'll throttle it out of ye!"

She groaned like a wounded animal, and weakly tried to push his hands away.

Suddenly there was thumping from outside the room. Ramsay heard it, and froze. The old woman continued her unearthly moaning.

"Shut up!" he hissed. "Shut up, and listen! They're here for God's sake! They're at the door!"

There was another set of knocks. They echoed through the empty darkness beyond the parlour door, and seemed to shake the very walls of the place. Rosalinda feigned a struggle to catch her breath. Ramsay stared into nothingness, his mind in a turmoil. At last he signalled to her to go and answer the door. She shook her head and stared at him, her eyes wide with fear.

"Answer it!" he whispered. "Keep them there. If they have to come in, I'll get out by the back. Say nothin' about me. You know what I can do to you, and I *will* come back. I'll claim what's mine, or we'll both perish from me tryin' it!"

He dragged her to her feet, broke the candle free from the table, and stuffed it into her hand. He pushed her to the door, and waited in the darkness, hearing her scramble through the debris piled up in the passage. There were voices. She cackled an objection, then very plainly the stern voice of Turnbull bellowed forth, suddenly nearer, suddenly just on the other side of the door.

Ramsay leapt back towards the rear of the room, scooped up a grimy pea-jacket from the floor, and cautiously edged open the door through which he and Emily Gilchrist had first entered. He slid outside and moved gingerly along the side wall. He stooped under the tangled branches of an overgrown bush and crept beyond to the open grass. He looked back at the old house, but there was no sign of anyone. He stood, frozen by uncertainty for an instant, then broke into a stiff trot, pushing his arms into the coat as he went, and straining his eyes to scan the way before him, desperate to get his bearings. There to the right were the barracks, a good way off, and further west, straight ahead of him, he could see the outline of the head-wheels of the Leazes pit. He quickened his stride and made towards it. As he ran, carefully dodging the tufts of thick winter grass and potholes, all he could see in his mind's eye, taunting him, glinting and winking at him with brazen mockery, were those damned glass beads that the old woman had worn strung around her scrawny neck for as long as he could remember.

CHAPTER 21

"We byeth gan belaw"

Turnbull and Piper took off at speed as soon as they were beyond the broken outside gate, running into the wind across the wide and empty Town Moor. They soon slowed and then halted as one, both of them straining their eyes against the gale and into the gloom. The tall jagged silhouette of the pit-head reached up like a black claw against the skyline. Turnbull suddenly jerked his arm towards it.

"There!" he pointed. "There's young Allen, the constable, by the spoil heap, on the right. Get over there, but do nothing!" He moved away. "I'll get a woman from the mill to go to the girl, and be straight back with you. I tell you, do nothing until I get there!"

Piper was already off at a pace, his eye on the tall hat of the constable, who seemed to be cowering down by the slates and stones that rose like a mountain in the distance. As he drew closer, he saw another figure nearby, surely Parrish in his old felt hat, standing upright, a short distance further around. Piper ran towards him, and soon Parrish caught sight of him and raised a beckoning hand. At last, breathless, he was at his side.

"Where is he?" Piper gasped.

"We've bloody lost him!" came the reply. "There's all those chaldrons and wagons lined up over there. He could be anywhere amongst them. If he's got any sense he'll keep away from the pit-head. That's closed-in with fencing all

257

around the back edge. And there are men working on the bank there, so surely he'll avoid them. He must be among the wagons."

"Can't he just slip around the far side and make off across the moor?" Piper said, anxiously.

"He could, but we'd see him plain enough on the open ground. Though if he twists about and makes for the barracks, we could easily lose him. Yonder bobby is watching for that."

"Turnbull bids us wait until he gets here. He's gone to get help for the girl. We found her in the cellar at the house. She's in some distress, I tell you! But how do you reckon it? I'm wondering if we shouldn't just move in straight away, to give him less time to consider his options."

Parrish shook his head. "Give it a minute. Once Turnbull is here we can cut three ways and try and force him out." He breathed heavily. "My God, I'm not as young as I was. That gallop across here has taken it out of me. That bastard Ramsay! I can't credit it. He's made fools of us all. But what is he to the woman at the house?"

"She claims kinship to him. The son of her brother."

Parrish looked puzzled at that. "Of Jack Leonard?"

Piper nodded. "So it seems. Leonard's name is on the list of the Four and Twenty Committee, and on the deeds of that family house on the Durham Road. The old woman must have legal possession of it now. She was the lynch-pin of the Corly Croons scheme, so she's no stranger to the skill of legal manoeuvrings. She's been holding Ramsay to ransom with talk of her fortune for years. He must have believed he was in line for a quite a sum. And then he saw it all set to be lost if John Selkirk spoke up and exposed them. It sounds like Selkirk was determined to do right by the son he had deserted, before his own bad health could finally take him. But Ramsay has obviously acted in panic. He's waited all these years, working right at the heart of the local justice system, with a watchful eye out, especially with regard to his own inheritance. And then for it all to come to this."

Parrish shook his head in dismay. "Well, he'll be lucky to get out of this with his life, never mind his inheritance!"

"I hope he does," Piper replied. "He's got a lot to answer for yet." He glanced over the other man's shoulder. "Here's Turnbull. Thank God!"

Turnbull ran over to them and halted, trying to catch his breath. "I've sent two women to see to Emily, and two carters to relieve my man who was watching the old witch. So then, where's our blasted quarry?"

Parrish repeated the state of affairs to him. Turnbull nodded as he spoke, but then stopped him short.

"Three ways of escape, you say," he exclaimed at last. "In fact there is another, a fourth, and I'd wager that's what he's making for. The tunnel!"

Piper looked alarmed. "To the coal mine? Surely not!"

"No!" said Turnbull, "Not to the mine. To the new Victoria Tunnel! It leads directly to the Tyne. It's where the full wagons are sent down, to unload at the staithes on the river. If he gets in there, he has a clear run for about two miles and then out into the open at the water's edge."

"He could be in there already," said Parrish. "Where is the mouth of it?"

"There, I think, by that line of chaldrons," Turnbull replied.

He led them away towards it. He whistled sharply to the constable across the spoil heap and beckoned him to follow. When they reached the trucks, two workmen appeared, their faces as black as night with coal-dust, trudging towards them, calling and waving at them as they did so.

"Hey! What do you think you're doin'?" one of them called out, a rough anger in his voice. "Them trucks'll be movin' along before ye know it, and you'll be under the wheels, ye stupid buggers!"

"Did you see a man here?" Turnbull called to them. "Did anybody go into the tunnel? He's on the run from the police!"

The coalmen looked at each other, and one responded, "We saw somebody run along past the timbers and into the tunnel about ten minutes ago. We've followed him into it, just a stone's throw, callin' out at him to stand fast, but he's away."

"Damn!" Piper shouted. "He's got a good start on us!"

The collier shook his head. "He won't be that far along it. It's pitch black in there, and he hasn't got a lamp. He'll find it hard goin'! He'll be exhausted by now, and it's two mile's length! It's a hell of a stretch, believe me."

Parrish stepped forward. "Can't we ride the wagon, that would be quicker, surely!"

Again the man shook his head. "You'd not last a hundred yards. They're all full tubs, and there's no clearance above for any more height, let alone a man perched on top, and if you cling to the side or to the coupler you'd be shook off in no time."

Piper looked back at the trucks, lined up and waiting.

"When will they move off?" he asked.

The other man shrugged, "At shift's end, to reach the staithes by dawn for unloadin'."

"So how long?" Turnbull demanded, desperation in his voice.

"They're fillin' now, so maybe there's an hour, maybe less."

Piper turned to Turnbull. "We've got to risk it." He spoke to the collier. "Can you give us a lamp of some sort, to at least light our way? And is there a bay, a siding or something where we'd be able to dodge the trucks if they come?"

"We can't give you anythin'!" said the collier, indignantly. "Aren't you listenin'? You'll be broken like firewood if one of those buggers hits you. We'd be out of our jobs if we let you go down there!"

Turnbull stepped towards him. "That man in there is a murderer. This is urgent police business. Now give me a lantern and step out of the way. I'll speak on your behalf at the end of this."

The man strode over to a low wooden hutch and pulled out a pair of lanterns.

"Speak on our behalf, ye say?" he muttered. "Ye won't have breath in your body to speak a last prayer if those tubs get on top of ye!" He lit the pair of lanterns in the shelter of the hutch, and then added, "Every two hundred yards there's a recess, on alternatin' sides, one to the left and then next to the right. Cower down in one of them if ye get the chance and wait until the full length of the line has gone past ye. They'll be at speed but it'll still take a good five minutes for them to pass. All ye can do is wait. But as ye go along, try and remember which side the last recess was at, in case ye have to reach the next one in a hurry."

"Is there another way out anywhere along it?" Piper asked anxiously.

"There's a ladder up to Westgate about half way down, but the gate is locked. Only the manager has a key for it."

The men looked at each other. Turnbull turned to Parrish. "I won't ask you to come with us. Can you make your way to the staithes at the river and I'll get constables sent there. Allen here can attend to that. If by chance Ramsay gets through, they're to take him. They'll know who he is."

Parrish nodded. "And you'll be right behind him anyway, am I right?" They smiled at each other and Turnbull nodded. He and Piper took the lanterns and set off down the tunnel.

Stepping inside it was like stepping into hell. The damp and dust-caked bricks arched to no more than a few inches above their heads at its highest, and the rails underfoot were wet and slippery, the timbers beneath them the same. An angry wind moaned through it, and the echo of tiny sounds, drips, creaks and scuttling vermin seemed close and almost upon the two men. They walked in file, Turnbull leading. The light from the lanterns was meagre, and seemed as if it was soaked up by the walls around them. But soon, by stepping dance-like, toes-first on the wooden sleepers, they began to manage a good pace. But it was heavy work. Piper felt his breath squeezing through his chest, and after a few minutes he was glad to see Turnbull raise his hand to halt their progress. They stood silently, stooped and cowering, waiting for the panting to cease, and then listened intently. There was no sound now, except for the incessant drip of filthy water. Turnbull set off again, and Piper followed. Soon, any feeling of distance or time ebbed away. Their lanterns lit their path only a few feet ahead of them, and now even the rats had deserted them. There was nothing here for any living being.

They halted for a second time. It took even longer for the sound of their gasps to subside, and then again they listened, longer again. There was silence still, but just as Turnbull made a move to advance, a sharp echo reached them from somewhere far in front. It could have been a footstep, it could have been a snap of wood, but whatever it was, it betrayed the presence of someone, but at a distance away that was impossible to fathom. The sound brought a faster pace from Turnbull, and Piper struggled to find his footing. He soon was at the other's back once more, and this time Turnbull went further, on and on, without stopping, until at last he staggered to a halt and cowered against the arch, his arm supporting him against the bricks, his lantern swinging wildly. Piper bent over double, his heart pounding, his belly muscles wrenched with cramp. But almost immediately, they heard it, surely no more than a hundred yards or so in front of them. It was difficult to tell. The steady but slow rasp of footsteps on gravel, long rasps, echoing like the distant drum-beat of a retreating army, but with no regular rhythm, just an incessant trudge of tired limbs, halting, stumbling, falling into themselves in this devil's darkness.

"Ramsay!" Turnbull shouted. The echo repeated it a thousand times. "The game is up. Stand fast where you are! Do you hear me?"

The steps ahead may have slowed for a moment, but then picked up again, at a steadier, more determined pace. There was no other response. Turnbull moved on, he too at a greater speed. Piper staggered again, and felt the sweat sting his eyes. Turnbull was beyond the cast of his lantern now, the light of his own bobbing and bouncing off into the blackness. Piper tried to quicken his step, but his legs felt like they had irons on them.

"Ramsay!", he heard Turnbull cry out once more, and he saw his shape ahead of him for an instant, but then it was off again. Piper had to stop for a moment, his eyes swimming in the gloom. Turnbull's voice rang out again, and suddenly seemed a distance away. Piper moved on again, picking up speed, and then heard an anguished cry, somewhere far ahead of him. Within a few seconds, he almost stumbled into Turnbull, standing with his lantern reaching out in front of him.

"He has fallen, it sounds like!" Turnbull said, and shouted again, "Ramsay, bring an end to this, man!"

This time there was a muffled, desperate-sounding reply, but unintelligible to the two pursuers. And then the sound of exhausted, misshapen steps started up again. Turnbull cursed the man and stepped into a slow, determined run once more. Piper pushed himself along in his wake, his whole body wet with sweat beneath his clothes. He peered ahead over Turnbull's shoulder, but there was only endless darkness. How was Ramsay forging his way through such complete blackness? Again Turnbull called out his name, and again a single, strained note of defiant response echoed back at them.

There was a sudden change in the wind, and for a moment Piper thought that the end of the tunnel must be in reach, but he slowed and turned his head to his rear. There was a low rumble, a scream of squeaking metal, and a harsh creak of straining wood. He felt the shudder of it through his own feet upon the sleepers. Powdered lime-dust drifted down from above them, into the glare of the lamp. Turnbull slowed and turned towards him. He had heard it too. The wagons were on their way.

"How far are we?" Piper shouted.

"I don't know!" he replied, "They could be on top of us at any moment!" He turned once again to the front.

"Ramsay!" he screamed. "The wagons are coming down! It's hopeless!"

By now the ground was shaking, and the metal rails were sounding off a high, howling scream of their own, growing louder by the second. Once again Turnbull called Ramsay's name, but by now it was all but drowned out by the relentless rumbling of the advancing army of chaldrons, full to their mighty brims with sparkling new coal.

"Where are the safety bays?" Piper cried out. "I haven't seen a single one!"

The two men rushed forward in desperation, swinging their lanterns to either side of the archway. The rumble of the rails was deafening by now, a mad echoing roar from the throat of the earth, hurtling wind and dust and filth all around them, as if the entire structure of the tunnel was about to fall around their heads. Piper took a chance to look back, but there was still only a black nothing. Then he felt Turnbull's hand pull at his arm, and in a moment the pair of them fell together, sideways into a cold pool of thick water, smelling of dank oil and coal. It splashed into Piper's eyes and he cursed loudly, in pain and alarm. Turnbull shouted back at him, but his words were lost in the din of it all. He crouched down, pulling in his long legs underneath him and buried his head into Turnbull's back.

Almost at once the wagons were upon them, snatching the lantern from Turnbull's hand. He gave a cry of pain as it did so, but after that, the thunderous, relentless noise of the wagons became everything. On and on it went, bringing a gale of freezing air along with it, its heartbeat on the rails pounding a thump into Piper's chest. It was never ending. His eyes were tightly shut. His ears felt like the very blood was being pumped out of them. The sound held no respite, and it was like each wagon had its own dreadful tale to tell, at ear-splitting volume, never ending, an angry reproach to mankind for ripping the earth apart to secure its black treasure. On and on and on it went. Piper tried to fight it back, but his body was wracked by the terror of it, by the fear of the immense power being unleashed upon them.

Then, with a mighty rush of air, it was over. The noise rattled off into the echoes beyond, and ebbed away. The two men lay there for a long moment, and then Piper felt Turnbull breathe deeply beneath him. He rolled over and off him, and heard a long groan coming from his vague shape that he could only just make out. They were in complete darkness now. The lanterns had been taken by the monster that had all but devoured them.

"Are you all right?" Piper said.

"Yes, I'm all right. I can move anyway. And you?"

"Yes, I'm in one piece, I think. What chance did Ramsay have in all that, do you reckon?"

"As good as our own, less perhaps without a light. We'll have to press on in the same direction I think. Can you manage it?"

"Yes, I can do it. At any rate, we can't stop here."

The two of them rose gingerly, and searched for a footing in the darkness. The sound of their steps was their only reassurance. Occasionally it felt like their eyes might become accustomed to such lack of light, but it was only their nerve-ends deceiving them. The rumble of the waggons still moaned in the distance. They staggered onwards in its dreadful wake.

They emerged, squinting and staggering, stretching their punished limbs into the late evening air, about an hour later. Parrish gasped at the sight of them, but breathed a long sigh of relief. They were both drenched in filth, their faces caked in it, their clothes like rags of mud, clinging to their bent bodies. Piper was retching a dust-filled cough, and Turnbull croaked in a high rasp when he finally spoke.

"We found him," he said, slowly. "What was left of him. There was much damage to the body, as far as we could fathom in the darkness. We'll need to halt the next run of waggons until we can get him out of there. I'm glad I don't have to do it. We'll get someone from the Leazes pit to tend to it. It won't be their first time at such a task, I'm sure."

Parrish nodded. "I reckon they'll have seen a lot worse," he said. "Emily Gilchrist has had a doctor tend to her. She's been taken home. The old woman Rosalinda is at Grey Street police-house. All your Pilgrim Street men are still waiting here, so she's being held there."

Piper cast his eyes heavenwards. "Just when I need a wash down, the rain in this town has finally ceased for the first time since I've been here."

"It sounds like your insides need as much of a wash down," said Parrish. "We'll pass some whiskey around once you're cleaned up, shall we?"

"Let's make a night of it," Piper replied. "I have a boat to catch to London in the morning."

CHAPTER 22

"Ho'way hyem now"

Alec Parrish shielded his eyes with his hand against the morning sun, and pointed to the tall schooner on the opposite bank. He allowed himself a nostalgic sigh.

"The Archibald," he said, "Out of my home port of Leith. It's shallow water thereabouts, but some fine ships came out of it. She's probably bound back there on the next tide."

Evan Piper nodded and then turned to him. "Time for you to follow in its wake, do you think?"

He laughed. "No, there's nothing for me there now. Tynemouth isn't so different from Leith anyway, though its big brother Edinburgh has more charm than Newcastle could ever have! You should visit it one day. You'd enjoy the pace of it. And the castle is much more impressive, high up there on the rock."

Piper shook his head. "This is as far north as I'll ever go, I reckon. I can barely understand the language here, never mind lashing it up in a Scots brogue as well!"

"So will you be back here, do you think?" Parrish asked, a slight twinkle in his eye. "You seem to have fitted in remarkably well. You even lamented the lack of rain yesterday, if I remember rightly. And there's young Emily too. I could tell you were sweet on her there. Yet you didn't get a chance to say goodbye to her."

Piper shook his head, as if to clear it of such thoughts. "I'm not sure she or her father would welcome me back, after all the mud that I've stirred up, even though old Gilchrist has no blame to share in the fate of the poor Corly Croons." He changed the subject, and Parrish noticed it. "I doubt too if Turnbull needs me back here, even if there are more prosecutions to deal with. He's an able man, and took good charge in the end. I'd best be out of his way when he tackles the rest of it. There's still much work to be done."

Parrish glanced at him, thoughtfully.

"And your own investigations?" he said. "They came to nothing, I know, but how will your superintendents and captains reply to that when you report back? They evidently had high expectations of you, sending you all this way. And it was your own suspicions that provoked such an errand in the first place, wasn't it?"

Piper laughed. "Luckily I'll have a night or two on board this damned boat to arrange my answers, and my excuses. This business that we've resolved here will hold little interest for them, I'm sure, when there are Prime Ministers and anarchists to juggle with on their own territory." He turned to face Parrish and continued. "It's been a rare week of it though, has it not? But mind you, exposing Ramsay in the way that we have, I think will do little to sweeten the reputation of the Peelers in the eyes of this town. I feel regretful about that."

"There are rotten apples in every barrel," Parrish replied, "But I have to admit, it was with some skill that Ramsay slid himself into the fellowship of so many, and not just the likes of Turnbull and the others. The people of this town knew him, and trusted him. I get the feeling now though, that he despised us all. And none more so than his own flesh and blood, old Rosalinda. She'd kept him dangling with promises for a long time. I would not have counted on him putting up with it for much longer, had things fallen another way."

"I think you're right about that," Piper said. "When his father was languishing in prison, Ramsay's hands were tied. He was in limbo, unable to lay claim to anything, lest his true identity was revealed. She had a hold over him. Once Jack Leonard was dead, he must have seen things a mite differently."

They walked on. Piper was deeply weary. The mention of Emily Gilchrist had unsettled him, and Parrish allowed him his own thoughts. Above them, an aimless gaggle of seagulls cawed out a shrill chorus, a mocking laugh perhaps, in the gleeful knowledge that they were untroubled by the trials of Man.

Then almost certainly, Piper heard one of them call out his name, clearly, purposefully, and he had an instant of mystified doubt as to his own wakefulness. Beside him, Alec Parrish had heard it too, and had already turned back in the actual direction from whence the call had come. Piper twisted about, and saw the familiar figure of Elijah Turnbull, striding, though somewhat stiffly, towards them down the quayside. As he reached them, Piper saw plainly what the last twenty four hours had taken out of him. His eyes were bloodshot red and his face grey, despite being scrubbed clean of the muck from the Victoria Tunnel. It was clear though, that the experience of it would take longer to wash from them both.

Piper smiled. "I'm touched that you've risen so early to come and see me off!" he said, brightly. Turnbull arched his brows and smirked in a familiar, friendly fashion.

"That's not exactly it," he replied. "There was much progress made yesterday, after you went back to your lodging. So much in fact that it's left us dizzy with all the twists and turns of the affair. It struck me that if I was to share it all with yourselves, it might become clearer in my own mind."

Piper looked squarely at him, suddenly alert.

"So, are you assuming that it was definitely Ramsay who did away with John Selkirk, as well as Doctor Rossiter? The old woman more or less stated that, I reckon."

Turnbull nodded. "She hasn't said much more since we took her in, but it does seem likely that he was responsible. He certainly wove a tangled web as he went about his business. There are those at the Pilgrim Street police house that have taken it very hard indeed, to be deceived so much for and so long, not least Sergeant Fitzsimmons. He's been ferreting away tirelessly ever since our first suspicions were raised."

"And with some result, I take it," Piper replied, seeing the keen look on Turnbull's face.

"Certainly that," he said, almost smugly. "We assumed, I think you'll agree, that Ramsay was the son of Jack Leonard, and nephew of Rosalinda, and that was the basis of his involvement in this whole business. Well, perhaps it really is as simple as that, but Fitzsimmons delved a little deeper into his background, and there could be more to it. His name, Ramsay, for example."

Parrish nodded at the mention of this.

"Yes," he said, "That's been preying on my mind. Not a random choice, I'd bet."

272

Turnbull shrugged. "Well, whose choice it was is open to question, but there is another trace of it in this affair, unexpectedly so. It turns out that Ramsay was the maiden name of John Selkirk's mother."

Piper stiffened somewhat. "That could be nothing but coincidence. Is it a common name around here?"

Turnbull shrugged. "Not uncommon, but it was enough to intrigue Fitzsimmons. The old dog burrowed further still. By the time I was back at Pilgrim Street last night, he had already put his hands on Ramsay's certificate of birth, issued by the infirmary at Forth Banks. That alone should have confirmed the high position of the family that he belonged to. No cottage bedroom birth for him. It was the details on the paper itself that stand out as interest for us. He was registered as Charles Ramsay Leonard."

Piper's eyes were alight. "And the father's name? Surely not John Selkirk!"

Turnbull shook his head. "No, there was no named father. But the mother's name was plain enough. And equally surprising. It was Rosalinda Leonard. He wasn't the old dragon's nephew. He was her son, left to be raised by her brother Jack and his wife, who herself was weak and childless."

Piper let out a loud laugh and shook his head in wonder at this. "But was Ramsay aware of it, that she was his mother? Surely he must've seen the birth certificate at some point."

"Perhaps, but perhaps not. It's only by chance that it survived for Fitzsimmons to locate it. He remembered that Ramsay had once worked as a waterman, and wondered if he'd ever been registered as such. It turned out he had not.

But a few years after, when Ramsay was involved in that accident at the mine, he was one of three to survive, and they were all taken to the Keelman's Hospital, in a poor condition. The nurses there located the birth papers at that time, in an effort to trace next of kin, and to alert them of the incident. And that document was still there, folded for thirteen years in a sheaf of accident reports. And I have to say, old Fitzsimmons was as surprised as I was by what he found on it."

Piper raised a finger to make a point. "Well, surely that all but tallies with what the old witch said, when we confronted her in that dreadful house. About how John Selkirk had neglected his son, Andrew, then adding that he had been equally negligent with his other children, or words to that effect. Do you remember that?"

Turnbull nodded, though cautiously.

"'His bastard progeny' is how she put it," he said.

"Tell me Alec," Piper continued, "How was the boy Andrew described to us? And how was Selkirk himself described to me, when I first met those who had known him? And his brother, George, what is his striking characteristic?"

Parrish stared back at him. "You mean, the thick curly hair, the 'corly croon', the tell-tale link in the whole matter?"

Piper nodded. "Exactly that. Now picture Charlie Ramsay, as he sat in the tavern last Tuesday when we first spoke together, the three of us, and he took off his cap and placed it on the table!"

Parrish threw back his head and laughed. "As thick a head of hair as I have seen, and as coiled as the spring in a rich man's fob-watch!" He shook his head in wonder. "Well, the notion is a far stretch, and it would take more than a crop of curls to convince me of it, birth document or not. It would mean that Ramsay took the life of his own father by doing away with poor John Selkirk. And likely he never knew it."

Piper turned again to Turnbull.

"Have you confronted Rosalinda with all this?" he asked.

"I haven't as yet," he said. "And I'll tell you why. There's been another matter to deal with, of equal significance. Something that has been on my mind since I first clapped eyes on the old crone. Something that I assume eluded Ramsay until the end, yet it leapt out at me straight off. There he was, desperate to get his hands on the profit of her wheeling and dealing, and it was there right in front of him, day after day, as plain as can be. Yet he was too blind to see it. It was hanging round her scrawny neck the entire time."

Piper frowned in disbelief.

"Not the hideous glass beads that she was wearing, surely?" he said.

"Exactly so!" Turnbull replied, smiling triumphantly. "But not glass. Precious stones in fact. It's hard to credit that she was displaying them openly to poor Ramsay, when he was so hungry for his inheritance. She was taunting him, teasing him, and he never realised it."

Piper shook his head. "Well I would never have realised it either, had I been in his place. They look like nothing but clouded glass to me."

"I recognised them for what they were almost immediately," Turnbull said, sighing heavily. "They have the same appearance as a bagful of gems found in the coat of a murdered man, a Russian as it happens, some ten years ago. It was right here by the dock that they found him, and then the gems were brought to the old courthouse for appraisal, which is where I remember seeing them."

Piper looked dumbfounded.

"Russian? Are you saying that the murder of a Russian sailor is also connected to all this?"

Turnbull smiled and shook his head. "No, not so likely, only as a link to the source of these jewels, I'd say. And he wasn't a sailor as such. He was one of a swarm of Russian exiles that came to Shields in the early part of this century. They brought with them pockets full of precious stones and jewels. It was a common-enough currency for them, as they traipsed around the world looking for somewhere to settle."

Parrish nodded. "I remember them coming here when I was a lad," he said. "You had to pity them, being so displaced, but they were a wild and savage lot. They spread those stones around like pennies, trying to buy favour and influence. I suppose it's no stretch to assume that some of them landed at the feet of the Four and Twenty, and that the old woman snatched them up before they had a chance to roll into the coffers."

Piper stared at them in turn, as he listened to this.

"And where are these Russians now?" he asked.

"They were eventually rounded up and shipped south," said Parrish. "It had been by pure chance that they were here, as I remember. Their boats were damaged in a gale and drifting off-shore, so they were pulled in for repair. As soon as they reached land, the fellows scattered. There were women too, wild looking wenches, dark and as tall as their menfolk. Eventually, they were herded together, and made to continue their journey, to islands off the south coast of England, or some such place, in preparation for the French Wars. But it's always been said that many hid away and managed to remain here. Those with cunning and enterprise. They melted into the darkest parts of this town, and blended into its population. Others drifted out into the countryside around and about, to Northumberland and the borderlands. It is harsh out there, but compared to their own land, no great hardship for them. Many are probably out there somewhere still, I'd wager."

Turnbull agreed. "And those gems of theirs were scattered like husks among the lowlife and scoundrels of Tyneside for years after. Few of them likely realised their true worth. It seems that Rosalinda and her cohorts did, despite the plainness of their condition. Precious stones retain their worth better than most things, regardless of the times in which they are proffered."

Piper took a long breath of the morning air, as if to clear his head of this web, and nodded pensively. But the twists and turns of it refused to untangle.

Turnbull yawned into the morning air.

"I can't help but feel that we started our journey towards justice a mite too late," he said. "Your remark yesterday on the coincidence of the hairdressers sticks like a thistle to me. What significance could that have had? An intrigue of conspirators maybe, places where information could be handed over? An outwardly innocent way of meeting up and exchanging idle talk, yet a perfect hidden network to smoothly enable the whole Corly Croons enterprise to carry on. And the snide use of that name, ridiculing the unkempt hair. Maybe that was minted by a coterie of wigmakers and powderers that thought themselves higher in society than those they were taking advantage of. And of course, each of them would be handed a portion of the bounty, in recognition of their efforts and discretion. I suspect though, that it may be hard to reconcile that theory after all these years."

Piper nodded. "Yes, I think the passage of time will draw many veils across this whole business."

The three men walked further along, each tangled in his own thoughts. The quayside was busy with its usual morning market, as it had been when Piper arrived ten days before. The sky to the east was clearing, but there was a dread in the pit of Piper's stomach for fear of another stormy journey. He kept that to himself, and tried his best to keep up an easy, casual conversation with the other men. At last they were at the ticket ledge, where a wide gangplank led to the London trader, The Barefoot, moored majestically at the water's edge. Her steam was already up, and the throb of her machinery brought back nothing but the memory of the battling engines of Piper's journey north into his mind, now with the added spice of the still-vivid roar of the coal wagons through the darkness of the Victoria Tunnel the previous day. At that thought, the swell of an open sea, fresh air and a wide sky didn't strike him as so bad after all.

He turned to them with a fond smile. "I'll have to leave the two of you to tackle the puzzle without me, I'm afraid. You have the makings of quite a team, I reckon."

Parrish raised a hand in objection to such a notion, and shook his head.

"You know that I've no stomach for the structure of the law, even as it's established in this town," he said, "and whatever friendship the three of us might have here and now, you are both still representatives of it." He laughed, "There are matters I could never discuss with you, concerning my long and somewhat varied life!"

"I believe it!" Piper replied, cautiously, but not without mirth.

Turnbull tried to ignore Parrish's remark, and took and shook Piper's hand in a firm grip.

"Your own business, when you get back to London, that's another concern entirely," he said to him, knowingly. "If there's anything I can offer in support for you to set before your superiors, just let me know."

Piper smiled, and with a nod to Parrish, turned to walk up the steep ramp to the waiting boat. He handed in his boarding paper to the attendant and, as he reached the decking, he turned back, only to find that Parrish and Turnbull were already gone and out of sight.

He walked along the length of the vessel, past the hatches and portholes, and to the blunt safeness of the stern. He leaned over the rail, staring long and hard at the green river, curling on its endless way seawards from up-stream, from beyond the heart of the town, past Sandgate, and the chares and wynds of this ancient, care-worn place.

Somewhere in the deep throng of all that, he thought, Emily Gilchrist was hopefully managing to cope with a new day, without too many of the clouds of yesterday's storms darkening her sky. Her outward fragility, Piper surmised, hid a steely determination, which he hoped would sustain her in the days ahead. He would have easily stood by her side as she faced them, but there had been no chance to make such an offer. He wiped from his memory the sight of her in that hideous cellar, and imagined her instead as he had first seen her, frail upon that stage at Balmbra's Music Hall. But try as he might, he could not remember the song that she had sung that night, about the waters of this River Tyne, lying between her and her true love. He closed his eyes, but still it escaped him. Neither the tune or the verse could he grasp. They would come back to him soon enough.